WHEN'S MUMMY COMING

RACHEL WESSON

LONDONGATE PUBLISHING

For MA1(SW) Cynthia M. Nipper, USN (Ret), a dedicated reader and cheerleader for many authors. Thank you.

CHAPTER 1

BERLIN, NOVEMBER 1938

*H*einz Beck walked to the train station, eyes and ears alert in case they were waiting for him. The attacks were increasing. What had once been an occasional beating or stones being thrown had turned into an almost weekly event. He wasn't about to show his fear. His heart raced painfully, his stomach clenching, not just from hunger. A combination of fear and frustration that he couldn't fight back. Not as he'd like to, anyway. If he inflicted any injuries on a Gentile, his family would be made to pay the price.

The hair on the back of his neck rose. Was he being followed? He turned quickly, almost colliding with his younger brother.

"Tomas, what are you doing here? You should be at home."

Tomas blanched at his brother's tone. "I want to go to school with you. Papa says I'm smart. I'm too old to stay home with Liesel and *her*."

Heinz took his brother's hand and considered what he should do. He couldn't blame the child for not wanting to stay home with their stepmother. He did everything to stay away from the house too.

"You can't come to school. You're too young. The school is overcrowded because Jews like us, have nowhere else to go. There's very little space for new students if the teacher even lets you in the class."

Tomas looked up, clutching his teddy bear, his almost black eyes begging Heinz to reconsider. "I'm not young, I'm almost five."

"But…"

"Please, Heinz. Brown-Bear will be as quiet as a mouse, I promise."

Heinz hesitated.

Tomas's shoulders slumped as he sighed. "I'll go home. Why does nobody like me anymore? First Mrs Fischer and now you."

Guilt seized Heinz, making his stomach harden. He bent down to his brother's level. "Tomas, I like you. I wouldn't worry about you if I didn't. I'm not Mrs Fischer."

"She used to like me," Tomas whispered. "She used to give me chocolate cake when I went to play with Max. Now she hurts Max by holding his arm too

2

tight if he tries to say hello to me. I don't know what I did, Heinz. Do you?"

Heinz suppressed the urge to take Tomas around to the Fischers' and ask the woman to explain her actions. Make her face the fact she'd broken a four-year-old's heart. Two hearts, if what he'd heard about Max being distraught over losing his best friend were true.

"Come on. Forget about Mrs Fischer. You'll make other friends." Heinz took his brother's hand and led him to the elevated train station. They lived about thirty minutes away from his new school. He kept his eyes open for the first sight of a brown uniform, chatting to Tomas to distract him.

What if the Hitler Youth got on the train, or worse, the SA? Those men, in their brown uniforms, took delight in tormenting Jewish men, women and children. Heinz usually escaped their attention, as he didn't resemble pictures of a typical Jewish male. Although he had dark hair, his eyes were blue, not brown. Still, a quick glance at his papers and the red J for *Juden* would surely get him into trouble.

When they reached the platform, he held onto Tomas's hand, not wanting him to be swallowed in the crowd. He smiled acknowledgment at Rachel Bernstein, the girl from the neighbouring apartment building, who was also waiting for the train. His heart beat faster and he could feel his cheeks flushing.

Always the same reaction, which was silly as she was just a friend. She was in love with Joshua Stern. Now, Stern, he looked like a poster boy for the Jewish congregation. Heinz had lost count of the number of times Stern had been picked on at their last school – by teachers and pupils alike.

"Morning, Tomas, are you coming to school too?" Rachel whispered, to avoid attracting attention from the Gentiles taking the train to work.

"Yes, and I'm so excited. I can't wait to show the teacher how good I am at maths. Papa's been helping me, and I can count all the way to a hundred. Want to hear?"

Heinz groaned as Rachel nodded her head. In his element, Tomas proudly recited the numbers. He then showed off his English abilities – their stepmother, Trudi, had taught them a couple of words. Trudi was insistent that he and Tomas had to leave Germany. She had been trying to get Papa to agree to send them to England ever since the Nazis marched into Austria. Or maybe even before then. Heinz knew she just wanted Papa all to herself.

"What's wrong with you? Bad breakfast?" Rachel asked. It took a couple of seconds for him to realise she was talking to him.

"What? Oh, nothing. I was just thinking."

"Do the world a favour and don't. Your expression would turn milk sour."

4

He didn't smile, even though he knew she was teasing. Trudi was winning; he knew she was wearing Papa down. Only last night, he'd said he would consider it but only if the three children left together. That had put a stop to Trudi's plans. She wouldn't let her darling two-month-old baby, Liesel, go to live with strangers in another country. Who wanted to live in Britain anyway?

"Have your parents been talking about the Kindertransport again?" Rachel whispered, having looked around first to check nobody could hear her.

Heinz nodded.

"Mine too. They say it's the only way we can leave but I want us to go together. So does Mama. She says we still have a chance with the Americans. Papa's brother emigrated there when the Nazis first came to power. He can sponsor us. He's rich."

Heinz thought Rachel was rich. Certainly, the Bernsteins had more money than their family did. Papa and Mother used to live in a large apartment, and he remembered having servants. But that changed when Mother died and Papa wasn't allowed to work anymore. The current regime had no use for Jewish doctors.

"Are you far down on the list?" He immediately regretted asking, as her face fell. She nodded but didn't elaborate. Everyone, even the children, knew where they stood on the emigration list. Everyday

5

conversations spun around theories of how fast the Americans would work through the quotas, what tricks could improve your chances, stories of how so-and-so had got out. It made him wonder what everyone had talked about in the days before Hitler. Heinz caught the fear in Rachel's eyes just as the train arrived. As they got on and took their seats, he tried to reassure her.

"Don't worry. Everything will be fine. They said some South American countries will allow us to live there."

"Heinz, Papa was talking to your father. He wants us to go on the same Kindertransport. He says you could look after us."

Heinz sat straighter. Mr Bernstein had really said that? But her next words made his chest fall.

"I told him I don't need looking after, and certainly not by you. You're never out of trouble. If anyone, Papa should have asked Joshua." At the mention of his name, Rachel's eyes took on a funny expression. It made Heinz's stomach crunch. He wasn't going to put up with being adversely compared to Joshua.

"I can protect you better than he can. The Nazis know he's a Jew just by looking at him. Sitting with him would put you in danger, not protect you."

Her eyes widened and her face flushed as she hissed at him, "Being on a Kindertransport train would tell them I was Jewish, regardless of who I sit beside. At least Joshua wouldn't start a fight. He only tries to protect himself. *You* would find someone to fight with, even if you were on your own."

With that, Rachel moved seats, going to sit nearer a group of girls. Ruth, her sister, whom Heinz hadn't even noticed, gave him a reproachful look before going to join Rachel. Tomas stared at him but remained silent.

He stared out the window, flexing his hands. It wasn't his fault trouble seemed to find him. He couldn't stay quiet and watch as old people were beaten up or made to scrub the street, or when younger kids were being picked on. But he knew Rachel was right. He was always angry, and he knew whose fault it was. Not the Nazis, although they were bad enough. It was *hers*. His stepmother's. She had stolen his mother's husband and her home, and now she wanted to send them away. But he would never consider that woman his mother. Never.

That day passed without incident. The master accepted Tomas's presence and his brother had a great day. Ruth Bernstein introduced him to some of her friends and the two of them had chatted non-stop the entire way home. Rachel had even smiled at Heinz when she caught him looking at the younger children. Maybe life wasn't too bad after all.

Trudi said you should always look for silver

linings. He missed his old school and some of his Gentile friends, but having to attend school with Rachel was definitely a silver lining, if ever there was one. Once she got to know him better, she would see he was perfect for her. Then she'd forget all about Joshua Stern.

CHAPTER 2

*T*he cuckoo clock chimed midnight as Heinz sat at the table trying to finish his English homework. He'd left it to the last minute, having spent most of the evening trying to persuade his papa and *her* that he was too old to go on a children's train to Britain. It wasn't only Trudi who believed the children needed to learn English. One teacher at school, Mr Stein, had attended Oxford and was fluent in English. He had spoken to the older children and told them they must learn the language to help their families if they emigrated to America or Britain.

"Why do I have to learn English?" Heinz had asked that day in school.

Mr Stein sat back in his chair, moving his chalk from one hand to the other. Heinz, squirming on his seat as the teacher stared at him, wished he hadn't drawn attention to himself.

"Tell me, what do you think the people are doing queuing outside the British and American embassies?"

Heinz flushed. "Waiting for papers to leave Germany."

"And how would these people survive if they were to be successful? Can the British and Americans speak German?"

The class laughed but a look from the teacher soon put a stop to that. "Those who know how to communicate in English will thrive. They may even get a chance to come back to Germany and push Hitler and his minions out of power. Do you see why you must learn not just how to speak English but how to write it? An understanding of their customs will also help you and your family settle in a strange country."

Heinz didn't much care about settling somewhere else. He loved Germany but hated Hitler and his party. He thrust his chin out. "Learning English is worth it if I can come back and get rid of the Nazis. Permanently."

The boys in the class cheered at Heinz's remark but Mr Stein hadn't smiled. "Don't give the Nazis control over your soul, children. They will win if they turn you into murderers intent on revenge."

Sitting at the table struggling with his grammar books, Heinz wondered why Mr Stein hadn't left Germany. Was it for the same reasons as Papa? He looked at his father, sitting in the chair staring at the newspaper in his hands, his mind miles away. Trudi sat opposite him, knitting. Heinz went back to studying.

A loud bang broke his concentration. He lifted his head and listened to a series of shrill whistles, followed by ear-splitting screams.

Tomas, in his night clothes, ran from his bedroom clutching his teddy bear to his chest. "Papa, what's that noise?"

Their father stood up from his chair but Heinz was already at the window staring at the street below. He couldn't see anything but the noise was deafening. He heard loud banging and the repeated sound of shattering glass. His nose twitched at the smell of smoke before he saw it.

"Papa, the synagogue's on fire."

Papa's face turned ashen against his salt-and-pepper hair as he moved to the window, pushing Heinz to one side to get a clearer view. Heinz heard his sharp intake of breath before he faced Heinz, his eyes clouded with worry.

"I have to help. You stay here and mind your brother and sister and your mama."

Heinz opened his mouth but, at a look from his father, he shut it again.

Trudi protested, moving closer to her husband and putting her hand on his arm, a begging expression on her face. "Please don't go out, stay here where it's safe. I don't want anything to happen to you."

"I can't stay here, hiding like a coward. People will be hurt, they will need my help. I have to go." Papa's lips pursed as he straightened his shoulders and moved over to the shelf where his doctor's bag was kept. Trudi fell silent and they all watched him quickly check the contents.

Heinz reached for his jacket. "I'll come with you."

"No! You stay here and look after everyone until I get back." His father's tone brooked no argument. He stared at Heinz until his hand fell away from the jacket.

"Yes, Papa." He moved to the window and stared out at the smoke.

Tomas flung himself at their father. "Please, Papa, stay. I'm scared. There is so much noise."

"I'm a doctor. I have to go."

His father's voice trembled slightly, making the hair on the back of Heinz's neck stand up. His father wasn't afraid of anything or anyone.

A few seconds later, hearing the bang of the door, Heinz squeezed his eyes shut for a couple of seconds before feeling Tomas pressing close to his side, clutching his hand.

"What do they want? Are they going to kill us?"

He didn't get a chance to answer, as Trudi intervened. "No, silly. Who'd want to kill you? Everyone loves you. Come away from the window, boys. Both of you."

Heinz stared at her, not moving.

"Heinz, I asked you to move."

Still he stared, and would have continued to do so, but the window shattered. A rock barely missed his head.

"Come away from the window and shut off the lights. Now!"

At her shout, he moved. He gathered Tomas in his arms and carried him to the bedroom, following Trudi. His stepmother carried Liesel, who had been sleeping in her room, into Tomas's room. Heinz pushed Tomas's bed as far away from the window as possible, and Trudi placed Liesel carefully beside Tomas, tucking her under the blankets so she couldn't fall out. Together they piled extra rugs on top of the younger children to protect them from any flying glass. The bedroom was off the main street, so perhaps they would be safe.

Tomas cuddled Brown-Bear; his eyes large in his face.

"Heinz, I'm scared."

Trudi answered. "We all are. I'll read you a story after I check the other windows."

Heinz spoke up; Papa had left him in charge. "I'll check them. You read the story." He went through their apartment, closing the curtains and turning off all the lights. Only when it was dark did he poke his head around the curtain to sneak a look out of the window and immediately wished he hadn't. *Sturmabteilung*!

They had invaded their street. It seemed like every SA man in the country was standing outside. He watched as the uniformed thugs burst into the apartment building opposite. In seconds, he could see them in an apartment on a lower floor, hurling furniture from the window. He recognised Mr Geller, a wonderful old man, a veteran of the First World War, who always had a supply of chocolate for the children in his building. Geller stood up, in protest, only to be knocked to the ground. Heinz held his breath. He couldn't see the old man anymore but the SA men were kicking something on the ground. Tears in his eyes, Heinz closed the curtains, wishing he hadn't promised his father to stay put. He wanted to go to Mr Geller's place and help him. But it was too late.

There was a knock on the door. He jumped, despite his bravado. Heart hammering, he moved closer but didn't answer it.

The knock came again. "Please, open the door."

He unlocked the door, his heartbeat thundering in his ears.

"Rachel, what are you doing here?" Rachel, Ruth and their mother almost fell into the hall, their eyes red and their faces tear-stained. He touched Rachel's arm.

Rachel held his gaze for a second, long enough for him to see her terror before her mother pushed forward. A wild expression in her eyes, Mrs Bernstein looked around her. "Is your father here?"

"No, Mrs Bernstein, he left to help at the synagogue. Come inside, please. We should lock the door." He took her hand to pull her inside, as she seemed incapable of understanding.

Her voice trembled as she glanced behind her. "But what if they come here? They will kill us all."

Heinz exchanged a glance with Rachel.

"Mama, please get a hold of yourself, you are scaring Ruth. They aren't going to kill anyone. They are just bullying us, trying to scare us like they always have. You're letting them win."

Heinz watched in awe as the strict Mrs Bernstein looked at her daughter. He thought she might slap Rachel but instead, she pulled her into a hug.

"You are right, my darling. I'm so sorry. But when your papa and your brothers didn't come back after the SA came, I thought … Well, it doesn't matter what I thought."

15

Trudi came out of the bedroom. "Mrs Bernstein, I thought I recognised the voice. Please, come in. You are shivering. Here, put this on." She went to the coat stand and took down her fur coat. "Would you like some coffee?"

Heinz's lip curled. Trust his stepmother to fawn over their visitor.

"Thank you, Mrs Beck, I don't know if we should stay. We may have led them straight to you. I wasn't thinking. I just had to get away, they broke up the whole house, every dish and..." Mrs Bernstein dissolved into tears. Trudi gathered the woman to her and half-carried, half-dragged her to the couch.

"Heinz, a glass of water please for Mrs Bernstein, and take the girls in to Tomas. They will be company for one another."

He handed Mrs Bernstein the glass of water before he escorted the girls and Tomas back to the bedroom. He wanted to hear Mrs Bernstein's story so asked Rachel to tell Tomas and Ruth a story. Rachel didn't argue back, she seemed content to be with the little ones. Heinz grabbed extra blankets for them, the thoughts in his head tumbling over one another.

He made some of what passed for coffee and headed back to the adults, a tray of cups in his hand. What about his Oma and Opa? They lived farther away. Were they safe?

CHAPTER 3

*T*rudi picked at imaginary threads on her clothes as Mrs Bernstein paced, sitting down before standing up again a few minutes later. Heinz wanted to glue her to the seat. Tempted to look out the window, Heinz sat on his hands. The waiting was awful; for a split second, he wished something would happen. The ticking clock broke the silence, each tick sounding louder than the one before.

The noises outside escalated as the sounds of stamping boots came closer. The children ran out of the bedroom, closely followed by Rachel cradling Liesel. The threat seemed to galvanise Mrs Bernstein. She stood up again but this time took off the fur coat and gave it to Trudi.

"Try to hide it. Together with any other valuables

you have. The stuff that is easy to carry. They'll fill their pockets with your gold, your diamonds."

Trudi flushed, her eyes looking at the floor, her chin trembling. "There isn't much left. I sold all our valuables to buy food. I had to buy from the black market or the children … they would have gone hungry."

Mrs Bernstein held her hands out to Trudi who clasped them. "My dear, we all have to do what we can to survive. We don't have much time. Get your jewels now. Ruth, Rachel, come here, please."

The girls, white with terror, moved nearer their mother, Ruth clasping Tomas's hand.

Rachel held her mother's gaze. "Sorry, Mama, we didn't stay in the bedroom as we wanted to be near you."

Mrs Bernstein opened her mouth but shut it immediately. Trudi ran to her bedroom and returned carrying some jewellery. Heinz recognised one piece as his mother's engagement ring. He'd never seen Trudi wear it and had assumed they buried it with his mother. Mrs Bernstein picked it up, the enormous diamonds sparkling against her dark clothes.

"Now, children, this is a game. You know how we play hide and seek? I want you to do that with Mrs Beck's jewellery. Ruth, put this ring in your shoe and don't take it off. Don't tell anyone you have it."

"Yes, Mama." Ruth put the ring in her stocking

and then put her shoe back on, wincing as she tried to put her foot on the ground.

"Good girl. You can pretend you hurt your ankle and that's why you are walking funny." She turned to Rachel. "Put these on, Rachel, hide them wherever you can think of." She gave Rachel a pile of jewellery, which the girl took with her to the bedroom. When she returned, there wasn't a piece visible.

"Your engagement ring, Trudi, take it off and put it somewhere else. Be quick."

"But I—"

"Quickly, this is no time for arguments." As she spoke, Mrs Bernstein undressed Liesel, causing the child to cry.

Trudi turned. "What are you doing?"

"They won't look in her nappy." Mrs Bernstein's voice had a hysterical ring to it. Heinz glanced at Trudi, who ran her hands down the side of her dress.

"Mrs Bernstein, stop. I won't risk my baby for the sake of some jewels. Give her to me, please. Heinz, hide this inside that cushion." Trudi almost flung the ring at him.

Mrs Bernstein hesitated but Trudi insisted. "This is my home, my ring, but most importantly, my child. I know you are trying to be kind but enough." Trudi took Liesel into her arms before putting her hand on Mrs Bernstein's shoulder. Tears ran down the older woman's face, her whole body shaking. "Please sit down, Mrs Bernstein. We won't let them see our fear."

Mrs Bernstein opened her mouth but, at a look from Trudi, sank back into a chair. Trudi addressed the children. "I want you to lie down in the bedroom and stay there, no matter what happens. I will tell you to get up if you have to. Otherwise, you are not to move."

Tomas flushed, his eyes darting from Heinz to Trudi. He stammered, "Not even for the bathroom?"

"No, Tomas darling, not even for that." Trudi bent to his level. "We need you to be little soldiers. Can you do that and obey the order to stay in bed? The girls need you to protect them, as you are the man."

Tomas pushed his chest out before taking Ruth's hand to lead the girl to the bedroom as if she was not his elder by at least six months. Rachel looked at her mama, an understanding passing between them, before she took Liesel in her arms and headed to the bedroom.

Trudi turned to him. "Now, Heinz—"

"I'm not hiding in the bedroom."

Trudi gave him a look that would have caused Hitler to rattle in his boots. He was about to apologise when the banging started on the door.

"Open up, you filthy vermin. Quick, or we will bash the door in."

Mrs Bernstein jumped out of the chair, moving towards the door, but Trudi put her hand out. "This is my home. I will answer the door. You take a seat and let's try to be as civilised as possible with these animals."

Mrs Bernstein fell into a seat, her face paling as she clenched and unclenched her hands. Heinz moved closer, putting his hand on her shoulder. Startled, she looked up at him before squeezing his hand in thanks. Both of them stared at Trudi.

His stepmother ran her hands down the sides of her dress and took a deep breath before she opened the door, just as a soldier attempted to break it down.

"Gentlemen. How can I help you?" Her voice rang out clear, confident and courteous.

Heinz stamped down a feeling of admiration for her. The uniformed men stopped as if surprised to be greeted with such politeness.

Then an officer stepped forward. "Out of my way. We are looking for Beck. He is to come with us immediately."

"My husband isn't here. It is only us ladies and the children. You are welcome to search the property." Trudi stood, straight as an arrow, still pretending that it was her choice to invite them in. It seemed like it was working too. The men lost their earlier swagger. Despite himself, Heinz couldn't help but admire her bravery.

The officer directed two of the men to search. Heinz watched, his fists clenching and unclenching as the intruders took apart everything in the room. Trudi blanched but remained standing as dishes crashed to the floor, ornaments were flung against the wall and books pulled out of the bookcase. The noises were too much for the children who started screaming but didn't leave the bedroom.

"Shut those kids up, or we will." The officer pointed a gun at Trudi. She didn't flinch but gave him a look of disgust before rushing to the room to comfort the children. Mrs Bernstein went to follow but she was stopped.

"You don't live here?" The officer grabbed Mrs Bernstein roughly by the arm.

She looked at the hand on her arm and then into the man's face. "Unhand me, you lout. I am visiting a friend. Since when is that against the law."

Heinz held his breath. The man's face twisted in anger before he drew his arm back and slapped Mrs Bernstein across the face, knocking her to the floor.

"It's late and after curfew. Your sort shouldn't be on the streets."

"I wasn't out on the street. I live…" but whatever she was going to say next was drowned out by a second slap. Heinz had seen enough. He stepped forward and grabbed the man's arm just as he was about to deliver a third slap.

"Did your mother bring you up to hit women, you oaf? Let's see how you like to be hit." With that, Heinz delivered a punch of his own, his hand connecting with the man's right cheekbone.

His moment of satisfaction was all too brief, pain exploding over his shoulder, as something heavy came down on his right side. Then a boot kicked him in the ribs as he lay on the floor. Darkness mercifully descended just as another kick was delivered.

He heard Trudi scream. "Leave him alone, he's just a child. Stop hurting him." He tried to open his eyes before the blackness swallowed him.

CHAPTER 4

"Water, please … water." His mouth was dry, his throat scratchy. When he raised his head, his body exploded in pain. He groaned and couldn't bear to move but his need for water superseded everything else.

"Heinz, try not to move. You've been hurt."

He knew that. But he didn't know where he was, only the smell and sense of overcrowding meant it wasn't home or even a hospital. The floor under him was cold and hard. He didn't care, the need for liquid was all-consuming.

Wait, he recognised the voice. "Papa." He'd help him. He repeated his plea, "Water, water."

His wish was granted, as a few trickles of liquid spilled into his mouth, most of it escaping, dribbling down his chin. He opened his eyes, quickly closing them again as the light hurt. Sweat dripped down his face.

"Heinz, wake up, son. You need to sit up. If you are still lying down when they come back, they'll take you to the hospital. We can't be separated."

Where were they? He tried to do as Papa said, gritting his teeth against the pain as he leaned into his father's arms. It was no use. He couldn't stand on his leg.

His father's eyes bulged as his grip on Heinz tightened. He hissed, "Try harder. I know it's painful. I can't send my son to his death."

Why would going to the hospital cause him to die? Why wasn't he at home? None of this made sense. He struggled to sit up, his father and someone else helping him. When he put his weight on his foot, he screamed in pain and the world went black again.

Water hit his face as hands roughly pulled him to his feet.

"I said stand up."

He knew that tone, his father was mad. "Papa, I can't."

Boots echoed against the cement floor, growing louder as the men around him fell silent. He tried to keep his eyes open, looking, as everyone else was, towards the wooden door. Tension rose around him as the men in the room seemed to hold their breath.

Papa's face was pale, and Heinz could feel him trembling slightly.

"What's wrong?" Heinz whispered, his stomach churning as he fought back the urge to vomit.

"Shush." Papa's grip on his arm tightened. A sense of foreboding filled him as he fought against the desire to close his eyes, to escape into sleep.

"Stand up as straight as you can, son. I need you with me," Papa whispered.

Heinz tried to answer but no words came.

He heard his father beg the men around them. "Help me with my son. Please."

His father kept whispering but Heinz couldn't hear every word. The pain was too strong to focus on anything else. He tried taking a deep breath but that only made it worse. His ribs ached. Gingerly, he tried to move his hand over them but his father knocked it back.

"Don't draw attention to your injuries. Just stand straight. It won't take long and then you can lie down again. I'll get you more water."

The promise of water did it. He could barely tolerate the pain but his thirst was worse. He stayed standing, rocking slightly in his shoes but he couldn't fall down, as there were too many people packed around him. Someone behind him whispered a prayer. You could almost taste the fear in the room.

The door opened, the sound of metal grating

against the metal doorstep, sending shivers through him. Men in brown uniforms pushed into the room, using batons to beat back anyone in their way. Heinz tried to stare at the floor, but his gaze travelled up from the boots, recognising the SA uniform and the hate in the men's eyes. Were they the same men who'd come to his home and hit Mrs Bernstein? What did they want?

CHAPTER 5

NOVEMBER 1938, SURREY, ENGLAND

ally Matthews stood at the war memorial in the heavy wind and rain. Wet rain, her friend Maggie called it. The type that got down the back of your neck even with an umbrella and a raincoat. Maggie was standing to attention beside her, tears mingling with the rain on her face. Sally turned her gaze towards the names inscribed on the war memorial. *Reginald Ardle*. Maggie's husband of two years.

When the two minutes' silence was over, Sally linked arms with Maggie as she held her umbrella over both of them.

Maggie's smile was forced. "Let's get out of this downpour before it washes us away. Enid and Doris said they would join us back at the vicarage."

* * *

SHELTERING in the porch at the back door, Sally shook her umbrella before closing it and putting it on the floor beside two others. She pushed open the door of the vicarage kitchen, savouring the warmth hitting her face.

"Sally, we thought you'd got lost." Maggie handed her a towel to dry herself.

"It's a lovely day, isn't it?" Sally smiled as her friends stared back at her with an incredulous expression on their faces. She continued, "For the ducks, I mean."

Maggie gave her a look. "Sally Matthews, I think you've lost your marbles. Come and sit down and get a cup of hot tea and a slice of my coffee-and-walnut cake into you. That will sort you out." Maggie bustled around her until Sally had a cup of tea and a plate in front of her.

Doris, her neighbour, winked at her from the other side of the table. "Maggie forgets you could walk here blindfolded, Sally."

Enid pushed her glasses higher on her hawkish nose. "Sally was practically raised here. If it weren't for Maggie and a few other people in Abbeydale, she would have died from neglect."

Sally smothered a laugh as Doris mimicked Enid's pinched expression. Sally and Doris had both been through school with Enid, until the older girl had left. Enid had always taken every opportunity to remind Sally she'd been born on the wrong side of the blanket. Doris protected Sally, despite being younger and smaller than Enid. But with her blonde hair and movie star looks, Doris could always look to the boys for backup if Enid took it too far. Sally didn't rise to the bait. She'd learned long ago there was no arguing with Enid. Nothing satisfied the woman, not even her lovely long-suffering husband, Arthur.

The wind howled as Sally bit into the cake and murmured with satisfaction at the combination of tart coffee with the sweet cake. Maggie baked the best cakes in Abbeydale if not in Surrey.

"This is delicious, Maggie."

"Thank you. I made it for the new vicar to welcome him to our town."

Before Sally could ask anything, Enid sniffed. "Don't you think he's rather young? Doesn't look to me like he should be out of short trousers."

Sally couldn't look at Doris, knowing she'd laugh if she did. Enid was only twenty-five yet she sounded like someone in her nineties.

Maggie defended her new boss. "He's young and has a lot to learn but his heart is in the right place. He's modest and open to suggestions. He thinks our Women's Institute is a great idea and said he was looking forward to our assistance in the future."

"What does he need help from us for?" Enid blinked rapidly, helping herself to another slice of cake. "It's nice cake, Maggie, but you've made better. A tad on the dry side, don't you agree?"

Sally stood to fill the kettle and put it back on the stove. Maggie was capable of fighting her own battles but it didn't stop Sally from wanting to tell Enid to button it, or better yet, suggest she go home. Why Maggie included her in their weekly meetups was a mystery.

"Shall we listen to the news?" Doris glared at Enid before turning on the wireless as she spoke. The large, brown, wooden case glistened from Maggie's daily polishing. None of her other friends had a wireless so Maggie was used to them gathering around hers to listen to music when they came to visit.

As they listened, Maggie and Doris were shocked into silence at the reports on the radio. The Nazis had attacked the Jewish population in Germany and in Austria.

Doris, a tear running down her cheek, said, "Oh, those poor people. Nobody deserves to be treated like that. And now, the Nazis expect them to pay for the damage to the properties. How can the German people stand by and let this happen?" She looked around at her friends, aghast. "We wouldn't let it happen here, would we, Sally?"

Sally shared her horror, but she had to be honest.

"I'd like to say no, but you saw the papers, Doris. When Hitler came to power and brought Germany out of their depression, people over here were calling him a saviour."

Doris tutted over her cup. "Hardly."

"They did, though. He created jobs, and people had money for the first time in years. You saw the newsreels. All the people out of work here, people struggling to get by, and yet in Germany they had jobs, food and homes. It wasn't so long ago people were saying our government could learn a lot from Hitler."

Enid finished off her slice of cake, dabbing her face with a hanky but missing the crumbs around her mouth. "Maggie, maybe add a little extra coffee next time. My dad told me you could never trust a German."

Maggie replied, "Enid, you can't judge people based on their nationality. There are hundreds if not thousands of Germans who don't support Hitler."

Enid wasn't listening. "You're Irish, Maggie. You don't understand how much we English hate the Germans. Things sounded too good to be true, and they were. Hitler and his friends have to be stopped. There will be war soon, I'd bet money on it."

"Enid Brown, I was born in Britain. My parents were Irish and proud of it. You watch your tongue." Maggie's rosy cheeks hinted her temper was up. "I lost my Reg in the last war, young lady. I wouldn't be rushing into another one, let me tell you."

Enid looked like she would burst.

Sally jumped up, pretending to notice the clock. "Look at the time. The lads will be home soon for their supper, and here we are sitting around when there's work to be done."

"My Arthur won't go hungry. I have a hotpot all sorted. I just have to heat it up." Enid gathered her things and left without a second glance.

Sally watched as the door closed behind her.

"When will I learn not to invite that poisonous witch for afternoon tea?" Maggie huffed, as she took the plates and cups and placed them in the sink.

"Can I help you with those, Maggie?" Sally asked, hating to see her friend upset.

"Relax, Sally, love." Maggie gave her a loving look. "Your Derek would eat a bare plate if you served it up to him."

Sally blushed at her friend's teasing. It was true, Derek would eat whatever she gave him. He was a lovely man, her husband. *Her husband.* They were married. A few months ago, she hadn't even known who Derek Matthews was, but a chance meeting and here they were, an old married couple.

"It must be love," teased Doris.

"You can talk," Sally quipped. "If Derek still looks at me the way your Ken looks at you when

33

we've been married a few years, I'll count myself lucky."

Doris pushed her blonde hair back from her face. "He's a good man, my Ken, even if he does have two flat feet and a dicky heart. Still, it'll keep him out of the army if we do go to war. I don't care what the government says, I don't trust that Hitler, not as far as I could throw him."

Sally sat back down. "You don't think there will be war, do you?"

Doris's cheeks reddened and she wouldn't meet Sally's eye. "For the love of God, don't be listening to me. What would I know? I'm only a housewife. You get along now and get that husband of yours fed."

SALLY RUSHED HOME, but Derek must have called into the pub for a quick half. Like Enid, she'd made a hotpot earlier and only had to heat it up. It was ready to dish up when the back door opened and her tall, raven-haired husband walked in. Her cheeks flushed at the sight of him. He still had the same effect on her, even after weeks of being married.

"That's a sight for sore eyes. My beautiful wife and a home-cooked meal. I really landed on my feet, didn't I?" His blue eyes twinkled.

She blushed scarlet as he pulled her to him and kissed her thoroughly.

"Derek, the neighbours. Someone might see."

Derek held her gaze, the expression in his eyes making her feel giddy. "So what? I'm allowed to kiss my wife, aren't I?" he said, grinning.

She didn't resist as he kissed her again. She loved him holding her, his arms around her making her feel safe.

"So, how's your day been?" Derek asked. "Did you get to see your friends?"

"Doris and I called in to see Maggie. Enid too. We listened to the radio. I wish we had a radio. I'd love to listen to music and the different shows."

"I'll get you one the next time I'm up in London."

"I wasn't hinting, Derek."

He washed his hands and sat at the table, waiting for her to join him before he picked up his knife and fork.

"I know, love, but it will be company for you. For when I'm away."

Her appetite fled. She knew he would have to be away from time to time, his sales job required travelling back and forth across the country.

"Are you leaving?"

"Today? No." He smiled but the smile fell when he spotted the tears in her eyes. "Sally, what is it? Who upset you?"

"There was something on the news about what happened in Germany. Doris said she was glad her Ken wouldn't be called up to fight. She thinks there will be a war." Being in the territorials, Derek would be among those first called up. Like Enid's husband, Arthur. What if Chamberlain was wrong. Many didn't agree with his speech about it being necessary to make an agreement with Hitler.

Sally waited for him to deny it but he kept his eyes on his plate as if the peas would take flight if he didn't mind them.

"Derek?" Her anxiety grew with the silence.

"Can we talk about something else? How about us going up to London for a night or two? Have another honeymoon? We could see a film or go to a show. What do you think?"

"We only just got back. Do we have the money for it?" Sally was always worried about money. She couldn't help it, having grown up the way she did.

"I have the money. I promised to look after you, didn't I? Now wipe away those tears and get your husband some pudding. I swear I could eat a horse."

Sally dished up his favourite: sticky toffee pudding. Maggie had taught her how to make it. It wasn't as good as Maggie's but Derek didn't complain. He said he liked it a bit crunchy on top.

Afterwards, he helped her clear the table. Most men didn't do housework but Derek said he wanted to enjoy chatting to his wife, not watching her skivvy on his behalf. She wondered how she'd got so lucky, marrying this amazing man.

They sat entwined on the sofa, chatting about their plans for the future.

"You'll need a gardener, Sally. To keep the front lawn looking as good as it does. We put so much work into getting it sorted."

Sally grinned, remembering the early days of their courtship when she and Derek had worked side by side in the garden. He'd employed a few of the local men to pull up the weeds and clear out the rubbish. Sally had helped them clean out Rose Cottage; it had been full of dust, spiders and goodness knows what else.

"What are you grinning about?" he asked her, kissing her smile.

"I was remembering how hard we worked to sort out the cottage. Do you remember all the spiders?"

He grinned. "I remember Enid screaming her head off. I never knew such a small woman could make such a racket. No wonder, Art, I mean *Arthur*," he winked, knowing Enid hated her husband's name being shortened as she considered it common, "says he'll be the first to join up."

The war again. Sally pushed that thought aside. She cuddled closer to him.

"Enid wasn't very nice to Maggie earlier. Told her she knew nothing about the Germans."

He rolled his eyes. "Maggie knows nothing? I thought she lost her husband in the first war."

Maggie didn't talk much about Reg, she said it was too painful. The sun went out of her world the day he died. Yet she wasn't shrivelled up with self-pity or bitterness and deserved better treatment. "She did. Maggie's lived here all her life but Enid insists on calling her Irish."

"She does have an Irish accent, especially when she calls everyone love." Derek kissed Sally again. "I don't think Maggie needs any help in keeping Enid in her place. I'd back Maggie any day of the week." He leaned closer to kiss the top of her nose. "Unless she was fighting with you, of course. Not that I want you to fall out. I would miss her."

Sally teased, "You love Maggie's cooking, so you're biased."

He tickled her ribs, making her laugh and squirm. "Anyone can cook better than Enid Brown. Do you remember that day you organised a picnic for all the workers? Even after a hard day pulling up rose bushes and whatnot, nobody was hungry enough to eat her hotpot. I can see why Arthur's so thin."

She slapped his hand playfully. "Derek! That's unkind. Enid worked hard getting our home fixed up." Only because Doris had guilted the woman into helping but Sally didn't mention that.

"She did, that's true." He nuzzled her neck, his breath making her senses whirl. She was finding it hard to concentrate on what he was saying.

"We should build an extension out the back, shouldn't we?" He punctuated his question with a kiss.

"Don't you think it's big enough as it is?"

"We only have four bedrooms, and one of those is tiny."

Derek nibbled the side of her ear, making it difficult for Sally to focus.

"We need more room for a family. I fancy having a boy and a girl but only if she looks like you."

She hit him with the cushion. "You can't say that. You're supposed to say you don't care what sex they are, so long as they're healthy."

"Who said? Nobody showed me the rule book."

She took his hand and massaged it between hers. "I'd like four or five children. I hated being an only child."

He kissed her neck and behind her ear, whispering, "Why don't you just go all out and have yourself your own football team?"

"I love children, don't you?"

"Yes, but I don't want to bring up my family

without being able to provide for them. Dad's money went to Roland; he's the heir and I'm the spare."

She playfully slapped him, hating the way he described himself. "You know your dad made that decision because Roland joined the family firm."

"I think Dad might have split his money but Mother wanted it all for her favourite, Roland."

"Marrying me didn't help the relationship with your mother." Her mother-in-law had refused to attend the wedding, telling Derek she would disown him if he insisted on marrying *a fatherless nobody*. Roland didn't come either. Derek said he didn't care but did he miss his family? Sally had offered to invite the Matthews to dinner but was relieved Derek had declined. From what Derek had told her, she wasn't in any hurry to meet her in-laws.

"Don't bring Mother into this. Although we should have a football team just to annoy her. Families with class only have two children, preferably boys to carry on the name, don't you know?" His posh accent dropped as he poked her playfully in the side. "With your plans, I'll have to earn a fortune. None of my family is ever going to go hungry or appear at school with their backside hanging out of their britches."

"Derek!" Her protests at his language died as he tickled her. He picked her up and carried her upstairs to their bedroom, lying her on the bed. She couldn't get over how happy she was. A chill ran through her. He must have felt her stiffen beside him.

"What? Something startled you. Was it a spider?"

"Yes, it crawled over there."

"You silly goose, I'll protect you from the big bad spider."

She let him laugh and tease her. She wasn't going to admit she was scared they were too happy and it wouldn't last. Derek didn't like it when she got all "doom and gloomy", as he called it.

CHAPTER 6

PRISON CELL, BERLIN, GERMANY

*A*n SA officer in a greatcoat read out their names. Everyone had to answer. Heinz missed his name but a poke from his papa made him answer. Those who hadn't answered were carted from the cell before the doors clanged shut loudly behind the uniforms.

Papa and his friends helped Heinz to lay back on the floor, his head on Papa's lap. Papa kept his promise and gave him a small drink.

Heinz found his voice. "Where are they taking those men? To the hospital?"

"To the morgue," came the reply, but Heinz didn't see who'd spoken. He gazed into his father's eyes and read the answer right there. No wonder his papa had prodded him to stand. He tried to smile, to remove the worry from his father's eyes, but the effort proved too much. He felt himself falling into the welcoming darkness.

THE NEXT FEW days continued in much the same way. The men clamoured for food and water. They were given something resembling watery soup and black, hard bread. There was never enough for everyone, and riots broke out when the food arrived. Papa stayed with Heinz but he still got his portion of food. The other inmates, possibly realising the benefit of having a doctor in their midst, made sure of it.

"Papa, how long have we been here?" Heinz asked, trying not to cry out as his father examined his leg, loosening the splint.

"A week, I think, it's difficult to keep track." Papa pressed the flesh. "The bruising is going down. You were lucky, Heinz, it isn't broken."

"When do you think they will let us go home?" His voice broke on the word *home* but he hoped his father wouldn't try to comfort him. He'd be mortified if the tears lurking behind his eyes spilled over in front of all these men.

Papa's silence told him everything. He looked into his father's eyes and caught the look of despair and fear. "Papa?"

"I don't know if we will be allowed to go home,

Heinz. That old man over there," Papa pointed to an elderly man holding his arm at a funny angle, "he was in the police force years ago. He served with one of the policemen from the station next door, who smuggled in some food to his friend. He told him we are marked for transport to Dachau."

Heinz's heartbeat pounded in his ears as he tried to breathe. *Dachau.* He'd heard rumours about that place. When his leg wouldn't let him sleep, he'd listened to some of the men as they whispered about a place they thought was hell on earth.

"Papa, why don't they just let us go home? We haven't done anything wrong."

His papa put his hands on Heinz's shoulders. "Heinz, look at me. We are innocent and in time we will be released. No matter what rumours you hear, keep faith in our innocence."

The next time the guards arrived with food, they were accompanied by an older police officer with a clipboard. Heinz stared at the man, who was looking ridiculous in his spiked helmet. What was the policeman doing working with the SA? His shiny boots clicked on the floor as he moved from one side of the room to the other, calling names as he went, but Heinz noticed he didn't look at the men before him.

"What's he doing, Papa?"

"Shush, Heinz."

The policeman repeated some names. The SA

shouted and gestured with their guns at some men to stand up.

Heinz watched the men, in their late forties and older, stand up and walk reluctantly towards the policeman. He checked their names against his list and pointed at them to go and stand by the door.

Heinz froze at the next name. "Beck, Ari Beck."

He grabbed for his papa's hand but missed it as Papa stood up. "Stay here, Heinz. No matter what. Do not move."

Heinz knew better than to disobey that tone. He couldn't tear his eyes from his papa's back as he walked to the front, his shoulders upright as if he were still the soldier he'd been in the last war. He watched as his father answered the policeman's question but then shook his head. The policeman glanced around him furtively before moving closer to Papa. He whispered something but Papa shook his head again. The policeman placed a hand on Papa's arm but, with a smile, Papa removed it and returned to Heinz's side. Heinz saw the disbelief fighting with admiration on the policeman's face. Before he could ask his father what had happened, a neighbour spat on the floor.

"You are a fool, Ari Beck. Anyone but a fool would have taken the chance to escape."

Escape? Papa could have left? Heinz looked to his father for an answer but he didn't speak.

"Papa, what did that man mean? Were you allowed to leave?"

"Those men who were called out all won medals in the last war. Your father did too but he … he decides he should stay here in this pigsty."

Heinz stared at his father, who wouldn't meet his eyes.

"Papa, you should have gone. You would have been free."

"Physically, perhaps, but I will not leave you behind, Heinz. Now rest."

"Is it true? Did you hit one of them?" men whispered to Heinz, as they passed over food to his papa. Heinz didn't want to talk about it. It had been stupid. But, if it happened again, he knew he'd do the same. He couldn't stand back while someone beat up a woman.

But now, he was stuck in here, and what was worse, so was his father. Papa could be at home now if it weren't for him. Rachel Bernstein had been right; his temper had got him into trouble.

CHAPTER 7

*H*einz shivered as the people slept around him. The temperature had dropped in the last few days. He wondered if the roads were covered in snow. Was it December yet? Surely they couldn't have been in this jail for three weeks already. Had they? He closed his eyes and pictured his family this time last year. They'd been looking forward to Chanukah, the festival of lights. Although neither Papa nor Trudi were religious, they did celebrate the main Jewish festivals. But Papa also let them have a Christmas tree. The best of both worlds. He sighed before inching closer to his father, comforted by his presence.

The next morning, the routine changed. The door screeched open, the metal noise vibrating through the crowd, who shrank back as if they would be safer by putting distance between them and the guards. But instead of taking people out, the guards pushed a crowd of men into the room, more and more until there was no room for anyone to lie down, only to stand. The door clanged shut behind them.

Silence lasted only as long as it took the sound of the guards' footsteps to disappear. Then, everyone seemed to speak at once.

Papa said to a newcomer, a rabbi whose beard appeared to have been half shaven, "Rabbi, when were you picked up? Where have you been held?"

The man didn't answer, just stared at them. A younger man put his hand on the rabbi's arm. "*Kristallnacht*. Rabbi tried to save our synagogue but those thugs pushed him out of their way. He was lucky they didn't push him inside the burning building. Instead, they made him clean the road with a small brush and they chopped off half his beard. He hasn't spoken since."

Heinz eyed the old rabbi. Maybe it was best his mind appeared to be gone. He didn't have to deal with their reality. Men crowded forward, shouting questions.

"Where have you been since *Kristallnacht*?"

"Do you know what the SA's plans are?"

"Will they release us?"

The newcomer held up his hand. "Speak quietly, please. We were held in the local police station. A few of the policemen knew the rabbi and others as they were prominent members of our community. They sneaked in extra food and water. Someone found out and they moved us here. Said we shouldn't get too comfortable as we would be moving on in days."

"To where?" Papa asked.

"I don't know. They didn't say, but from their gleeful expressions, I doubt it's somewhere as nice as this." The man's sarcasm caused the questions to falter.

Heinz studied Papa's face, waiting for him to reply. Papa kept his head bowed for a second, before responding, "Let's not get ahead of ourselves. They can't mean to keep us all prisoners. Surely the newspapers will have told the world what happened."

Another newcomer spat on the ground, barely missing Heinz. "They told the world, so what? Nobody cares. If they did, they wouldn't have made us wait in lines for visas and quotas. They would have given us passports. You think they will do something for us now?" The man spat again.

Heinz waited for Papa to respond, but he said nothing. The rabbi muttered something sounding like a prayer. Heinz didn't pay any attention, prayers bored him. He pushed his jacket under his head and fell asleep.

Sometime later, he woke up to see Mr Bernstein and his sons.

"I thought they were bringing us to a camp, not another detention centre, although I am glad to see friendly faces." Mr Bernstein looked around, then settled his gaze on Heinz. "My boy, I heard what you did for my wife. Thank you. Was she alright when you saw her last? What of my girls?"

"Yes, they were all fine," Heinz muttered, not wanting to tell the man his wife had been beaten up. "Mrs Bernstein was very brave."

He didn't know what had happened once he'd passed out but he hoped he'd told the truth. He could still see the man hitting Mrs Bernstein, his whole face twisted up with hate.

"Did you get any information about what will happen to the women? Nobody will answer my questions about Trudi and the children. Will they be left at home? Have you seen any women prisoners?" Papa whispered to Mr Bernstein.

"No, I don't think so. Nobody saw women being taken away. But other things happened. Things I don't want to discuss."

Heinz had no idea what the man was talking about but Papa paled even more, if that was even possible. Heinz reached up to hold Papa's hand.

"They are together. Mrs Bernstein will look after Tomas and the baby."

"And Trudi. My darling, brave, fearless Trudi. Who will look after her?"

Heinz dropped his Papa's hand. Always Trudi.

"We should have listened to your wife, Mr Beck. She was right. We should have done everything to get out. Now my boys and I ... what will happen to us?"

Heinz wanted to shout at the man to pull himself together. He was fit and healthy, wasn't he? He looked at the Bernstein boys and saw his anger reflected in their faces.

Izsak, the eldest, spoke firmly, "Papa have faith. We will get our chance to fight back. They will not defeat us."

Mr Bernstein threw his hands up, his tone scathing. "My son, the fighter."

Izsak rolled his eyes, before replying in a tight voice, "If you had listened to me, we would be in Palestine now, not locked up like animals. You couldn't be wrong, could you? Even Mama wanted to leave but you ... you knew better. You knew all the answers. But you were wrong. So wrong."

Mr Bernstein's eyes widened at his son's tone, his face flushing, but it was Gavriel who spoke up. "Izsak, that's enough." The nineteen-year-old was Rachel's favourite brother, the peacekeeper in the family. "Papa did what he thought best. We can't turn on each other now. We have to stick together to get through this and back to Mama and the girls."

Izsak shrugged but stayed silent.

Gavriel patted him on the back, then turned to his

father. "Papa, enough defeatist talk. We won't last long if we believe we are beaten. Together we will survive, at least some of us. We have to live to tell our tale. Make people listen."

Papa put his hand on Gavriel's shoulder. "Well said. You will make a fine leader one day. Tell us what you have heard."

Gavriel glanced around, before lowering his voice to a whisper. "They intend to take us to Dachau and keep us there. Some of the elders believe they will hold us for ransom. Others believe we will be freed after a certain time period. There is no way of knowing who is correct."

Papa concurred. "I suspected as much. I've heard about Dachau and other similar places from friends and colleagues. At least it is not the Gestapo prison in Berlin."

"True. Mama and your wife will work to help us on the outside. Mama knows some of my Gentile friends," Gavriel whispered. "We must do everything we can to survive, by sticking together. We know how the SA minds work. They prey on the weakest link. The old, the sick and the in—"

Papa cut him off. "We must agree to share resources. Food and water. To help each other get through. Agreed?"

Gavriel and Izsak nodded but Heinz saw Mr Bernstein eye him doubtfully. He tried to stand but gave up, as the exertion brought him out in a cold sweat. "I can handle myself." But the words came out in a whisper rather than a roar.

Papa put his arm around his shoulders, and Gavriel moved closer. It was Gavriel who spoke. "We are in this together. We, the whole Bernstein family, owe you a debt for protecting Mama."

Heinz attempted a smile, but even that took more effort than he had. He hoped it would be a few days before the Nazis took them to this new place. He couldn't march anywhere just yet.

As HEINZ RECOVERED, he grew more interested in the men around him. The only thing they seemed to have in common was their Jewishness. Some men wore tailored suits and jackets with leather shoes, whilst others wore torn trousers and slippers. Some men had no shoes and looked like they had been dragged from their beds.

The stench became unbearable, as the slops bucket overflowed. Some men gave up moving to the corners and peed where they stood. Heinz could see others try to keep themselves clean, using a portion of their drinking water to clean their faces and hands. Others stared into the distance, unseeing, the shock of the change in their circumstances too much for them.

Gavriel moved from group to group, trying to keep their spirits up. "Please keep the centre of the room clean, move to the corner to relieve yourselves. They may keep us locked in like animals but we don't need to behave that way. We can't give up hope. Our salvation will come. We must be ready when it does," Gavriel said, over and over.

Some men listened but others turned their faces away. Some grew belligerent. "Who are you to tell us what to do? Your fancy clothes and nice accent don't mean anything in here. Your money didn't help you, did it?"

A man wearing clothes so dirty he had to be homeless, spoke up. "Ah, leave the youngster be. He's obviously losing his mind. The men in white coats will pick him up if the guards don't kill him first."

Gavriel didn't listen. Izsak moved to the younger men, keeping his voice low. Heinz watched as he spoke using his hands and drawing things on the ground; was he planning an escape?

An elder man, holding himself up straight, his long grey beard and sidelocks marking him as a Hasidic or Orthodox Jew, said, "We should pray for deliverance."

"You heard the guards. That's forbidden."

The rabbi pierced the speaker with a glare. "I don't answer to anyone but God." With that he began to chant in prayer, others moving closer to join in.

Papa administered whatever help he could to the sick. Heinz watched as his father spoke softly. "If you men move closer to this side, you will free up some space to let this man lie down."

"Why should he get to sleep?"

"He's older and ill, what other reason do you need?" Although Papa spoke gently, the determined set of his chin showed he expected to be obeyed. The men moved back, if grudgingly.

Izsak, Gavriel and some of their friends had to protect the food rations. As more people arrived, the rations grew smaller and fights broke out.

Gavriel pulled a man off another. "Stop it. It's only a crust of bread. We have one enemy to fight, don't waste your energy fighting each other."

Heinz saw a man approach a sick man lying on the floor muttering to himself. With a furtive glance around, the thief stole the sick man's shoes. As he did so, he looked up and caught Heinz staring. Furious and impatient with his own injuries, Heinz could only stare as the thief pulled his finger across his throat, sending a clear message: Speak and you die.

Heinz tried to close his eyes to rest. "Papa, why are they making so much noise? I can't sleep."

Papa glanced around at the men arguing over the most random things. "It helps them to talk about release or being moved to a work camp. Believing the Nazis need them to work means they can hope for better conditions. More food and water. Showers to wash in, clean clothes to wear. If you take away people's hope, what's the point in living?"

"Do you think they want us as a workforce?"

His papa didn't answer but moved to Mr Bernstein's side to examine him. The man was breathing heavily, sweat pouring off his forehead.

Gavriel held his father's hand. "He didn't bring his medication with him. For his heart. They smashed the bottle on purpose."

"I will ask for some."

* * *

PAPA PUT in a request every day but nothing happened.

"Papa, please don't keep asking. You shouldn't bring attention to yourself."

It was the wrong thing to say. Heinz couldn't bear the look of disappointment on his father's face. "I am a doctor. They will never take that away from me."

CHAPTER 8

*E*arly one morning, the thunder of marching boots woke them up and the doors were flung open.

"Out now. *Schnell! Schnell!* Into lines, all of you. You will have a new home this evening. Those of you who survive the trip."

Izsak whispered, "Ignore them, Heinz, they like to brag. I wish I could get one of them on his own." He stood on one side of Heinz, Gavriel on the other. "Walk like this, in time with us. We will help you."

Heinz did as they bid, ignoring the wave of dizziness as he put all his weight on his foot. He would find a stick as soon as they were outside, to use as a crutch.

As they marched, that thought fled as he saw crutches being kicked out from under those using them. If the men fell, the other prisoners were ordered not to help them. The men had to get to their feet alone, or they were shot.

Heinz flinched as another shot rang out behind them.

"At least it's a fast escape," Gavriel growled.

Heinz didn't want to die. He was too young; he hadn't even kissed a girl. When they got a chance to rest, he would close his eyes and picture Rachel's face. Not that he would tell Gavriel and Izsak he dreamed of their sister.

They marched for over an hour, down main streets. People stopped to stare but nobody offered any help or support. Some even threw stones at them. Heinz heard the sounds of trains whistling, then saw the steam. They were going to the train station.

When they got there, the train wasn't a passenger one but one used for transporting livestock. The men took a seat where they stopped, figuring the Nazis wouldn't shoot all of them. They were right.

Gavriel said, "Dachau is near Munich, isn't it? Always wanted to see that part of the country."

Heinz appreciated Gavriel's attempts at humour. He was trying to distract them, his father most of all. Mr Bernstein wasn't doing well and had struggled to keep up with the march.

At a roar from the Nazis, they stood up and marched towards the train.

"They can't be putting us in there?" Izsak commented.

The group were ordered into the cattle cars. "Looks like we're travelling first-class," Gavriel replied.

Heinz gagged, the smell worse than anything he'd ever known. The dirt of the animals had been left behind, scenting the air with a mixture of urine and animal dung. Heinz stumbled forward as the man behind him knocked him. Ahead of him, the Nazis kept forcing them inside, using their rifle butts to club them over the head or back, whatever was closest.

Heinz held tight to his father with one hand and Gavriel with the other, hoping they would end up in the same car. The pain in his leg made him dizzy. He'd have fallen over many times if it hadn't been for Papa and the others helping him. Relieved at last to stop marching, he tried to take comfort in the fact he could rest. Not that there was room to sit down, as the men continued to pile aboard, including Izsak and Mr Bernstein. Then the door was slammed shut and locked. It was worse in the dark. They inched their way towards the side of the car to try to be near a gap. At least they would have fresh air. There was no water and only one bucket for the entire car to use.

* * *

A TRAIN JOURNEY between Berlin and Dachau should have taken, at the most, about five hours. Instead, it took them over a day-and-a-half, with the train constantly stopping to let other trains past. During these stoppages, nobody opened the cars to provide them with water or food.

Mr Bernstein started raving the first night, finally slipping into a coma the next afternoon. Heinz was guiltily relieved at the silence. His own thirst was the only thing he could concentrate on.

Disorientated and exhausted, most fell out of the carriage when the door was finally opened. Gavriel helped Heinz down before trying to return to help Izsak with their father, but a club from a guard stopped him. Izsak couldn't carry his father. Papa had said he was dead, but his sons hadn't believed him. The body was kicked out of the car, and the sound of it hitting the ground would remain with Heinz for a long time.

"Get in line. March."

They staggered into a line, Papa and Heinz following Gavriel and Izsak. They stumbled along the route, passing a few curious onlookers who turned away in disgust. They spotted a town in the distance as they marched for about thirty minutes.

"We should be there soon. I can see smoke up ahead." Gavriel's commentary was cut short by the uniformed men's screams demanding silence.

Heinz forced his legs to move, despite the urge to give in to the pain. One foot in front of the other, left, right, left, right. He couldn't even look up, just stared at his feet willing them to behave.

He walked into Gavriel when they were ordered to stop. Heinz looked up and saw the sign over the gates into the camp. They waited in silence; any attempt to speak was met with a beating.

The guards saluted, as an officer, his hair cut close to his ears under his cap, made his way towards them. Heinz watched his friends turning ashen, saw his father's sharp intake of breath, his own heartbeat racing as he recognised the black uniform with the skull and crossbones motif. The SS was a relatively new part of Hitler's forces but their reputation for cruelty and barbarity was already well known. In comparison, the SA were a group of boy scouts. Heinz stiffened.

A prisoner in the line ahead of Heinz made the mistake of looking the officer in the face, and got a rifle butt in the face in response. The sound of the beating, the heavy thuds followed by a high-pitched scream, eventually replaced by whimpers then silence, went on as the officer addressed them.

"Welcome to Dachau. It is my job to see you behave. You have been imprisoned for your own protection."

Heinz felt Izsak stiffen beside him but he remained silent.

"If you behave, you will be set free. *Eventually.*" The officer sneered as he raked the crowd with his eyes. Heinz could feel them burning a hole in his head, and it took all his restraint not to look up. "If you don't, there will be consequences. Not just for you but for those who share your quarters. Please line up. We have a welcoming committee waiting to show you to your new home."

The camp guards formed a guard of honour on each side of the group. Heinz didn't have to wonder why for long. As they marched through, the line of guards struck them with whatever they held in their hands: truncheons, whips, rifle butts. The victims screamed, which only seemed to increase the frenzy of the attack. Men started to run as if by doing so they could get through the horror unscathed. A number fell over those already on the ground and didn't get a chance to get back up again. Papa staggered under the force of a blow and momentarily lost hold of Heinz. Heinz stopped, but he could do nothing – he watched Papa try to stay upright, but another belt sent him flying to the floor.

Heinz would have dropped too, but for Gavriel catching his arm and dragging him through. He glanced behind him, catching a glimpse of Papa's face, bloodied, holding his hands over his head in a bid to protect himself. His father opened his eyes and looked at him once. Heinz looked up in time to see a guard, a distinctive scar running down one cheek, raise a club. "No!" he screamed, but the crowd surged forward and he lost sight of Papa.

Gavriel put his arm under Heinz's jacket and pulled him through the last couple of steps until they were past the guard of honour and free from attack. Only then could they breathe. They were through. He hadn't been hit once but Gavriel hadn't been as lucky; a whip had caught him across his shoulders, cutting through the fabric of his shirt. Heinz noticed Gavriel's jacket was missing. He'd given it to his father in an attempt to keep the man warm.

They waited for Papa and Izsak to make it through. Izsak arrived, his eye streaming from where a rifle butt had smashed into it. But there was no sign of Papa.

"Where's Papa? Where is he?"

Izsak couldn't look him in the eye. Gavriel's hold on his arm tightened. Heinz fought to escape, trying to return the way they had come.

Gavriel hissed, "No, Heinz. You can't go back there. Wait. He may yet turn up."

Heinz still tried to escape but Gavriel would not release his hold.

More guards arrived, and Heinz could do nothing but go with them as they escorted the crowd to another building. The guards screamed at them to undress, ready to go to the showers. Prisoners dressed in camp uniforms shaved them, their blunt razors causing nicks on their head. Heinz followed Gavriel's lead and undressed quickly, hoping the prisoner shaving his head would be gentle. He flinched as the blade nicked his scalp, but compared to some he got off lightly. His feet barely registered the cold cement floors as they were marched into the large room, bare but for the shower heads hanging from the ceiling. Heinz tensed, gritting his teeth to prevent a scream as the ice-cold water hit his body. He could see the guards laughing, hitting some of the prisoners close to them. He locked eyes with Gavriel; he wouldn't do anything to give the guards extra satisfaction.

Water still dripped from his skin when he was forced to put on some ragged clothes. No consideration was given to how well the clothes fit, and he had to hold up the trousers with his hands. He grabbed some shoes and, between Rachel's brothers and himself, they got shoes that almost matched in size by swapping with other prisoners.

"Have you seen my father? Dr Ari Beck? He's about this tall?" Heinz asked those around him, using his hand to show his father's height – but it was useless. Some shook their heads, others stared at him as if he was speaking a foreign language.

"Someone must have seen him." Heinz looked

this way and that, before spotting some men he recognised from the first place they had been held. "Did you see my papa? He was the doctor who helped you?"

He grabbed one man by his shoulders, almost shaking him, determined to get an answer, but the man stared through him. The total lack of expression in the stranger's eyes was frightening.

Gavriel urged him to move on. "Heinz, enough. Come and eat."

Heinz joined the queue behind Gavriel. When they got to the top, a prisoner handed him a bowl containing what looked like dishwater and motioned him to move on towards another prisoner holding a basket of bread.

He glanced in the bowl. It was soup not water, with globs of fat congealing on the surface. The bread was rock hard.

"Dip the bread in the soup and eat."

Heinz ignored Gavriel. He couldn't stomach the food.

"Are you eating it? I'll take it." Another prisoner held out his bowl, allowing Heinz to pour his soup into it. He turned away as the stranger lifted the bowl to his mouth and drank the liquid in one gulp.

Gavriel said, "You can't do that every day. You starve, they win."

Heinz ignored him. He didn't care if he died.

The camp officer appeared once more. This time, silence fell immediately and everyone's head remained down. Heinz couldn't restrain himself; out of the corner of his eye, he glanced at the black-uniformed man. To his surprise, the officer's face, with it's perfectly chiselled clean-shaven features, resembled that of a Prussian guard. He was tall and slim; if not for the uniform, he could easily have sat in a gentleman's club. This man wasn't built like a tank of muscle like a lot of the SA personnel. As Heinz watched, the man took off his cap to smooth his blond hair before replacing it. His eyes roved the crowd and settled on Heinz. A second too late, Heinz recovered his senses enough to look away. But not before he had seen the palest, coldest blue eyes ever. Heinz shivered. The hair on the back of his neck stood on end as he waited for the punishment for being caught staring … yet it never came.

"Schnell, schnell." Rifle butts helped the prisoners into lines. The officer's assistant read out a roll call.

"Amos Aaron."

"Ben Aaronson."

Prisoners responded 'yes' when their name was called.

"Ari Beck."

Heinz caught his breath as the officer called his father's name. There was no answer. His heart beat faster as he tried not to scream *Papa*. He wanted to run to the guard and make him tell him where they'd taken Papa.

"Heinz Beck." He responded to his name and waited. The roll caller hesitated, causing beads of sweat to appear on Heinz's lip. The silence seemed to last minutes but it was less than a couple of seconds before the roll call continued. Heinz's legs trembled so he pushed his feet into the ground in an effort not to move.

"Gavriel Bernstein." Gavriel responded.

"Izsak Bernstein."

"Moses Bernstein." Silence.

The officer's assistant made a note before continuing. And so it went on for almost an hour. Heinz remained standing as straight as possible, staring at a point in the distance.

When the roll call was over, a prisoner further down the line in front of Heinz stepped forward. The tension among the prisoners rose as all of them seemed to hold their breath at the same time.

Heinz glanced at the man, under his eyelashes. He looked older, a father perhaps, although with the shaved head it was harder to tell.

"Excuse me, sir." The man's voice trembled. "You didn't call out my son's name. "Noah Adelman. He is…" The man's voice trailed off as the guard moved towards him.

"You shall see him soon."

The man smiled in reaction to the guard's comment. That's what Heinz remembered long after they had marched away, leaving the man behind on the ground, his life bleeding into the earth.

WHEN THEY FINALLY REACHED THEIR assigned barracks, they met a group of prisoners who told them that they had been there a few months. Heinz couldn't believe the state of them. They looked like scarecrows, and the smell of vomit, urine and excrement was eye-watering.

One walking scarecrow looked at the newcomers and said, "Gavriel, Izsak, I would say it's great to see you but…" He looked around him and shrugged.

Heinz watched Gavriel's reaction. Visibly shaken, with tears in his eyes, Gavriel put his arms around the man and hugged him.

Izsak joined them. "What happened to you, David? Mama said you disappeared from the university. Aunt Sophie tried to find out where you were but she couldn't. We thought you were safe. Your father?"

David shuddered, his lip curling. "Don't talk to me about him, I think he finally got rid of his Jewish son. He divorced Mama years ago. I continued going to university, I think your father may have helped with money. I joined the Jewish groups. We weren't violent but we did protest when teachers were banned or classes cancelled. The SA came to the university. They took us all out to the courtyard. The Jews were shot – for resisting arrest. With their hands in the air! They didn't kill me because of my father being a Gentile. The rest of us arrived here, on October the first."

"But that is only…" Heinz's brain caught up with his mouth and he shut up.

"I know it is a short time but believe me, in here, it is the equivalent of a thousand years of hell. Do I know you?" David asked, turning towards Heinz.

Heinz shook his head.

"He is a neighbour from our building. Dr Beck is his father."

The man's eyes opened wider. He recognised the name. Heinz moved closer. "You know Papa? He was with us when we arrived but he disappeared, before the showers."

"He's dead. We were part of the burial detail. You're younger than the usual collection."

Heinz reeled in shock. Papa dead? He couldn't be. He shouldn't even be in the camp. Not with his war record. "It's my fault – I shouldn't have been so stupid. If I hadn't hit that Nazi, Papa would be at home now with Tomas…" *And that woman and her brat.*

"Heinz, don't." Gavriel spoke, his tone gentle. He

put his arm around Heinz's shoulders. "Heinz struck an officer who hit Mama after she went to Dr Beck's house for shelter. So, the story goes."

David stared at Heinz for a couple of seconds. "You are either very brave or very foolish."

"Heinz, David is our cousin on Mama's side. We haven't seen him in a while, as his mother married a Gentile. Once, he was nice and polite but today he has forgotten his manners." Gavriel swiped at David's head but Heinz knew he didn't intend to hit the man. Even a gentle push and David would fall over.

"Forgive me. I've been here too long. Here, use this to hold up your trousers." David produced a short piece of rope and gave it to Heinz. "Take these bunks, the top ones. You don't want to lie on the bottom. Sit down and let me give you some lessons on how to survive."

Heinz only listened with half an ear; his mind preoccupied with thoughts of his father. He lay down on his bunk and let the tears flow, under cover of darkness, as the men whispered around him. He vowed to make his papa proud; to live through this and, in time, to avenge his death.

CHAPTER 9

DACHAU, MARCH 1939

" *L* ooks like it's your lucky day."

Heinz groaned as Stucker grinned at him, his eyes lit up with malice. The stocky guard's belly fell over the top of his trousers. Heinz was tempted to stare the guard in the face, he had learned not to, and stared at the ground instead.

"Your mother must love you a lot." Stucker poked Heinz with his stick and sneered. "The things she was prepared to do just to get you out of here."

Heinz clenched his teeth as the other guards laughed. Counting backwards, he focused on the numbers rather than the offensive comments. His mother was dead, so they could hurl insults at him all day, he wouldn't react. His headache worsened from the effort of ignoring the guard's taunts.

Glancing out of the corner of his eye, he saw

Gavriel eyeing him with concern. Rachel's brother had kept him sane in the months since their descent into hell. He'd done his best to keep Heinz out of trouble, arranging the best jobs for Heinz in the kitchens, away from the hard-manual labour most prisoners were subjected to. This had given Heinz the chance to heal, physically at least.

The prisoners were dismissed from roll call. Heinz went to follow them but Stucker stopped him.

"I told you, it's your lucky day. You should show your appreciation. Get down on your knees and thank me for saving you."

Heinz hesitated but only for a second. His time would come for revenge but he wasn't physically fit enough to take on the guard now. He got on his knees and thanked the guard.

"That's better. Have a shower and get changed. Your papers are waiting."

Heinz risked looking up. Was the guard serious? Was he really being released?

He got a belt on the shoulders. "Can't leave marks on your pretty-boy face. Not when you will be seen in public. You will tell everyone you meet of the wonderful holiday you had in this camp. And, if you are not out of Germany within eight weeks, I shall look forward to seeing you again." The guard fingered his stick. "Go on."

Heinz almost fell as he staggered towards his hut.

Gavriel was waiting. "What's going on? Is it true? You're being released?"

"I've no idea. That's what Stucker said. I have my mother to thank, apparently. Only, she's dead." Heinz shook his head. "Are you getting out too?" He regretted the question the moment he'd spoken, as Gavriel's shoulders sagged.

"Not today."

"Gav, I swear, once I am outside, I'll do everything I can to get you out."

"Heinz, you have to get out of Germany. Don't waste time on trying to help lost causes. You have to live. For all of us. Tell the world what's happening here. You promise?"

Heinz choked back the lump in his throat despite the tears in Gavriel's eyes. They both knew they couldn't lose control.

"Go to the showers. There are some others being released today. You know the drill; shower, shave and a final beating. Mind your head, don't let them hit you there. And your leg."

"Gav, stop trying to protect me. I owe you my life. One day I will repay you."

"Live, Heinz. Find Mama and tell her we are alive and well. Don't tell her how it really is. You promise?"

Even now, Rachel's brother was protecting his family.

"I swear." Heinz embraced Gavriel. "I will see you again."

"Not if I see you first," Gavriel replied, but his trembling voice told of his fear. He walked away without looking back.

With one last look around the hut that had been his home for the last three months, Heinz headed for the shower block.

* * *

TRUDI WAITED in the village not far from the camp. She had walked near enough to see the watchtowers in the distance. The camp itself was surrounded by electric fencing. She didn't want to risk going closer in case they changed their minds about letting Heinz go. Herr Hoess had given her his word, in return for most of the remaining jewellery Mrs Bernstein had saved, but everyone knew how little that meant.

She chose a café near the train station. She wanted to get away from Dachau as soon as possible after Heinz was released. She'd heard too many stories about men being released and then re-arrested as they took the train back to whatever city they lived in.

She grimaced at the taste of her lukewarm coffee, or what passed for coffee these days. People were staring at her. Taking her copy of *Völkischer Beobachter* out of her bag, she pretended to read. She scanned the pages, resisting the urge to tear it into shreds. The pro-Nazi content disgusted her but it was a form of protection. The people who'd helped her get Heinz out had recommended taking the paper as a means of blending in.

Two hours passed. The owner of the café asked her a few times if she wished to buy something else. She couldn't afford to waste money, so she picked up her paper and walked outside. Should she walk in the direction of the camp? She didn't have much of a choice, as Heinz didn't know she was waiting for him.

She walked along, noticing that her surroundings looked just the same as any other Bavarian town. The townspeople walked about their business as if they weren't aware of the horrible camp or its purpose on their very doorstep. Yet they had to know. The Nazis had been incarcerating people there since 1933.

She spotted a small group of people walking towards her, noting their discomfort. None of them interacted with the townsfolk they passed, who also seemed to be ignoring their existence. She quickened her step.

As she got closer, she had to squeeze her eyes closed a few times to stop the tears. They all looked as if they hadn't eaten for weeks, and they were dressed in suits far too big for them. They shuffled rather than walked. She searched their faces, until one of them looked up. Their gazes locked; he came to a sudden stop, and the man behind him walked into him.

"You!"

Trudi tried to hide her shock. Heinz was a boy, fifteen years old, yet nobody would believe that to look at him now. He looked older than she did, and not just because of the shaved head and eyes that were too large for his face. She'd heard the rumours of how badly the prisoners were treated and she'd witnessed the beating that Mrs Bernstein had endured. She wasn't prepared for Heinz's facial expression, though. Her limbs shook with fear as she wiped her clammy hands on her coat.

She stepped closer to embrace him but he put his hands out to stop her. "What are you doing here?"

"Isn't that obvious? I came to collect you. To take you home to Berlin. Tomas and Liesel miss you. I miss you."

Heinz glanced behind him. Surely he wasn't thinking of going back there. Did he really hate her so much?

She said, "The train to Munich leaves shortly. We must hurry. We can't afford to miss the connection to Berlin."

She begged him with her eyes to come quietly and not make a scene. The rest of his group had walked on, and it was just the two of them, strangers among the townspeople. She didn't want to risk a confrontation, feeling all too sure the local police would throw him back in Dachau. She didn't let her mind dwell on her potential fate.

"Heinz Beck. Come on now. For your father's sake."

"You know he's dead."

Trudi nodded. "They told me. Tomas needs you. He hasn't stopped crying since you left."

Heinz glared at her. Yes, she had used his brother, but given what this had cost her, she wasn't above using anything. She tried to keep her anger in check. He wasn't being ungrateful; he couldn't know the price she had paid for his release. He was in shock and possibly in pain too.

"I'll buy some food at a café near the station. I have our train tickets already. Let's walk. You set the pace."

"I'm not an invalid, Trudi."

She didn't answer but held his gaze. He was the first to look away as he began to march off, the beads of sweat around his forehead showing the effort this took. But, if that's the way he wanted to play it, so be it.

They stopped at the café and she bought some food. She charmed the assistant into wrapping it up for her, explaining she had to catch the train to get to Berlin. When they got on the train, she gave him the food, ignoring his lack of response. She took her paper out of her bag and opened it.

"Since when do you read that?" he asked, frowning.

"Since it stops questions. Now shut up and eat." The look she gave him dared him to say something but he seemed to get the message. Their journey passed without incident, and they changed at Munich onto the Berlin train.

They had only travelled for an hour when trouble came, in the form of a group of SS soldiers. Despite the relatively empty carriage, they pushed into the seats beside them. Trudi thought Heinz was asleep but she didn't dare to look at him. She continued staring at her paper.

"What's a pretty *Fräulein* doing with a convict?"

Trudi raised her eyes to look at the man who'd spoken. He was of a similar age to her, blond-haired and blue-eyed, a model for Hitler's Aryan look. Shivers ran through her as she looked into his eyes, the palest shade of blue she'd ever seen. She put the paper down and smiled her sweetest smile.

"Doesn't he look just dreadful? If the hospital had told me he would be so emaciated, I would have taken his suit to the tailors and had it altered. But there wasn't time. Do you think it will take us long to reach Berlin?"

She saw the curiosity mingling with surprise in

his eyes. He'd expected her to be nervous and perhaps scared.

"Hospital?"

"Why yes. What did you think was wrong with my husband?"

The soldier looked from her to Heinz and back. "Husband?"

"We married just over six months ago. My beloved wanted to join the SS. I insisted we got married first as I didn't want him to go away without first becoming a father. You know how our amazing *Führer* loves families. But he failed his medical. He has TB, probably from back when he was a child and his widowed mother had to live in such squalid accommodation."

Trudi was almost enjoying herself now, as the SA men moved away from her stepson. She sensed he was awake but hoped he would keep his eyes shut, as well as his mouth.

"TB?"

Trudi forced some tears and scrambled in her bag for some tissues. As she wiped her nose, she bit her inside lip hard enough to draw blood.

"It's just horrible and so unfair." She pouted, batting her eyelashes at the man. He paled, taking a step back. She moved forwards, enjoying for a second having the upper hand. "You should have seen him in our wedding photos. He looked rather like you, but not as good-looking."

The man jumped away as if she could contaminate him by flirting. She sighed, trying her best to keep her voice steady.

"Now we're married and I'm stuck with an invalid. I can't divorce him. Isn't much point as I probably have it too. I never knew it was so infectious, did you?" She coughed delicately into a tissue, seeing it turn slightly red. That sent the SS men fleeing, with a mumbled "Heil Hitler".

Trudi sank back into the chair, feeling weak and shaken. The other passengers had already fled, some having left as soon as the uniformed men sat down. Others had left during Trudi's tale. She was thankful they were alone. She could feel Heinz watching her.

"You should take up acting. You had me believing you at one point."

His scathing comment pushed her over the edge. "Shut up, before I denounce you myself. You have no idea what I've had to do over the last few months to protect my family. Don't you dare sit there in judgment of me. Grow up."

She closed her eyes and feigned sleep until they reached Berlin. She couldn't wait to feel her child in her arms. Liesel, the light of her life. She didn't want to waste any of the time she had left with her one-year-old baby. Her cuddles over the next few days, weeks if she was lucky, would have to last Trudi a lifetime – or at least until the war was over.

She'd tried to escape, planned different routes, but always her husband had said no. Why had she listened to him? It was too dangerous now for her to leave with the children. She didn't have enough money left for bribes.

The only option was to get the children out first and then try to follow them.

CHAPTER 10

BERLIN, MAY 1939

*H*einz stood opposite his stepmother, holding his arms by his side, his hands fisted, trying to keep his temper under control. They were having another argument about leaving Berlin. Trudi had secured tickets for him, Tomas and Liesel on the so-called Kindertransport – a train taking Jewish children from Berlin.

"I'm not going on some kid's train. I'm the man of this house now."

"You're a child, at least in the eyes of the Nazis, and we should thank God for that."

He swallowed, trying not to raise his voice. He'd wake Tomas and Liesel. Tomas found it hard to fall asleep, terrified of his nightmares. He clung to Heinz during the day and whimpered like a beaten-up puppy if Heinz went out of the apartment. Heinz found it claustrophobic, despite Trudi and Rachel telling him his younger brother was reacting not just to the loss of his father but to the loss of his childhood. It wasn't safe for Jewish children to be on the streets anymore.

"I'm not running away, Trudi. I promised Gavriel I wouldn't leave him to rot in Dachau."

"Gavriel will be fine. I have friends working on getting him and Izsak out. You have to go to Britain. Tomas won't go unless you do. He can't protect himself, he's too small."

He turned his back on her. She was right. Tomas was scared of his own shadow. "Tomas likes Ruth and Rachel Bernstein. Ruth mothers him, despite only being six months older. He can go with them."

Tomas surprised both of them by yelling, "No! I won't go. I'm not going anywhere without you. You're my brother."

Heinz recovered first and turned to his brother, who was standing in the doorway. "Tomas, go back to bed. You'll do as you're told."

"You're not Papa and you're not my mother. I don't have to do anything you tell me. I won't go. You can't make me. I'll just run away. So there!" Tomas stamped his foot, waving Brown-Bear in the air as if the toy was a weapon.

Heinz took a step towards him, his arm raised. Not that he would hit his brother but he hoped Tomas would take the hint. The child didn't move, and kept eye contact too; his determination to prove he meant what he said was obvious.

Trudi spoke up. "You will both go. I'm not your mother but I am your guardian and responsible for the pair of you. I won't stand by and let the Nazis get you. You will get on that train on Saturday and you will take Liesel with you."

Heinz snapped, "You aren't offloading your brat on me." His cheek stung from the slap she gave him.

"Don't you call your sister ugly names. Isn't it bad enough that everywhere we go others do just that? I'm glad your papa is dead. He'd die of shame if he heard you now."

Trudi turned and ran in the direction of Liesel's room, her sobs audible to both children, who stared after her.

"She loves Liesel. Why is she giving her away, too?" Tomas asked.

Heinz couldn't answer, as the truth would terrify Tomas even more.

He stared out the window into the street below. All around him were memories. Some happy ones, but those had been crowded out by bad ones. He could still see Mr Geller standing up to the uniformed thug, his papa racing to help at the synagogue, Rachel and her mother coming to the door. Since his return from Dachau, he'd seen things had grown even worse than before. People they once knew avoided them on the streets. Papa's patients, some of whom owed their lives to his father's skills, just walked past him now, as if he didn't exist.

Tomas came over and held his hand. "You won't let them take me away, will you?" He gulped, his voice trembling. "I know you don't like me being scared and acting like a baby but I can't help it. I feel like I don't belong here anymore. Everyone hates us and I don't know why."

Heinz squeezed Tomas's hand. He was torn between wanting to stay to fight with the resistance, limited though it was, and doing his duty by his brother.

"Heinz, please don't leave me. I'll do everything you say. I won't talk, or get on your nerves. I won't touch your stuff. I'll even give you Brown-Bear. I hear you walking around at night, I know you find it hard to sleep. He'd help you."

Heinz bent down and picked up the younger boy. "Papa gave Brown-Bear to you, Tomas. You keep it, but thank you. You don't have to bribe me to stay with you. I'm your big brother. I won't leave you. Ever."

Tomas wound his hands around Heinz's neck, his tears wetting his shirt collar. Heinz couldn't say a word, his own tears were flowing too. He knew he had to leave, but one day he'd come back and have revenge on all those who tortured his family. They would pay, the Dachau guard with the scar on his face, most of all.

* * *

THE NEXT MORNING, he had breakfast laid out on the kitchen table before Trudi appeared. She ignored him as she took her seat, Liesel on her lap.

Heinz said, "Tomas and I will go on the Saturday train. I will see what food I can gather before we go. Aunt Chana will help me."

"You will take Liesel too?" Trudi asked. She held her baby so tight the child protested loudly.

"I think she should stay with you." He walked out of the apartment. He had to visit Aunt Chana and say goodbye.

CHAPTER 11

"*H*einz Israel Beck."

"Here." He moved closer to the man with the list standing behind the row of desks. He stared straight ahead of him, despite his stepmother's pleas to remain invisible. It wasn't possible for a boy of his height to hide behind the crowds, particularly in this sea of infants and children. He'd seen Rachel and Ruth Bernstein queuing some distance behind him.

The man's gaze flickered over him, his mouth twitching, but whether in amusement at Heinz's bearing or annoyance, he wasn't at all sure.

"Your papers."

Heinz handed over the papers with the red J stamped on the front. The man glanced at them before staring at him, a challenging expression in his eyes.

"It says here you are sixteen years old."

Was that a question? Heinz didn't know, so he stayed silent.

"Jewish pig, I am speaking to you. I asked you a question."

"Actually, you stated my age," Heinz said, then staggered back with the force of the blow.

"Be careful, boy, or I will have you thrown on the train to Dachau, not put on this children's day trip." His lips curled over the word *children*. Heinz squeezed his hands, the nails biting into his palms. How he longed to hit the man square in the jaw. He heard the voice of his stepmother carrying across the crowd.

"Excuse me, please, sir. Heinz, take Liesel." She was pushing her way towards him, Liesel in her arms.

"Yes, take the baby. A nursemaid is all you're good for."

Heinz bristled as the Nazi gloated. He couldn't believe Trudi had shown him up like that in front of this Nazi thug. He didn't want her brat.

He took a step forward but then saw that this was exactly what the man wanted. He was looking for a fight, so he could mash him into a pulp and then blame the Jewish community for not behaving. If it was just the two of them, he stood a chance. He was well-built, although, given the starvation rations at Dachau, he had lost muscle. Still, he would give everything he had and die trying.

But he had to think of the children. The little ones around him who waited to get on this train to safety. If he fought back, others would follow his lead and the Nazis would send the train away empty. He couldn't do that. Not to Tomas, his five-year-old brother now staring at him, a combination of awe and abject terror on his face. It was this that brought him back to his senses.

Trudi, clutching Liesel to her chest, pushed through to his side, her tear-stained face staring at him, a begging expression in her eyes. How had she managed to get in, when the parents were detained outside the platform? Probably flirted her way through; with her dyed blonde hair and blue eyes, she didn't look Jewish. Yet she wore the yellow star, just like the rest of the adults.

"Heinz, take her, please." Her voice trembled, her hands shaking as she held the baby out to him. Liesel screamed in protest, grabbing a length of her mother's hair. "Heinz, you are her only chance. She has a ticket so will travel on the train but I don't want her with strangers. Forget what you think of me. She is your baby sister." Tears now rolled down her face as she pleaded with him. Her voice dropped to a whisper, "Please, for your father's sake."

Papa. That was low. He closed his eyes, determined to block the last image he had of his father from his mind. His bloodied scalp, the...

89

"Heinz, the train. Go, now."

"The baby needs papers too." The man held out his hand, his gaze assessing Trudi. Heinz saw the same expression on his face as the SA men had on the train back from Dachau – admiration fighting with disbelief. Trudi defied the stereotype of the ugly Jew that men like him wanted people to believe in. She was only twenty-one and, despite the lack of food, still looked young and very attractive. Heinz knew his friends fancied his step-mother. Even calling her that seemed ridiculous; the woman was barely five years older than he was. Far too young to have taken the place of his darling mother.

"Papers."

Trudi looked directly into the Nazi's face. Her bravery was inspiring but then Heinz remembered he hated her. Trudi's voice shook slightly as she said, "Her name is Liesel Beck."

"Liesel Sarah Beck, you mean." The Nazi watched Trudi's face for her reaction, his delight in his power evident. One of the many Nazi decrees was that all Jewish people were to add Israel or Sarah to their names, depending on their sex. Heinz didn't glance at his stepmother. He kept his eye on the Nazi, not liking the way he was looking at Liesel. She was an innocent baby but he'd heard of what some soldiers did to Jewish babies.

"Yes, sir, pardon me."

He listened scornfully as his stepmother acted the part of the downtrodden Jew. Her eyes flicked at the soldier before looking at the floor, making him think he was her master. Her acting abilities were so good, she should volunteer to be Goebbels' next film star. She looked desperate, as if she was prepared to do anything to get her child on the train.

He glanced around at the row of tables lined up, Nazis with lists, children waiting in lines. She wasn't the only one.

He saw more than one bribe flow across the table, discreetly pocketed by the Nazi who would blame the Jew if it was discovered. He knew, from neighbourhood gossip, what lengths the women of his community were prepared to go to, to get their children on a train out of Germany. His mother would never have done something like that. She would have remained dignified to the end. Mother would have spat in this animal's face, not played up to him as if he was God's gift to creation.

Heinz ignored Trudi and her pleas and yanked Tomas's arm forward.

"Ouch, that hurt. What did you do that for?" Tomas complained, but in a whisper. He was terrified, and who could blame him. He held on tight to Brown-Bear. Nothing would separate him from the stuffed animal, and if he was too old for bears, so what? He knew nothing of a time when the streets were safe for Jews.

"Tomas Beck. He's five." Heinz pushed his brother forward. He wasn't leaving him behind. Tomas was all he had of his mother and the one person Heinz admitted he loved. Everyone else had died. Mother, from cancer. Oma and Opa, distraught at the loss of their only child and the nightmare engulfing their country, had taken their own lives only two weeks previously. He could see Opa's Iron Cross lying on his unmoving chest. Papa … he didn't want to think about Papa. There was only him and Tomas left.

"You can go." The man indicated he take Tomas onto the train. Heinz pushed his brother forward but Tomas wouldn't move.

"Liesel has to come too. We have to look after her. She can't stay here without us. She needs her brothers to protect her. Papa told me it was my job when she was born."

Heinz said firmly, "Tomas, leave Liesel with her mother. Come on, the train will go without us."

But it was no use. Tomas refused. Heinz was pushed forward, losing his grip on his brother, leaving the child to run back towards the row of desks where Trudi stood. Heinz called, "Tomas, come back. Get back here now."

A guard shouted at Heinz. "Get on the train, boy,

or face the consequences."

The Nazi guard pointed to a crumpled body on the other side of the tracks. He hadn't noticed it. He didn't move until the truncheon came down across his shoulders.

Then Rachel Bernstein was behind him, pushing him forward. "For goodness' sake, get on the train. Now is not the time. Our time will come but for now, we must do what they say. Move. If you don't, you will upset the little ones. They look up to us. Stop being such a selfish sod and move your backside, or I shall move it for you."

Astonished that Rachel even knew street language, he moved forward onto the train, almost in shock. He took a seat in the carriage, craning his neck to see what had happened to Tomas. Where was his brother?

He scanned the crowd. He saw Trudi, standing at the door to the waiting room, back with the other parents not allowed on the station platform. Trudi. Yet she didn't look like his stepmother now. Her face was ravaged with pain, her expression tore at his heart, not that she saw him. Her gaze was focused on a bundle being carried onto the train. Tomas was carrying the baby.

Rachel moved forward to the doorway to help his brother onto the train.

The next thing Heinz knew, the bundle was thrust

into his hands.

"Your sister, I believe." Rachel stood in front of him. "Take her. I don't want to hear it. She's a baby and she needs you. Now take responsibility. I have enough to do with the others." Rachel turned her attention to Tomas. In a much warmer tone, he heard her say, "You are a real man. Your sister is a lucky little girl to have such a hero for a brother."

Despite the circumstances, Tomas beamed at the praise and immediately straightened his shoulders, wiping his sleeve across his nose. Liesel began to squirm, protesting about being held on his lap. She wanted to climb out of the window back to her mother. Heinz held her tighter, causing her to squeal in protest.

A Nazi spat in their direction. "Shut that Jewish brat up, or I will."

Tomas put Brown-Bear on the seat beside him before he held out his hands for Liesel. "Give her to me. I know how to keep her quiet."

Despite Heinz's misgivings, he let his brother hold the baby and watched as she immediately gurgled and smiled. It was almost as if she knew Tomas adored her whereas he ... he didn't even like her.

No, that wasn't true. He'd been all set to attack the Nazi guard when it looked like he might hurt the baby. Papa had treated Liesel like a princess. At first, he'd thought it was because of Trudi but it was more than that. Liesel was such a joyful child, always laughing and smiling at people. She brightened up any room. Papa thought she was a gift from God. He snorted. God would have been better sending them their exit papers, then Papa would be alive and they wouldn't be sitting all alone on this train.

"What do you think will happen to Trudi?" Tomas asked. "She was so sad when she gave Liesel to me. I thought she was going to jump on board too. Why didn't she?"

Heinz said, "She is too old to travel with us. You know the rules." He didn't want to think about his stepmother having feelings. Once, though, they had been close. Mother had engaged Trudi as a nanny to Tomas when she'd first fallen ill. She wanted Tomas to be brought up properly, as befitted the son of a doctor. Trudi was the orphaned daughter of friends of Mother's. Her family could trace their history right back to the early days of Cologne. Had Mother known Trudi wouldn't wait but a couple of months before she took up all the roles Mother had held, including warming her husband's bed?

Papa had only married her when Trudi trapped him by getting pregnant. That's what Aunt Chana said, and he believed her. Chana was his father's eldest sister and shared his adoration of his father. Papa could do no wrong in Chana's eyes. Chana had liked Mother and often said she was the perfect mate for her brother. "A proud lady, your mother, she could give the best dinner party in the whole of Berlin. Her table settings were just perfect, and the food she provided, *Oy Vey,* it was always cooked to perfection. Your mother was part of the reason your Papa was so successful. Martha could charm honey from the bees. Of course, she was part of the Rothschild family, you know."

Once, when he was younger, having listened to stories of Mother's relatives, he had walked into a Rothschild bank and told the staff he was a part-owner, much to their amusement. Mother hadn't been in the slightest bit amused and had sent him to his bedroom without any food. He couldn't understand why she'd been so angry until later Papa explained she was, in fact, only distantly related to the Rothschild family, by marriage. They didn't even know who Martha Beck was.

"What are you thinking about?" Tomas asked, squirming in his seat.

Heinz looked over at him. The baby seemed to be sleeping. "Just stuff. What's wrong with you? Sit still."

"Can't. I have to go pee."

He rolled his eyes. He should have guessed. His brother's bladder was always full, no matter how many times he went to the toilet.

"You will have to wait."

Tomas turned white and then his cheeks flushed. "Can't wait. Been waiting since before we got on the train. Trudi wouldn't let me go. Said I could get lost. I can't hold it much longer. I'm going to wet myself."

Heinz stood up, looking around. He couldn't see any toilets.

"What's wrong? Sit down for God's sake, they will come back," Rachel hissed.

"Tomas needs to…" Heinz caught himself in time. "He needs the bathroom."

"Oh." Rachel gave Tomas a sympathetic look, and then one of the girls sitting with her said, "I need to go too."

"Me too," another girl added. Soon it seemed as if everyone in the carriage wanted to go.

"I'll take them." Rachel stood up, patting down her skirt. "Look after Liesel."

"No, you take the baby. I will take Tomas and the others."

Her eyes flashed with temper. "Sit down and shut up. Things are bad enough without you spoiling for a fight. Not all of the guards are as bad as the one at the station."

Rachel's tone told him to listen. He held out his hands for Liesel.

Tomas gave him a serious look. "Take good care of her and don't wake her. She doesn't like that."

With that advice, Tomas disappeared in Rachel's wake.

Heinz sat back into his seat, shifting slightly to get comfortable. Liesel was surprisingly heavy for the size of her. He glanced at the bundle and his heart caught. Liesel was staring straight back at him, not smiling or crying or anything. Just holding his gaze, her big eyes seeming to assess him. She had Papa's eyes and his thoughtful expression. Then she put her hand out and grabbed onto his finger, squeezing it tight. His heart turned over, despite all his efforts to harden it. She kept squeezing, gave a contented little sigh and, closing her eyes, started to snore very softly.

TRUDI BECK WATCHED as the train pulled out of the station, taking her heart with it. Her arms ached for Liesel, her precious baby, but she also ached for the loss of Tomas and – despite Heinz's reaction to her now – him too. She walked slowly, her shoulders slumped, back to her now-empty apartment. She wasn't alone, other mothers walked with her, some fathers too, although many were still missing after *Kristallnacht*. She closed her eyes, not wanting to think about that night, that awful night when everything changed.

CHAPTER 12

*T*here were some Jewish chaperones on the train but Heinz paid them little heed. He knew they would accompany the train to England and then return to Germany. Why didn't they leave the train too and make a break for freedom? That's what he would do in their position.

He watched the scenery as the train moved swiftly along. The tension in their carriage rose as they drew near the Dutch border. They knew from stories passed around the community, they faced another Nazi inspection before they reached the relative safety of Holland.

Rachel came back with Tomas and the other children. To his surprise, she slid into the seat next to him.

"Do you have any valuables?" she whispered.

He shook his head. What was she thinking? He glanced around him to check nobody had heard.

"I'm certain you do. Your stepmother wouldn't have let you make the journey without something. Hide them well, not in anything that can be searched. They will tear everything to pieces in their bid to steal. A friend told me they even stole a Star of David necklace from a child on the last trip. What could they possibly want with that?"

Heinz replied, "Gold, what else? The Nazis take everything they see, from gold to paintings to whole apartments. They even charged the Jews for the cost of cleaning up after *Kristallnacht* – and you're surprised they took a necklace."

Rachel pursed her lips but didn't take him to task for his sarcasm.

"Mama gave me some diamonds. But just in case anything happens to me, I want you to know I sewed some into the hem of Ruth's dress." Rachel leaned closer, the scent of her hair tickling his nose. "She's too little to know, as she would give the game away."

He nodded and then realised what Rachel had said.

"Nothing is going to happen to you. I won't let it. You are coming to England with us and that's final."

She gave him a sad smile but didn't argue.

Instead, for a second, she leaned in closer, leaving no distance between them.

"You will be a good man when you get control over that temper." She kissed his cheek. "I never thanked you for what you did for Mama."

And then she was gone. Back to caring for the younger children, soothing their cries for their mothers and fathers. He glanced around; it was the children who didn't cry who bothered him the most. The ones who sat as still as the Catholic statues Trudi had shown him when she'd taken him to see a Catholic church one time.

He remembered the funny smells in the church and the paintings in the windows made from glass. The priest had been nice enough, patting him on the head before moving Trudi away, to speak to her in private.

He'd thought Papa would be annoyed when he told him about visiting the church, but he had instead exchanged a small, secret smile with Trudi. He'd told him not to tell anyone about the church visit, particularly Aunt Chana.

Later, he heard Papa ask Trudi if the paperwork was possible, but he hadn't known then what Papa meant. It was only in Dachau, listening to the stories of how other Jews had tried to leave, that he had heard about Jewish children being given fake Catholic papers, in a bid to hide from the Nazis. Had that been what Trudi had been trying to do?

Suddenly, the train screeched to a stop. Rachel glanced at him, her face turning white. They heard loud German voices and the barking of dogs. Some children began to wail but most were stuck silent to their seats, in terror. The compartment doors were thrown open.

"Luggage inspection!"

The older children scrambled to take their cases and haversacks from the luggage racks above the seats.

"*Schnell! Schnell!* Open up," the Nazi soldiers screamed, as they moved along the carriage. Any bag that wasn't opened up fast enough was torn apart.

Soon the carriage was strewn with clothes and possessions, as the men searched for anything of value. Just as Rachel had predicted, nothing escaped their eagle eyes. When they caught a young child with twenty marks, he got a vicious clout across the head, even though his protests about not knowing it was there rang true. Necklaces were yanked from around girls' necks. Heinz held his breath as a soldier ordered a young girl to remove her earrings. The girl's hands were shaking, as she tried but failed to do what he said. He nudged her with his rifle, terrifying her even more. The child stared, tears rolling silently down her face.

"Schnell or I will tear them out." The guard motioned what he would do with his arms as she didn't seem to understand him. She tried again, but her hands were shaking too much.

Rachel stepped forward. Heinz wanted to scream at her to sit back down but he didn't utter a sound. Rachel removed the girl's earrings calmly, before handing them to the soldier. The look he gave Rachel made Heinz's hair stand up on the back of his neck. It wasn't the look one gave a child.

Heinz moved so suddenly that Liesel, sitting on his lap, protested with a squeal and then roared. It got the man's attention, giving Rachel a chance to dart back into the crowd of children.

A soldier stopped in front of Liesel. "What's wrong with that rat? Trying to hide something valuable in its clothes?"

Before Heinz could react, the man grabbed Liesel from his arms. Liesel's cries soared as her arms flailed about, in protest at the rough handling. The soldier shook her as if she was a small dog. Heinz stepped forward but it was Tomas who came to the rescue.

"Stop that. You're scaring her, you bad man. Adults don't hurt babies. Go pick on someone your own size, you big, fat meanie."

His breath caught in his chest. What on earth had

got into Tomas? What would the Nazi do to his brother?

Heinz said, "Sorry, sir, my brother gets a…"

"Silence." The man thrust the protesting Liesel at Heinz. "Undress her. I want proof she is hiding nothing."

He did as he was bid but kept an eye on the Nazi and his brother at the same time. The Nazi held the back of Tomas's neck, making Tomas stand on tiptoe to try and remain on his feet. Tomas's face was white, his large blue eyes taking over most of his face.

"There." Heinz held up his naked sister, who stared at the Nazi too but in silence this time.

The Nazi dismissed Liesel with a wave of his hands, his attention falling to Brown-Bear, clutched in Tomas's hands.

"Give me that bear."

Tomas paled, cuddling the bear closer. "No. He was a present from my papa. Papa died and it's all I have left."

"Give it to me or I will throw you off the train." The soldier lifted Tomas further off his feet. Despite this and the continuous threats, Tomas kept an even tighter hold of the bear. The Nazi's eyes gleamed.

"Give the man the bear, Tomas," Heinz hissed. "Now!"

Tom glanced at him, his eyes wide and filled with tears. "Do I have to?"

Heinz nodded. Tomas hugged the bear and then held it out to the Nazi, who let Tomas drop immediately to the floor. Rachel sprang forward and picked him up, cuddling his face to her neck so he couldn't see the guard produce his dagger. Heinz held his breath as the man used the dagger to rip the toy apart. Not content with removing the head, the soldier cut and ripped off the arms and legs, his temper rising as he found nothing but stuffing inside. Heinz didn't know what would have happened next but for a whistle summoning all the soldiers off the train.

"One day, you'll regret the fact some Jewish cow gave birth to you," the man snarled, as he grabbed pieces of the bear and took them with him. Once he'd gone, Tomas broke free of Rachel's arms. He gathered the leg and arm left behind and tried to put them back together.

"Why?" Tomas sobbed. "Brown-Bear didn't do anything."

Rachel cuddled him, tears running down her own face as they sat down. Heinz couldn't move, his voice wouldn't work. Liesel held her hands out to Tomas, trying to touch his face. Heinz moved closer to his brother and watched as the baby put her arms around Tomas's neck.

Liesel stuttered something that sounded close to, "Liebe, Tomas."

Tomas sat and took Liesel in his arms and cuddled

her close. He didn't speak another word, not even when some lovely Dutch ladies got onto the train and gave them baskets of food. They smiled and tried their best to help the traumatised children. But nothing could console Tomas.

CHAPTER 13

June 1939

"Mrs Matthews!"

Sally turned at the sound of the local vicar calling her. He was new to their parish, a much younger man than they were used to. He pushed his glasses to the top of his nose and ran a hand through his hair, but only succeeded in making it look more untidy. Reverend James Hilton had passed away a few months previously and it had taken time for the parish to find a replacement.

Sally couldn't remember his first name. "Yes, Reverend."

"Would you have time to have a cup of tea with

me at the vicarage? I have something I would like to discuss with you and some of the other ladies in the village." He pulled at his collar, making her think he was nervous.

"Now?"

"Well, I know your husband has already left for training and you must have a lot of chores but if you have the time, that would be wonderful. Time is against us, you see, and I must find some families. Would you mind?"

Sally thought of all the chores she had planned for today, but nothing was so urgent it couldn't wait. Intrigued by the reverend's nervous energy, she said yes and headed into the vicarage.

"I just hope you don't want us to knit more socks. I wasn't blessed when that skill was doled out."

He laughed, and she relaxed. He seemed much easier to get on with than old James Hilton had been. That man had been cranky, even before his arthritis had crippled him. God forgive her for thinking that way of a man of the cloth.

"I think Mrs Ardle may have made some of her buns today. Let me just see. Why don't you hang up your coat and make your way into the study? You know where it is, I assume?"

He saved her from answering by pointing to a door on the right-hand side of the house, while he headed straight on.

She opened the door and gasped; it was such a mess. There was paperwork everywhere, not just covering the desk but the chairs around it as well. There were papers on the small sofa and on the coffee table. She wasn't sure where he meant her to sit.

He followed behind. "Mrs Ardle will bring in the tea. Oh my, what a mess! It looks worse than I remembered. Forgive me, Mrs Matthews, let me take those." He removed some papers from the couch and indicated for her to take a seat.

Sally grinned at him calling Maggie, Mrs Ardle. She couldn't remember anyone doing that before, not even Reverend Hilton.

Maggie waddled in, carrying a tray with some china cups, saucers and a plate of her famous buns.

"Morning, Sally. Don't you look lovely in that gay-looking dress! Don't tell anyone about the mess in here, will you, love? I'm ashamed to be associated with it. Wasn't like this in Mr Hilton's day, may he rest in peace. But Reverend Collins, he spends more time with the people and less at his desk. I wish he'd let me in to tidy up but he says it's confidential. As if I would tell anyone..."

The woman was gone almost as fast as she came in. Sally and Reverend Collins exchanged a smile. Maggie was very caring and would do anything for anyone but she never stopped talking. Always asking questions but never stopping to wait for an answer.

"She treats me like a wayward son."

Sally bit back a smile. She didn't think this man would be amused to find many of the local women wanted to take him in task. His trousers were so long, the hems brushed the ground so were constantly dusty. His hair needed trimming, his glasses cleaning and his suit jacket looked worn at the elbows. He resembled a boy trying to wear his father's suit. If anyone needed a mother figure, he did.

"She must like you. Maggie is kind, sensitive and loyal. She looked after me when my mum couldn't." Sally hesitated, not knowing what the vicar knew about her background.

"So, you think I should let her tidy up in here?"

Sally paused, not wishing to speak out of turn.

He filled the silence. "Please, Mrs Matthews – Sally, if I may. I need all the help I can get. This is my first parish, you see, and I have rather big shoes to fill."

Any reservations Sally had felt fell away. "You're doing a great job already. I've heard nothing but good things about you. I would say, take every bit of help you can. With the war coming – and please let's not pretend it isn't – I think people will lean on the clergy even more than they do already. Anyone can deal with paperwork. It takes a special person to ease another's burden."

"That's exactly what I wanted to speak to you

about, Sally. You're just the kind of person I was looking for."

"I am?" Sally hoped she hadn't landed herself in a whole load of voluntary work. She did her bit, and more, but she didn't have time to deal with some of the ladies who lived up on the hill. Those who sat around for hours on various committees without making any progress – or none that she could see anyway. She preferred to get things done, not sit around drinking tea.

"What did you have in mind, Reverend, because it's only fair I warn you, Mrs Shackleton-Driver is the volunteer commander in this town." And the surrounding county, if truth be told, but Sally didn't want the vicar to hear her speaking ill of her neighbours.

He didn't mask his expression of distaste in time. "Mrs Shackleton-Driver is a formidable lady and her ladies do great work, I'm sure. What I am looking for is someone closer to the ground."

"The ground? You make me sound like a root vegetable," Sally replied.

He turned red and began trying to apologise.

She waved it away. "What you are trying to say, politely, is that I'm working class. That's what I am, and no reason to beat about the bush. I don't move in the same circles as Mrs Shackleton-Driver and her friends."

He flushed again at her frankness, shuffled some papers and then spoke.

"I am looking for ordinary families who would consider an extraordinary gift. The gift of a home to a child who has left everything behind. A German or Austrian child. One from a different religion."

Sally put her cup down to stare at him. "Jewish children. Coming here to Abbeydale?"

He looked surprised. "You've heard of the Kindertransport?"

Sally nodded but remained silent.

"That's a relief. Then I don't need to tell you how urgently we need to find families. As you rightly said, war is coming and time is running out. I've spent time in Germany, and I can't quite believe how bad things have become. The whole Jewish people are in jeopardy and we must save the children. We just have to."

"But how can I help?"

"We need people just like you. People who have a home of their own and could offer shelter to these poor little mites. Do you know, many who are travelling on their own are only five or six years old? Some are even younger." He took a gulp of tea, his cup rattling against the saucer. "Some have seen things no person should see, let alone a child. The events of *Kristallnacht* have left lasting scars."

Sally sat up straighter and frowned. "But surely

they would be better staying with their families? Children that age need their parents, their mothers."

"They do, and in an ideal world we would take the whole families. But immigration is proving difficult. There are many, including those representing our church, who believe mass immigration of the Jewish people will lead to problems. They are also worried about Nazis coming over here."

"Can't they tell the difference between Jewish people seeking safety and Nazi supporters?"

"They should ... But to be frank, I don't think the objections are always rational. The Nazis don't hide their dislike for the Jewish race but there are some people here who share their appalling views," he leaned in closer and whispered, "even some in our own royal family."

Sally's eyes filled up. The thought of any children being hurt always made her angry. She knew a few families in town where the fathers, and sometimes the mothers too, used to beat the children just because they could. She hated to see a child scared or hungry.

"So, you want me to volunteer to look after a child until you can find a Jewish home?"

"Not necessarily. I could lie and say yes, that's exactly it. I guess that might be what the Jewish organisations here would wish. But there are simply too many children and not enough places. I would like you to offer your home to a child for as long as that child needs one."

Stunned, Sally studied his face. "You mean until the war is over."

"At least until then. And I need your help to convince other women to do the same. Do you think there are many in this village who would help?"

"I haven't said yes, yet."

"But you will, won't you? I have been listening to what people say about you, Sally. I don't think I have misjudged you. You will take in a child, won't you?"

Sally couldn't answer that. If she was alone, of course she would, but she was married now. What would Derek think? He wanted children of their own. She'd been secretly hoping she had already fallen pregnant but that hope had been dashed a few days earlier.

He stood, pushing his mousy brown hair back from his forehead, and taking his glasses off to peer at her, an earnest expression on his face. He looked even younger without them.

"Why don't you come and meet the train with me. It's my turn to meet the next one at Liverpool Street Station. You can see how everything works."

She didn't want to disappoint him but nor was she sure she was ready to take on children. "I don't know, Reverend Collins. I'll have to ask my husband, and

Derek is in the army now. I don't know when he'll be back."

"Ah, yes. You're recently married. How do you think your husband would react? Would he want the children to be housed in dormitories at the seaside? That's what's happening. They are taking these poor unfortunates to live in what were supposed to be holiday prefabs. It is freezing cold and not ideal but where else can we put them?"

She hesitated, not wanting the man to think badly of Derek but unwilling to commit herself either. She needed time to think.

"But I thought they had to come to relations? I mean, that was part of the agreement to take these children in." She rubbed her forehead, her temples becoming painful. Her first instinct was to help but this was a bigger commitment than gathering food or clothing for those less well off. This meant opening her first real home to strangers.

"Yes, Sally, some do come over to those who've sponsored them. And in some cases, the children are reunited with parents who arrived here first."

His words pierced her heart. With disbelief, she repeated what he'd said. "You mean the parents came to England and left their children alone at home?"

He put his glasses back on, taking a slight step back as if to show disapproval. "Nothing is ever as simple as it seems. In many cases, fathers and mothers have come to England as a means of saving their children. Only when they have found a home and work here can their children qualify for emigration. A few have aunts, uncles or older siblings living here but few immigrants can afford to provide shelter for someone else's children. They are finding it difficult to survive themselves."

Chastened for having judged someone she didn't know, she remained silent. How often had her mum told her not to judge someone until she had walked a mile in their shoes?

She nodded. "I'll come with you to Liverpool Street and I'll speak to a few of the ladies I know. They might come with us." His face brightened but she hastened to set him right. "Please, don't get your hopes up. I want to help, I do. But these are Germans. I know they are Jewish and, hopefully, that's what people will see first, but there's a lot of anti-German feeling around here. Maggie and her generation lost so much in the last war. My own father died before I was born." She didn't add that her mother hadn't been married and had paid the price for it. He would find out soon enough when the gossips in Abbeydale caught up with him. "It may prove more difficult than you think to persuade people to put aside those views and just see the children for what they are: innocent victims."

"I am a good judge of character, despite my youth

and relative inexperience in this role. I had a wonderful mentor at my last parish. He taught me to try every solution I can think of. I might fail over and over again but every failure means success is just around the corner. Now, forgive me, I have to go. I seem to have a lot of weddings to plan."

Sally drained her tea and gathered the cups together. "I'll carry the tea tray through to Maggie. She'd be upset if I didn't pop my head in and say hello, now that I'm here." She stood up, but then she hesitated.

"What?" His eyes widened with curiosity, not censure. "Please, speak freely."

"Have you considered asking Maggie to help?" She could tell from the look on his face that he hadn't. "Maggie Ardle is well-known and respected in Abbeydale and beyond. She has a big heart and is just waiting to fuss over someone. That would be why you might feel a little henpecked." The flush on his neck told her she was right. "I've known Maggie my whole life, she was a godsend when Mum died."

He nodded as she spoke, a small smile lighting up his face before it disappeared and he looked almost like a scared child. He couldn't be afraid of Maggie, could he? She was a formidable woman but she didn't have a bad bone in her body.

He put his hands in his pockets before taking them

out again, shuffling slightly. He reminded Sally of a small boy.

"Um, perhaps you could ask her to tidy up, too, will you? I don't know how best to approach her."

"I thought you were a grown-up, Reverend."

"Ah, whatever gave you that idea." He laughed, picking up his briefcase before making a sort of salute as he walked out the front door.

Sally giggled as she gathered the cups, saucers and plates and took them into the kitchen. Maggie looked up as Sally came in.

"Gone running, has he? He's always late. Forget his head if it wasn't stuck onto his shoulders. Not a bit like Mr Hilton."

Sally leaned against the counter, facing Maggie. "I thought you didn't like Reverend Hilton, Maggie."

Maggie scrubbed the already-clean table with a cloth. "I couldn't stand him, as well you know, but beggars can't be choosers. I had to keep this job, I had nowhere else to go." Maggie stopped scrubbing and glanced up, a guilty look on her face. "But I wish I had stood up to him years ago. He had a mean streak in him and there's no mistake about that."

For some reason, Sally felt the need to protest even though she had often been the recipient of the vicar's spite. "He was ill."

"Ah, he was towards the end and in so much pain, the poor old devil. Didn't do his mood any good either. But that wasn't it. His father forced him into the church when he wanted to marry and have a family. But the woman he fell for didn't have the inclination to be a poor vicar's wife. She had a different future all planned out. Poor man, I felt sorry for him, to be honest. At first, anyway. Until he said those unforgivable things about your mam." Maggie walked to the sink and rinsed out the cloth. "Now, less said the better, the man is dead, after all. So, what do you think of the youngster?"

Sally didn't blink at the change of subject; she was used to Maggie.

"He means well and has some very ambitious plans, but..."

Maggie rolled her eyes. "You think he might be a little naive."

Sally laughed, as Maggie had hit the nail right on the head. Nothing got by this dear woman.

"I think he may have underestimated the anti-German feeling around here. You know of his plans for the Kindertransport?"

"I do. Sure, aren't we taking in two of the children? Not that he knows it yet. I haven't told him." Maggie put her hand up to her mouth. "You mustn't repeat it, Sally."

"Don't worry, I won't. He asked me to do the same." Sally glanced at Maggie.

Maggie's forehead wrinkled. "What's on your

mind? I didn't think you would hesitate to open your heart to some poor unfortunates."

Sally paused before she answered. "They're German, Maggie. Doesn't that bother you?"

"Me? No, why should it? Because of my Reg? He'd be the first one to take in a child, had he got the chance. These children aren't anything but innocent victims of that madman Hitler. I'd take in the whole lot if I could. How do we teach our children to love thy neighbour if we put conditions on it? I didn't think you would care, Sally Preston."

Sally held up her hand, not bothering to correct Maggie on her use of her maiden name. "Don't get upset with me. I don't care, but I'm a bit worried Derek might. He's going to be fighting the Germans."

"And you think the man you married would hold that against children?"

Shame flooded through her. Her Derek, who helped the old servicemen begging on the streets, who slipped food to the local children when nobody was watching. "No, of course not. Oh, ignore me. I'm just scared, I guess. I don't know anything about raising kids. There was only me." Sally stared at the floor, hating herself for admitting being weak. Maggie moved closer to her, putting her arm around Sally's shoulders.

"You're a born mother, and don't let anyone tell you different. Those children don't want perfection.

They just want what we all do. A warm bed, a roof over our heads and food in our bellies. And someone to love them. To hold them close when they're scared or worried." Maggie put her finger under Sally's chin and gently forced her to look into her face. "That's all anyone wants, isn't it?"

Sally saw the loneliness in the older woman's eyes. She'd been denied those very things when Reg had died. Sure, she had shelter and food but she doubted Reverend James Hilton had provided good company, let alone a shoulder to cry on over the long years of widowhood.

"Maggie Ardle, you are one in a million. That's what you are." She gave the other woman a cuddle. "Those kids who come here are getting a real treasure."

Maggie held her close for a couple of seconds and then broke away, taking out her hanky. "I can't believe we're marching into another war. We didn't learn anything from the last one, did we? That was supposed to be the one to end all wars. What did my Reg, your da and all those other men die for, would you tell me?"

Sally couldn't answer that.

CHAPTER 14

*S*ally, Maggie and Doris sat together on the train from Abbeydale to Waterloo, and then took the Underground from there to Liverpool Street Station. Maggie groaned as Beryl Dalton, a farmer's wife, joined them at the last minute. The reverend had gone on an earlier train, to meet various representatives of both the Jewish congregations and other churches.

"I can't imagine being forced to give up my children, could you, Sally? I mean, when you have one?" Doris swiped a hand across her cheek, but Sally had seen the glistening tear. She squeezed her friend's hand to comfort her. "The women in London had to do the same thing last year. Remember? When they thought bombs would drop on London." Sally took a breath. "You would do the same if it meant keeping your baby safe, Doris."

Maggie nodded in agreement. "At least we only had to send our kiddies out to the country. Those poor women in Germany and Austria are sending their little ones to a totally different country, across the sea."

Beryl sniffed perpetually. Sally was tempted to give her a hanky. The woman moaned about everything, from the price of the train ticket to the cost of sheltering the children. "I reckon some of the mothers are glad to get rid of their children, do you?"

Sally glanced up, realising the woman had addressed her. But before she got the chance to respond, Maggie answered.

"What does that mean? How could you think any woman would give up her own child?"

The woman shrugged. "My Ben says they will be good on the farm. Hard workers, Germans, no matter what else you say about them. I hope Reverend Collins lets us have the pick of the crop, so to speak."

Appalled at what she was hearing, Sally turned to stare out the window. She didn't want to get into an argument with anyone from the village.

Maggie spoke for both of them. "You tell your Ben those children are looking for kindness and shelter from an evil man and his disgusting regime.

They aren't workhorses or unpaid labour for his farm."

"Ben knows that, Maggie Ardle. Don't you go laying down the law to me. Never had kids of your own, did ya? So, what would you know about raising them?"

Sally bit her lip at the woman's unkindness. Thankfully, the train trundled to a stop and they all headed for the exit. Sally took Maggie's hand and squeezed it tightly. She'd seen the tears in her eyes. She knew how much her friend had wanted children, but God had different plans.

"Any child will be lucky to go to the vicarage to live with you and Reverend Collins," she whispered. Maggie squeezed her hand in return. They made their way up the rickety escalator to the main railway-station concourse. Crowds swarmed past them, parents yelling at kids to stay close, the air full of announcements for trains leaving from different platforms, the screech of trains arriving, their drivers applying the brakes, steam filling the air. Train doors opening and banging shut. The noise was too loud for conversation. Sally linked her arm with Maggie's as they followed the directions the reverend had written down.

Sally stopped in her tracks at the sight that greeted them, all background noise from the station fading away. She stared at a crowd of silent, bewildered-looking children, staring wide-eyed around them. Some had tear marks on their faces, some had their thumbs stuck in their mouths, other hands gripping an older child. She saw Maggie pale, tears filling her eyes.

Sally coughed to clear the lump in her throat. "There must be over two hundred of them."

"Look at those children, carrying babies. It's disgraceful." Maggie sniffed. "Look at the poor dears trying to be brave, they must be terrified."

Sally frowned. "They look like they haven't slept in days or had decent food. Some of them are just skin and bone. I'm going to have a word with the reverend."

Maggie pulled her back. "Don't jump to judge. Let him explain."

Sally tried to curtail her anger at the state of the children, instead forcing a smile at the flustered-looking vicar.

"Morning, Maggie, Sally." He ran an ink-covered hand through his hair, the other hand clutching some papers. "Things are a bit chaotic. My German is a bit rusty. Most of the children don't speak English."

Sally swallowed the lump in her throat. The children hung back in a group, as if there was safety in numbers. She spotted a number crying but almost without sound.

She heard Beryl Dalton before she saw her. Her

strident tones rang clear, despite the general noise of the station, as she shouted at one of Reverend Collin's female colleagues.

"I want three boys, about fourteen to sixteen years old. That one, that one and him over there should do nicely."

The reverend blinked a couple of times, muttered something and moved towards his colleague but then seeing the woman had things under control, he turned back to Sally.

Sally tried to keep calm. "I wish she wasn't going to be given any children, but that's unlikely, isn't it? I thought there would be more volunteers."

Reverend Collins smiled weakly. "Not everyone has your kind heart, Sally, and some can't afford to feed another little one. Now let's get to it, shall we? Do you have a preference for a boy or a girl?"

Sally shook her head. She'd written to Derek, telling him of her plans to come to Liverpool Street and maybe offer a child a home for the duration. She'd asked him if he had a preference but he'd never answered. She thought he'd be happy with either a boy or a girl.

She let her gaze roam over the crowd before she spotted a little boy not far off, tear stains marking tracks on his face. Something about him called to her.

She stepped forward and bent down to his level.

"Hello."

The boy stared at her, his eyes widening.

"Do you speak any English?"

He nodded but didn't respond. He looked up at the young man by his side.

The young man said, "My brother Tomas is shy. Papa taught us a little English. My name is Heinz. Are you taking us?"

"Us?" Sally queried. She'd assumed he was one of the group leaders but, looking closer, saw he was only about sixteen years old.

"Me and my brother. We stick together."

The smaller boy said something in German. His brother answered but it wasn't the right reply, as the little boy stamped his foot. The older one tried to reason with him but it was no use. The small boy crossed his arms, a mutinous look on his face.

She intervened. "What's wrong? Is he scared?"

The contempt in the boy's face took her by surprise. "No, he is happy to be in a new country with strangers."

His sarcasm rattled her. "Less of that, young man." Her response did nothing to ease the situation, with the younger boy now crying. Feeling helpless, she looked around for Reverend Collins and motioned him over.

"Sally, what's wrong?"

"I don't know. Tomas, the little boy, wants something but Heinz can't tell me what it is. I wondered if you could translate."

Reverend Collins exchanged a couple of words with Heinz, getting a similar reaction. But Tomas wasn't staying silent. He broke in, speaking rapidly. The reverend bent down to speak to him. He nodded as the child spoke, a little slower by then and accompanied by a lot of gestures. The boy kept pointing at a girl holding a baby, but she was deep in conversation with another English lady.

"Is that his sister? The girl holding the baby?" Sally asked.

"No, I don't believe the older girl is but I think the baby might be. She's some relation to him, and he won't go to a family without her."

Sally noticed Heinz wasn't looking in the baby's direction but staring at a point above the reverend's head. "Why wouldn't the older brother want that too?"

"He says the baby has nothing to do with them."

Sally met Heinz's eyes and knew instinctively he had understood what they were saying. For a second, she saw anger warring with guilt or shame in his eyes. She wasn't sure which.

Reverend Collins motioned her to move slightly to one side.

"Sally, you only intended taking in one child. You might want to pick someone else."

But Tomas seemed to have other ideas. He'd moved to her side, putting his hand in hers. She looked down at the look of trust on his little face, before he gazed towards the baby.

"I don't think I can say no, Reverend. I have the space, and looking after a baby will keep me occupied." Having two children in the house might make the evenings pass quicker. That was when she missed Derek the most. She bent down to the young boy's level.

"Tomas, would you like to come with me. To my home?"

Tomas looked at the reverend, who translated. The boy nodded but said something.

"He said, you must take Liesel, the baby, and Heinz, too. Sally, three children is a lot."

But the decision was taken out of her hands. Heinz spoke to his brother and Tomas replied. Heinz's eyes widened in surprise at whatever Tomas had said. For a second, Sally saw his pain before the mask went up once more.

"Take care of my brother."

And with that, Heinz moved back to the circle of children who had yet to be placed. Tomas started to cry but didn't try to follow his brother. Sally itched to drag the older boy back by the scruff of his collar. How could he walk away and leave such a small child alone with strangers? She'd have taken in the three of them even if Heinz did seem like more than a handful.

She bent down to take Tomas's hand. "Shall we go get your sister?"

Tomas looked in Heinz's direction, sighed deeply and then pulled Sally by the arm over to where the girl carrying the baby stood. Sally spotted another girl, about the same age as Tomas, hanging onto the older girl's coat.

Tomas spoke rapidly in German. Sally watched the older girl's face as her concerned expression turned to anger and she cast more than one dirty look in Heinz's direction.

Maggie and the reverend came over to Sally's group.

"Have you found someone, Sally?"

Sally nodded. "You?"

"Not yet. The reverend and I thought we would wait a bit. Maybe give a home to some children that might not otherwise be picked."

Sally knew what her friend meant. The angelic-looking children, those with nicer clothes and cleaner appearances, had been approached first. Also, siblings, who didn't want to be separated, were harder to place. Most people coming forward had room for only one child. Tomas pulled at her hand to attract her attention, pointing to the baby.

Reverend Collins spoke to the girl.

"This is Rachel Bernstein and her younger sister, Ruth. The baby is Liesel Beck, Tomas's younger sister."

Sally smiled. "Pleased to meet you, Rachel, and you too, Ruth."

Rachel smiled but Ruth just stared. Rachel kissed baby Liesel before handing her over to Sally, speaking as she did so. "She likes to look around when you hold her. See?"

Sally glanced at the baby, who was staring at her with the widest, blue eyes she had ever seen. She felt like she was being assessed, which was just silly as it was only a baby.

"She is hungry and needs a change. I did not know where to go," Rachel added.

Sally moved to take the child in her arms. "I can take care of that. You have done a wonderful job. Your English is very good too."

"Thank you. Mama says it is important we learn a little. We not have much time. Not enough."

Rachel put her arm around her sister's shoulders and pulled her closer. Rachel's bravery made Sally's eyes sting. Liesel held out her arms to Rachel but she simply kissed the child on the head and turned to go back to the crowd. Liesel started crying.

"Rachel, wait." Sally turned to the reverend. "Can you ask her why she hasn't found a family yet? I saw a few women speaking to her."

Reverend Collins tried his best. She could see by Rachel's facial expression that she found the reverend hard to understand but they made the best of things with hand signals and gestures.

"She says many have asked her what skills she has. If she can run a household and how good she is at sewing or baking. One lady wanted to know if she could make cheese." The reverend's anger was barely contained. "She said she will work hard but Ruth has to come too. She won't be separated from her sister."

Maggie put her hand on Rachel's shoulder. "Nor should she be. The poor child has already been torn away from the rest of her family."

Sally could only imagine what the older woman would do if someone asked Rachel those questions in front of her. Then an idea came to her. "Why don't you take Rachel and her sister, Maggie? You can teach Rachel new skills. Ruth and Tomas will have a friend nearby, and Rachel can teach me how to care for Liesel."

Maggie beamed but the look on Reverend Collins's face took her by surprise.

"I don't think that is a good solution. People will talk if I live in a household of women."

Maggie and Sally exchanged a look, before bursting out laughing. Reverend Collins's cheeks grew redder, making them laugh more.

Mr Collins's lips closed tightly at their laughter.

Through clenched teeth, he said, "I hardly think my concerns are amusing."

"Sorry, Reverend. It's the thought anyone would think living with an old woman like me would compromise your reputation. I am hardly a man-eater." Maggie laughed even more. The children just stared at them.

Sally knew she had to get him onside and assure him they weren't making fun of him.

"We're sorry, Reverend. We didn't mean to embarrass you but I think our community would see your actions for what they are. Those of a caring individual, showing by example what our community can do."

He was slow to smile. "Do you really believe that?"

"Yes, of course. Some people may talk about you but you can't live your life trying to please everyone. That's a losing game."

Reverend Collins looked thoughtful but didn't get a chance to think for long as Liesel decided the matter for them. She wriggled and held her hands out for Rachel, as she started to scream. Sally almost dropped her in shock. Where had the angelic baby of five minutes ago gone and what was this bundle of rage in her arms? She didn't know what to do. It had been years since she had looked after neighbours' children.

Rachel moved fast, taking Liesel from Sally and

holding her close, singing to her. The baby settled, her wails soon lessening to loud sobs.

"She's very wet," Rachel said. "I have one clean nappy left in her bag but I…" Her voice trailed off as she looked around, biting her lip.

Fed up with waiting for Reverend Collins to make a decision, Sally took control. "Maggie, please look after Tomas and Ruth while I show Rachel where to change Liesel. Reverend, can you tell Tomas we'll be back?"

Reverend Collins attempted to explain but Tomas and Ruth weren't being left behind. Tomas held onto Sally as Ruth grabbed her sister's coat.

"I could use the facilities too. Why don't we all go? The children should go to the bathroom before we get on the Tube." Maggie turned to Reverend Collins. "Will you please mind their luggage?"

Sally led the way, with Maggie bringing up the rear behind the children. They found the bathroom, and soon Liesel had been changed, everyone had used the facilities and they arrived back to find Reverend Collins. Sally happened to see Heinz with the farmer's wife. Her heart ached for him despite his previous behaviour. She smiled but he looked away.

"Let's go home, shall we?" Maggie suggested. "We can have our picnic on the train to Chertsey. Everywhere here is too busy and crowded. The children look tired and I'm not a young woman."

Sally smiled at that. Maggie had more energy than most women half her age.

"What will happen to the children who aren't placed?" Sally asked.

"They will go on to children's homes for now. They will find jobs for the older ones. The younger ones..." Reverend Collins paused before changing the subject, "Can you manage the journey home by yourselves? I have to deal with some administrative matters."

"We don't need babysitting, do we, Sally? Let's go." Maggie marched off, the children following her in a line like ducklings.

Sally smiled at the reverend's expression. "She's a diamond, isn't she?"

THE JOURNEY HOME WAS AN ADVENTURE. They spotted Heinz and two other boys with the farmer's wife further down the Tube platform but he made no attempt to interact with the children, despite Tomas calling out to him. Rachel had put her arm around Tomas and whispered something to him, while Sally wanted to thump Heinz for hurting the poor child.

The children weren't keen on the Underground but they stared out the windows when they got on the train to Chertsey. Sally spotted Heinz approach their carriage but at the last minute get into the one next to them. She glanced at Tomas, but thankfully he didn't appear to have noticed.

Rachel told them a little about their journey from Germany to England but they both sensed the young girl was keeping the worst of the details to herself.

Maggie stood up and shook the crumbs of their picnic from her dress. "Next stop is ours. Come on, everyone."

Tomas hesitated, shooting a question at Rachel. She answered him, before translating.

"He wanted to know if Heinz is getting off now, too."

So, he had seen his brother get on the train. Sally smiled at Tomas before answering, "Yes, he'll be staying near our village."

"Will we get to see him?" Rachel asked.

Was there an understanding between Rachel and Heinz? They appeared to be of a similar age.

"The farm is quite far from the village but the farmer brings his family to church on Sunday. There's the farmers' market too, on Saturday."

Rachel bit her lip, her cheeks flushing. "Church? You will make us go to this place?"

Sally hadn't given it any thought. She glanced at Maggie for guidance but the older woman shrugged.

"I think you should discuss it with Reverend Collins, Rachel." At the paleness of her face, Sally added, "I don't believe you will be forced to attend if that's something against your beliefs."

Rachel sighed. "I don't think Papa would like it."

At the abject misery in her face, Sally risked giving her a hug. "Sweetheart, you'll be well looked after at the reverend's. Maggie is a wonderful woman."

She didn't know if Rachel understood everything that she'd said but the girl looked a little relieved, giving Sally a small smile. Sally put her head back on the seat, closing her eyes, thinking of Derek. What would he say to the fact she had taken in two children, not one? She'd write to him as soon as they got back. Maybe he could get leave and come and meet them.

The whistle announced they'd arrived. Rachel carried Liesel, so Sally gathered the bags together, taking them down from the luggage rack. Ruth took Tomas's hand and led him off the train, following Rachel. Sally glanced around their seat to check for anything left behind.

She heard a voice say, "Shouldn't be bringing those foreigners over here. Got enough kids of our own, don't we?"

Sally looked up but the man who'd spoken wasn't speaking to her. He was talking to the person sitting opposite him.

"Germans, they sounded like. Never forget that

language. Heard enough of it in the trenches. What's a bunch of Jerries doing, coming here, then?"

Sally had heard enough. "Those children are on the run for their lives. The least you can do, sir, is have a little heart."

With her own heart racing, Sally stepped down from the carriage and slammed the door shut behind her. The satisfaction didn't last long. Was that the welcome that awaited these poor children? Couldn't people understand Hitler was *their* enemy too?

CHAPTER 15

Teeth chattering with the cold, Heinz tried to get comfortable on the lumpy bed. The thin wool blanket, covered in animal hairs, itched his chin. He'd heard the weather in England was worse than Berlin but how could it be so cold in August. The wind and rain rattled the window, and every so often a streak of lightning lit up their room, highlighting the patches of dark mould on the walls.

"Heinz?" one of the boys sharing the freezing cold bedroom whispered.

"I told you to call me Harry. Heinz was German, I'm English now."

"Can't see how you think changing your name makes any difference," Leon said.

"Hitler took my family and my home—"

Leon interrupted. "Yeah, we've heard it all before. What are we going to do? Run away? If we stay here, that grumpy old git will kill us. Between the cold and the lack of food and the work he wants us to do, being in a camp seems better."

"You've never been in a camp."

"You have. Is it much worse than here?"

"You've no idea what you're talking about. Go back to sleep."

"Heinz, what do you think happened to Manfred? Wasn't he brave to hit the farmer?"

"Shut up and sleep." Heinz turned on his side. Manfred was probably in prison, although the four-teen-year-old had only hit the farmer after being belted one too many times. A uniformed guard had arrived at the farm last night to collect him.

He heard Leon sniffling, trying to block out the sound of his tears with his pillow. Despite feeling bad for being short with his roommate, he wasn't about to admit he'd thought about running away. But Tomas was close by. Regardless of what he'd said to his brother in the train station, he'd made a promise to look after him, and that was one promise he was going to keep.

The farmer insisted the boys join the family at church on a Sunday. Harry didn't protest. Not that he was interested in prayer or converting, but it took him into town. He wondered if the woman would make Tomas go to church, but the first couple of times, his brother wasn't there.

* * *

ONE DAY, all his hours of boredom finally paid off.

"Heinz! Heinz!" Tomas had broken away from the woman and raced across the street. "Rachel and Ruth live with the reverend so I get to see them every day. Rachel helps *Tante* Sally with Liesel. *Tante* Sally doesn't have a baby of her own but she's learning." Tomas took a breath before adding, "I knew you'd come into town someday. I told *Tante* Sally you wouldn't stay away. How are you?"

Harry picked up his five-year-old brother and threw him into the air as he had done in the past. Tomas giggled, saying, "more, more," as Harry repeated the action.

Then he set him on his feet. "It's only been three weeks but you've grown," Harry exclaimed.

"*Tante* Sally feeds me all the time. The food's not as nice as home but she tries. She's really nice. Heinz, why can't you come live with us?"

"Because I can't. My name is Harry now. Don't call me Heinz anymore, and speak English."

Tomas drew back at his tone. Harry wanted to

kick himself. He reached out but Tomas pushed his hand away.

"Papa wouldn't like it." With that, Tomas strode across the street without looking back.

Harry called him but he didn't stop. The farmer shouted at him to get into the church.

Harry glowered at the reverend the whole way through the service. It was his fault for bringing them to this village. They should have left him and Tomas alone. They could have gone to Dovercourt Camp with some of the older boys. Then he might not ache all over, his hands cut to shreds. But most of all, he might still have a brother.

After the service, the reverend greeted everyone as they left. The farmer shook his hand as did the wife, both thanking the minister. Harry walked past the outstretched hand.

When they got back to the small cart the farmer used to save on petrol, Harry got a cuff around the back of the neck. "Treat your betters with more respect, boy. Englishmen are gentlemen."

Harry stared sullenly into the distance. Nothing this man did could come close to the pain inflicted by missing his brother. Only when the farmer was deep in conversation with his wife did Harry close his eyes. Then he allowed the memories to come. Papa laughing by the fire, Papa gazing at Liesel, his eyes lit up in wonder. Liesel looking at him on the train, the protective feelings that she raised in him. He'd let Papa down. The last thing Papa had said was to mind his brother and sister. A sole tear ran down his cheek. It was pointless thinking of Papa. What did one promise matter, when everything had changed beyond recognition?

CHAPTER 16

3RD SEPTEMBER 1939

Tears filled Sally's eyes as she turned off the radio to the sounds of "God Save The King". Her hand caressed the top of her prized possession. She remembered Derek's smile as he'd presented her with the gift that last June morning before he left.

"Derek, darling, be safe. I love you," Sally whispered, before saying a quick prayer to keep her husband safe and make the war short, so he could come home. She wished he'd write but as yet there had been no reply to her letter asking him about taking in children, nor the second telling him what she'd done. Was he annoyed? Disappointed? She pushed those thoughts to the back of her mind. Derek would want her to help.

Her back door banged, and Maggie came in, closely followed by Rachel and Ruth.

"I know we expected the news but I can hardly believe we're officially at war. The girls wanted to be near Tomas and Liesel." Maggie's look spoke volumes.

"Rachel, you know the way." Sally forced her voice to sound cheerful. These children had been through enough already. They didn't need to see her crying. "Off you go while I make Maggie a cup of tea. I made some cake yesterday so I'll give that to you later."

"Thank you, Aunt Sally."

Sally smiled. Tomas had started calling her *Tante* Sally. She'd corrected his German automatically. Soon all the children called her Aunt Sally.

She closed the door behind Rachel, and Maggie took a seat at the table, picking at imaginary crumbs on the tablecloth. Sally knew Maggie was just agitated and not finding fault with her housekeeping.

"What will happen now, Sally? To those poor children? They won't be able to send letters to Germany or get any from their parents. Rachel's had a couple from her mother. She doesn't say a lot but always asks Rachel to try to find her a job in England. We were working on it but now it's too late, isn't it?"

"Maybe she got out before they shut the borders?"

Sally knew it was unlikely but she hated to see Maggie upset.

"I don't think so. Reverend Collins was in tears earlier. They had another train ready to leave from Prague. I don't know why it was delayed but it was. Now it's too late. All those children are stuck under the rule of the Nazis. Oh dear God, Sally, what's to become of them?"

Maggie broke down and Sally pulled her into her arms. She hugged the older woman, letting the storm of weeping pass.

"Maggie, dry your eyes. We can't let the children see how upset we are."

"I'm so selfish. You are much stronger than me, and you, with your Derek at war. I should be comforting you, not the other way around."

"You support me every day of the week and twice on Sundays." Sally smiled through her own tears. "It's true. Who taught me how to look after two youngsters? I couldn't cook for them if it hadn't been for you teaching me when I was younger. I owe you a lot, Maggie Ardle, and you know it. Derek will be fine, just as those amazing children will be too. At the end of the war, we'll find their parents and reunite them. In the meantime, we just have to keep them fed and watered and give them lots of cuddles."

"You make them sound like farm animals."

Maggie gulped some tea, then said, "Reverend Collins is worried about something else."

"What?"

"Tomas's older brother and the other boys at the farm. He said he saw him at church on Sunday. The boy was barely civil to him. Not at all like the well-mannered young man Tomas is. He says he's very pale, with large, dark circles around his eyes. He looks thinner than he did when he arrived on the train. He implied he might be working too hard."

"Working at what?" Sally's legs wobbled. "Are you saying Reverend Collins thinks those boys are being mistreated on the farm?"

"He didn't say that, as such." Maggie wouldn't meet her eyes, her hands fiddling with the sleeve of her blouse.

Sally's stomach turned hard with dread. "But he implied it. We have to do something, Maggie. We can't let that horrible woman mistreat those boys. They've suffered enough."

Maggie's pinched tension-filled expression matched her frustrated tone. "But what can we do? I can't offer Harry or any of the boys a home, not when we have the girls living with us. It wouldn't be proper, especially as the vicarage isn't big enough and they aren't related by blood."

Sally stirred her tea. She could still see Tomas's brother, as clearly as if he stood in front of her. So proud and brave, trying to hide his pain. Rachel had confided in her about Tomas meeting Harry on the street.

"Tomas is upset at his brother changing his name to Harry. Did Rachel say anything to you about it?"

Maggie shook her head. "The poor lad, he must be trying to fit in. There's a fair bit of anti-German feeling around from the last war. It's not going to get any better. We have to do something for them, Sally. One of us should take a trip out to the farm."

"And do what? We can't make trouble. Constable Cooper would have our guts for garters."

Maggie picked up her cup, cradling it in her hands. "I remember Jack Cooper when he was smaller than your Tomas. Leave him to me. Now, what reason do you have for visiting?"

"Me?"

"I can't go. Reverend Collins wouldn't like it."

Sally choked on her tea, causing it to spurt out of her mouth in a very unladylike manner. "You've never let that stop you before."

Maggie wouldn't look her in the eyes. Sally stared at her friend until she gave in.

"Okay, you got me," Maggie admitted. "I'm afraid if I go and find the boys mistreated, I won't be able to control my temper. You know Beryl Dalton winds me up just by looking at her. She's a horrid old bat."

Sally knew the two had history; the comments the farmer's wife had made about Maggie never having children were just one of many snide remarks made over the years.

"I'll go, but can I take Rachel? I don't know how much English Harry can speak. I know he understands more than he lets on."

"Yes, take Rachel. I'll mind Liesel and Tomas. That's settled. You can go tomorrow if it's dry."

Sally glanced at Maggie's innocent expression. Yet she was left with the feeling Maggie had planned this outcome before she'd even walked into Sally's house.

CHAPTER 17

*T*he next morning, Sally dropped off Liesel and Tomas at the vicarage, then she and Rachel set out on the walk to the farm. Sally had planned on riding a bicycle but Rachel wasn't keen as she'd never learned how to cycle. Still, it was a bright, dry day, and Rachel had long legs so could keep up with Sally. A walk would do them both good.

She smiled at the girl as they set off. "I love how you do your hair, it's naturally curly, isn't it? I have to sit for hours in pin grips to get mine to go even slightly wavy." Sally slipped a hand through her straight dark hair.

Rachel smiled shyly and touched her hair self-consciously. "I would like to have hair like yours. Mine is so … what do you call it when it puffs up like this?" Rachel pushed her hair up on both sides of her face. "I look like a wet dog."

Sensing Rachel was trying to be funny, Sally giggled before telling the young girl she looked fine. "So, how are you settling in? Are the children nice to you at school?"

"Yes, most are. The teachers too. It is some parents who find it hard to be pleasant. They do not smile."

Rachel wasn't smiling much either. Sally guessed she was worried about her mother. They walked in silence for a few minutes until Sally plucked up the nerve to ask Rachel about her family.

"Maggie said you were waiting on news of your mother."

"Yes." Rachel sighed as she picked a leaf before shredding it to pieces. "But the letter did not come. No telegram either. Now the borders are closed. She won't get out. They will take her away," the girl caught her breath before adding, "like Papa."

Sally rushed to reassure her. She wanted to put her arm around Rachel's shoulders but something told her the girl wouldn't appreciate it. "It might be different for women, Rachel. Your mother is likely to have lots of friends. Maybe some will be able to help her. Don't lose hope."

Rachel picked another leaf and stared at it. She bit

the inside of her cheek before looking at Sally, her eyes full of doubt.

"You are kind, but it is hard. I try to tell Ruth everything will be fine but I am old enough to understand. Mama and Mrs Beck wouldn't have sent us away if there was no danger." Rachel kicked at the ground. "Trudi – Mrs Beck – she knew some people. They warned her to leave years ago but nobody would listen to the women. The men like Papa and Dr Beck, they were blind. They do not see until it is too late. Trudi tried everything but it cost money. She didn't have enough for everyone. She had some jewellery she managed to hide from the Nazis; they sent their soldiers to take everything we had, from fur coats to gold, diamonds and food. Trudi spent it all on the children. Mama did the same."

Sally didn't know what to say to comfort the girl. She didn't want to make false promises. Rachel was not a child. At her age, most English girls were out working. Rachel's command of spoken English was getting better. She still missed words out of sentences. She needed to brush up her written skills before she could land a well paid job.

"What would you like to do, Rachel? When you are older, I mean?"

"I would like to be a doctor but that dream will cost too much money. Maybe I could go into nursing. I think they will need nurses in Palestine."

"You want to go and live in Palestine?"

"Yes, among my people. My brothers, Gavriel and Izsak, they planned to go there. If they got out of Germany." Rachel took a deep breath. "We will be safe there. I wanted to go there for years but my father wouldn't listen to me. He didn't like to listen to children. He thinks he knows everything. Now he is dead."

Sally knew Rachel wasn't as heartless as she sounded. It was her way to stop the hurt from destroying her. She'd seen how well the girl cared for Ruth, as well as Liesel and Tomas.

"I think your parents did a wonderful job with you, Rachel. I would be proud to have a daughter like you. What do you think of Heinz changing his name to Harry?"

"I think he is running away from himself. He is so angry. He has been since his father married his nanny. Heinz, I mean Harry," Rachel flashed her a shy smile before continuing, "he idolised his mother and thinks Trudi took her place too quickly. Trudi, Liesel's mother, was a young girl without a family. She didn't steal Heinz's mother's place. If anything, his father is to blame for what happened. I don't believe Trudi saw Heinz's father as anything other than her boss until he, he … what you call it when men give you flowers and perfume?"

"Courted her?" Sally was going to use the word

seduced but quickly remembered Rachel was only fifteen. She didn't correct her use of Heinz instead of Harry. That would come in time.

"Yes, he courted her. She loved the boys, not just Tomas. She and Heinz were very close but that changed when she fell pregnant with Liesel. Trudi married his Papa and that was when he started being angry with everyone. The Nazis, we can understand." Rachel shrugged. "You cannot find a Jew who likes Hitler, but with Heinz, he hates everyone."

"Except Tomas and you…" Sally prompted.

Rachel coloured. "He loves Tomas. Tomas loves him too but also loves his sister. How could anyone not love Liesel? She is a baby. Totally innocent of everything. Heinz is stupid. Trudi sacrificed a lot to get him out of Dachau and onto the Kindertransport train. She was hoping to get my brothers out too. I don't know if she was successful."

"Dachau? What was that?"

Rachel's face whitened. She bent to pick up a stick and snapped it in two. "A camp where they sent the men after *Kristallnacht*. Some boys too, including Heinz and my brothers. Heinz doesn't talk about it. Bad things happened there. My father, Dr Beck and other men we knew didn't come back. My brothers, they were still there when we left. Mama was told to collect my father from the police station. When she arrived, they gave her an envelope full of ashes."

Sally stopped walking, horrified at what she was hearing. Rachel spoke in such a monotone voice – as if this was something that happened every day.

"Rachel, that's horrific. Your poor mother, and you girls. I'm so sorry."

"They said he died from his heart condition, but we heard rumours of people murdered, beaten up, tortured." Rachel threw her hands up. "I don't know what happened to him but he is dead. At least we know that for sure. Some people just disappeared."

Sally put her hand out to comfort the girl but withdrew it as Rachel kept talking.

"Rumours. That is all we have. My brother, they were alive when Heinz left Dachau. So, he says."

"You don't believe him? He'd have no reason to lie about something like that, Rachel. Would he?"

Rachel shrugged. "Person lie all time. Sometimes to protect you but it is still a lie. Like they said that Mama and the women would be safe. Why would they send us here if that was truth?"

As Rachel got more agitated, her English got worse. *How can I tell her things will improve?* Sally wondered.

"It was better when I could get letters. But now, nothing. I hate not knowing where Mama is." A tear fell from Rachel's eyes, and then a second one, but she swiped them away and kept walking.

Sally wanted to hug her but didn't, sensing the

girl was close to breaking point, and she didn't want to push her over that edge.

CHAPTER 18

*T*hey walked along the lane in silence. Sally glanced at the blackberry bushes. She should bring the children up here at the weekend to collect the ripe berries. They could make a crumble or blackberry-and-apple tart. She smiled, as memories of her own childhood hit, the taste of the berries squishy on her tongue, the juice running down her chin. Her mother warning her to watch out for thorns, and Maggie telling her mother to leave the child be.

"You have a nice smile," Rachel commented, breaking the silence.

"I was just thinking of my childhood; we used to pick blackberries up this lane. Me, my mum and Maggie."

Rachel looked around her. "Your mother lives near here?"

"She did but she died when I was twelve. We lived with my grandmother but Maggie was the one who looked after me. She taught me how to cook and keep house and got me a job up at a big house in Virginia Water. That's not too far away from here."

"You couldn't stay with your grandmother?"

"No." Sally didn't add that her grandmother had never wanted her, seeing her as a constant reminder of her daughter's shame.

They walked in silence for a while before Rachel asked, "What was she like, your mother?"

"Mum smiled a lot, even when she had little to smile about. She worked very hard, even when she was sick. She dreamed about buying Rose Cottage, the house I live in now. Derek – my husband – his father was born there but his family moved away when his dad was young and the house was left empty. Mum used to keep it clean, ready for when the family wanted to come down from London but they never did."

"My mother is not like yours. She is very strict and always has to know best."

Despite the words, Sally heard the sadness behind them. "Rachel, your mother loves you. If she didn't, you wouldn't be here. It's normal for children to think their parents are too strict. You must miss your family so much."

Rachel gave a slight nod but remained silent for a

while as they walked on. When she did speak, she changed the subject.

"So, how did you meet your husband?"

Sally's cheeks turned red.

Rachel looked at her curiously. "I'm sorry, I didn't mean to make you shy."

"You didn't. I always go red when I think about it. I thought Derek was trying to break into Rose Cottage, and I ran and got the village policeman."

"Break into…?" Rachel looked puzzled.

"Steal things from the house," Sally explained. "I came back with Constable Cooper. He tried to arrest Derek, who, in fairness, had broken a window trying to get in. He couldn't find his key. It took a while to convince us he owned Rose Cottage. His father had died and left it to him in his will."

Rachel looked a little confused. Sally wasn't sure how much she understood.

"It was his cottage and he wanted to see what it was like inside. He told me I had to agree to go to lunch with him to make up for thinking he was a criminal. We got engaged three months later and married three months after that."

"He is a good-looking man. I see his photograph in your house, you are a lucky woman."

"He is handsome, isn't he? But, Rachel, he is kind and has such a big heart. That is more important, don't you think?"

Rachel wasn't listening; she'd stopped walking and was staring into the distance.

"Harry is there, in the field." Rachel pointed to a group of boys ahead of them. They were picking or planting something, it was too hard to tell from this angle.

They kept walking until the boys called out to Rachel. Harry came running down to see her. He spoke rapidly to her in German but Rachel answered in English.

"Don't be rude, Harry. Sally came to see you today. She doesn't understand German."

To his credit, he apologised. In halting English, he asked her how his brother was.

Sally smiled. "Tomas is wonderful. Such a clever young man and so good with his sister. Liesel is finding her feet and is a joy to look after." She couldn't resist talking about Liesel even though he hadn't asked about her. She glanced at Rachel and spotted approval in her eyes.

Harry muttered something, to which Rachel reacted by hitting him on his arm. It was a mere tap, really, but to Sally's surprise Harry flinched.

She looked at him curiously. "Roll up your sleeve," Sally asked. When he hesitated, she glanced at Rachel, who said something in German. He shook his head and went to move away but Sally stood in front of him.

"Pull up your sleeve now, or I'll call the farmer."

Harry scowled but did as he was told. Rachel's gasp mirrored her own feelings. Every patch of skin was covered in bruises, old and new.

"Is your whole body like this?"

Harry refused to answer.

"I'm talking to you. Answer me," Sally shouted, getting the attention of the two other boys. "Has someone been hitting all of you?"

Harry glanced at the other boys, both of whom looked younger than he did, before he nodded.

Sally almost vomited. She couldn't believe what she was seeing.

"I'm not having it. That's not any way to treat a child." She set off in the direction of the farmhouse, calling back, "Rachel, stay with Harry until I get back." She'd seen the way he looked at Rachel. He wouldn't let any harm come to her.

Chickens shrieked and fled from her path as she stormed towards the house. A couple of horses stared at her from their stalls in the barn, but the pigs didn't look up from their trough. She could smell the cows, the unpleasant tang of dung in the air, but she didn't see them.

Rage surged through her as she marched into the farmyard and up to the back door. Knocking, she didn't wait for a reply but stormed into the kitchen. Beryl Dalton screamed and dropped the bowl she'd been carrying into the sink, putting a hand up to her ample chest. Sally noticed she didn't spill any of the bowl's contents. The smell of just-baked bread mingled with fried liver and onions.

The farmer jumped up from a table that was almost covered in plates of food. "What on earth, woman! You've put the fear of God into the missus. Are the Germans chasing you?"

Sally couldn't control her fury. "Do you think that's funny, Mr Dalton? As funny as leaving bruises all over those boys out there in that field of yours? You wouldn't treat an animal the way you've treated those children."

Dalton sat back down, picking up a slice of bread to mop up the gravy on his plate. He took a large bite before speaking with his mouth full, spraying her with bits of food as he spoke.

"Germans. Those boys are nearly grown-up. You stay out of it."

"I won't stand by and let you treat anyone like that, you miserable old windbag. And as for you, Beryl Dalton, you should be ashamed of yourself. You heard what the reverend asked for. A warm house, good decent food and shelter, for victims of war. Victims, not enemy agents. And the two of you sitting in church as if butter wouldn't melt in your mouths."

Dalton stood up and growled, "Who the heck do

you think you are, marching into my house and attacking my wife? Get out before I throw you out."

"You can huff and puff as much as you like, Dalton, but you'll not lay a hand on me. My Derek would have you in a box before you knew what hit you."

He took a step towards her, his hand slightly raised.

Sally felt the first flicker of fear. What was she doing? She should have gone for the constable and the reverend, not let her temper get the better of her and try and tackle this pair of bullies alone. She resisted the urge to flee, holding his gaze.

His eyes narrowed. "He isn't here, though, is he? Think he'll come back from France? Anything could happen."

His words, said in such a normal voice, chilled her. She'd expected him to rant and roar but this was more frightening. Seconds ticked by.

"Get out of my house and go home where you belong, while you still can."

Sally's heart hammered, thunder ringing in her ears. He wouldn't hit her, would he? He knew she'd have the reverend and the constable back at the farm before he could sing "God Save the King".

"Aunt Sally, are you fine?"

Sally's heart slowed, her breathing returning to normal at the sound of Harry's voice next to her, his heavy shoes stamping across the stone floor. She almost sagged in relief as he gripped her hand. Rachel slipped in silently, standing behind Harry. She glimpsed the other boys through the doorway but they stayed outside.

The farmer's attention swung to the young man.

"Aunt Sally? What are you calling her that for? She's no aunt of yours."

Harry stayed silent, his eyes never leaving the brute of a man.

Sally found her voice. Pushing aside her fear, she spoke quickly. "I know you're dealing on the black market." Sally pushed her hands closer to her skirt and crossed her fingers as she lied. "I have proof. You should be careful who you trust as it's easy to get thieves to turn on one another. I'm offering you a deal. You let Heinz, I mean Harry, come with me. Today. I won't say a word."

Beryl glanced at her husband, who had stiffened at Sally's comments.

So they *were* dealing on the black market. Would her threat to report them work?

Harry spoke up. "You come to take me home. I pack."

His declaration was as much a surprise to her as it was to the Daltons. Mr Dalton glanced between them but Mrs Dalton was faster to recover.

Beryl strode over to Harry, her finger pointing at

him. "You're not going anywhere," she said. "We signed papers for you to stay here and that's where you will stay."

Sally saw the doubt in her eyes, despite her aggressive tone. She took a step closer to the woman, speaking directly to her. "Harry didn't sign himself into slavery, Mrs Dalton. He's coming with me now and I suggest you make no attempt to stop us. If you do, I will return with the constable, the reverend and someone from the Ministry of Food."

At this, Beryl took a step closer to her husband.

Sally pushed her point home. "We both know the Ministry would be very interested to examine your books and the entire farm from top to bottom. I'm sure they will also inform the school board of the conditions in which you're keeping children, using them as slave labour."

She knew she'd won then, from the look Dalton gave her.

He hissed, "Get out and take that dirty kraut with you. Don't darken my doorstep again." He turned his back on her but Beryl stepped forward.

"You'll be sorry for this, Sally Matthews. I've seen you strutting around like you are somebody, not the result of that slapper of a mother of yours dropping her drawers for any Tom, Dick or Harry."

Sally gasped. Her mother may have been pregnant and unmarried but she was far from what Beryl suggested. She'd been walking out with Sally's father for years when the Great War broke out. She'd fallen pregnant when her fiancé came home on embarkation leave in 1918. They were supposed to get married but didn't have time to have the banns announced or get a licence. Her dad never came back and her mother had paid a high price.

Sally clenched her palms into fists by her side, her voice shaking. "Don't you say another word, Beryl Dalton." She'd love nothing better than to slap the woman across the face, but violence was never the answer. She held Beryl's gaze until the other woman looked away. Only then did she move towards the door.

But Beryl wasn't finished. She snarled, "Just you wait. I'll pay you back for this."

Gritting her teeth, Sally refused to let Beryl see her threat had upset her. She turned on her heel, leaving the kitchen to stand waiting for Harry to come back. She wished she could take the other two boys with her but she didn't have anywhere to put them. "I'll send the police to help you," she said to the scared-looking boys. If possible, they looked more terrified at this than they had before.

Rachel put her hand on Sally's arm. "The German police took many men away. They don't trust police."

Shaking, she asked Rachel to reassure them she would send help up to the farm. Rachel rattled off something in German but the boys clearly didn't believe her. Sally spoke again, "I promise I won't leave you here another night."

She'd insist Reverend Collins find a new place for them. Anywhere was better than this farm. The boys turned and walked away, shoulders slumped. She bit down on her lip, determined not to lose control. Not here, while Dalton was probably watching her.

Harry seemed to take forever but it was only a few minutes before he arrived with a similar brown suitcase to the one Tomas had, although his was more battered and worn-looking.

They walked out of the farmyard in silence. Sally took several deep breaths to slow her racing pulse.

Once they got to the farm boundary, Harry asked, "Where now?"

Sally slammed the gate shut behind her, although part of her was tempted to leave it open. So what if Dalton lost a couple of animals? "You're coming home with me Hei– sorry, Harry. I want to speak to the constable and the reverend but regardless, I am not leaving you here."

"There will be trouble."

There most likely would be but she didn't care. She couldn't turn her back on this boy. She already loved Tomas and Liesel like her own, and he was their flesh and blood.

"Don't you worry about trouble. I can handle the

Daltons. Now come on, let's get out of here. The place gives me the heebie-jeebies."

Rachel scrunched up her face. "The what?"

"Oh, it's just a made-up word for something that gives you the shivers or a bad feeling."

"Heebie-jeebies!" Rachel repeated the phrase a couple of times. "It is a good word. It gives me the heebie-jeebies too."

hey returned to the village without any further incident. Rachel and Harry spoke the whole way home in German and Sally didn't stop them. She needed time to think. What could Dalton do to her? She wouldn't put anything past his spiteful wife.

Sally had never been happier to see the red phone box on the outskirts of the village. Almost home. They would call into the vicarage first.

Sally stopped just before they reached the vicarage gate and turned towards Harry. "Harry, there's one thing you must do for me."

"Yes, Aunt Sally."

She smiled but then turned serious. "If you come to live at my house, you must treat Liesel the same as you treat Tomas. Both children need a happy home.

We have a nice time together and I don't want anyone to ruin that. Do you understand?"

Harry kicked at the ground before a quick reprimand from Rachel made him speak.

"Yes, I understand. I wish to thank you for looking after my brother. Ouch!" Harry glared at Rachel. "And my sister. I will take some of the burden now. They are my family."

"Glad to hear it. Right, let's get inside and collect the young ones. No doubt Maggie will be dying to hear everything. Then we will go home and you can have a bath and find new clothes. I want the doctor to examine you."

Harry paled.

"I don't need a doctor."

"Yes, you do. If only to give me a witness who can testify as to why I removed you from the care of the Daltons."

Rachel hissed something at him in German. He sent a beseeching look at Sally, but although she wondered at the fear in his eyes, she wasn't to be dissuaded. "You must see the doctor."

Rachel spoke again to Harry, who finally shrugged his shoulders before nodding.

Sally asked, "What did you say, Rachel?"

"I told Harry to shut up and do as he was told. If he'd done that from the start, he would never have ended up on the farm. Sometimes boys can be so stupid."

Sally hid a smile, and Harry turned scarlet. He'd obviously understood every word. She sensed Rachel's opinion of him carried more weight than anyone else's, so stayed silent.

Young love was a powerful emotion and she'd bet her life on it, Heinz or Harry, as she must remember to call him now, was head over heels in love with young Rachel.

THEY DIDN'T GET a chance to walk too far before Tomas and Ruth came running, with Maggie, carrying Liesel, trailing behind them. The younger children threw themselves into their siblings' arms. Sally saw Harry wince from the impact but he didn't let on to Tomas. He swung the younger boy right up in the air, who by now was speaking rapidly in German.

Harry put him back down on the ground, saying gruffly, "English, Tomas."

Tomas grimaced but did as he was told. "Maggie made cake. Ruth and I helped. We had icing."

Sally glanced at Maggie, seeing the questions in her eyes. "Rachel, could you take the children into the vicarage, please? I just want a quick word with Maggie."

"Yes, Aunt Sally."

Maggie gave Liesel to Rachel and watched as the five children went indoors, before turning to Sally. "What happened?"

"Maggie, we have to get the doctor, the constable and the reverend. You'd never believe how they are treating those poor children. Beating them and starving them by the looks of it. All the while, Dalton stuffs his mouth and Beryl gets fatter. I swore the two other boys still on that farm would have new homes tonight."

Maggie put her arms around her friend's shoulder. "Sally, love, calm down, you're not making sense. Who's beating the children?"

"Dalton. And maybe his wife too. You should see the poor boys we left behind. They look worse than they did in Liverpool Street. Can't blame them, can you? They've lost their families, their home and now they are being treated worse than animals."

Maggie pushed Sally towards the vicarage. "You go and help yourself to tea. I'll call in to the constable and get him to round up the troops. Can't have the likes of that going on in Abbeydale. This is England. We treat people properly."

Maggie bustled off in the direction of the constable's house. Sally didn't know why she didn't use the telephone but maybe she felt this needed airing in private. The operator wasn't above listening in on calls.

Sally went in to join the children.

Dr King arrived before Maggie got back, explaining he'd had a call from the constable. The old doctor had brought Sally into the world. He'd come out of retirement when war was declared. He never looked happy, but was good at what he did. He treated every call like it was an inconvenience, but underneath the gruff exterior, Sally knew the old man had a big heart. He'd always treated Sally exactly like the other children – unlike Reverend Hilton and many other adults in Abbeydale.

Harry blanched, taking a step back when Sally introduced them but after a quick word from Rachel, he allowed the doctor to take him away to examine him in private. Maggie arrived back as they were waiting.

"Constable is calling in some reinforcements from Chertsey Station and then he'll call here. Did Dr King arrive and is the reverend back?"

Sally nodded. "The doctor is with Harry now. Haven't seen the reverend."

It wasn't long before Harry came back downstairs looking relieved. Sally resisted the urge to cuddle him. Instead, she gave him the key to her house, sensing he might need some time alone.

"Go on home, love. That's my house over there."

She pointed to the house from the window. "I'll be there soon. Don't worry, nobody will hurt you now."

He didn't say anything but squeezed her hand when she gave him the key. Without looking at the doctor, he left.

Rachel glanced at Sally, then said she would take the children for a walk to the park. As she and the children were leaving, Reverend Collins arrived with the constable.

The doctor barely let the door close behind them before he burst out, "That young man has obviously been mistreated by the Daltons. It hasn't helped his old injuries."

Sally couldn't help but stare at Dr King. His uncharacteristic distress made her worry more.

"Old injuries?" Maggie asked, sending Sally a look, but Sally shook her head. She didn't know anything. The doctor continued.

"I believe he was tortured or at the very least given a savage beating, not just once but over a number of days, maybe weeks." He pressed a hand against his breastbone, taking a deep breath before he continued, "He has a number of marks on his torso, upper arms and legs. Cigarette burns and other things I would rather not mention in present company."

Sally couldn't believe her ears. Who had done that? "The Daltons?" she asked.

The doctor shook his head, glancing at Sally

before shifting his gaze to the reverend. "No, it looks like they were content to just beat him. These injuries were inflicted some time ago. Perhaps six months to a year ago. Has he said anything about what happened before he came here?"

"No, but I haven't spoken to him much." Sally shook her head and then remembered. "Rachel said he was in a place called Dachau, in Germany. She said her father died there, after he and her brothers and other Jewish men were rounded up and sent to live there. Harry and his father were sent there too."

"That would explain it. I've heard about Dachau. Although I didn't believe the worst of what I read." The doctor shook his head, his hand stroking his grey beard. "That young man is lucky to have survived, never mind been released, and even luckier to have made it onto the train. Most survivors of the camps don't stay free for long. They disappear or are locked up again. The Nazis don't like examples of their handiwork walking the streets."

Sally told them what Rachel had said about her mother collecting her father's ashes.

Maggie burst into tears. "Those poor darlings. Such lovely girls," Maggie sobbed. "What sort of animals would do something like that?"

Sally handed her a hanky. The doctor coughed before he continued. "I'm hearing similar stories when I go to London to visit my club. Most hope it's lies or exaggerations. I have met many German doctors, fine men. I can't imagine they would condone anything remotely like that. What's been happening in Germany since the early 1930s is a disgrace. What's worse is nobody has done a thing about it, and now we find ourselves in the middle of a war. Another one."

Sally didn't want to discuss the last war. She quickly steered the conversation back to the matter in hand, addressing the reverend. "Those other boys, the ones I left on the farm. What will happen to them? I promised them a new home by tonight. They can sleep on my couch if there's no alternative." Sally was determined not to break her promise.

"We," the reverend glanced at the men, "will go there now. I am very disappointed with the behaviour of two such regular churchgoers. I will appeal to their better natures."

"Good luck with that, Reverend, but you still need to move those boys," Sally muttered. She sensed he heard her, as his eyes widened, though he didn't argue. She had to be alone. To grab a couple of seconds to process everything before she had to put on a smile for the younger children. But she had to speak to the constable first.

She said, "I'd best get home and get some water on for that young man's bath. Thank you for looking after the children, Maggie."

"Pleasure. They were darlings, all three of them. Ruth played mother, Tomas was a soldier, and Liesel was her usual happy self. A little ray of sunshine."

Tears of frustration made Sally's voice shake. "Thank you all. Reverend, be gentle with those boys, they're terrified. Constable, I need to tell you that Mr Dalton threatened me."

The constable's eyes darkened under his raised eyebrows, his jaw clenching, and for a second Sally glimpsed why he could strike fear into those on the wrong side of the law.

"What did he say he'd do?"

"He said Derek wasn't here to protect me so I should go home and mind my own business." Sally didn't add what Beryl had said about her mother. She'd tell that to Maggie when they were alone.

The constable stuck his stomach out as he straightened his shoulders. "I shall remind Dalton that your husband is away fighting for our country. If you have anymore trouble from him, Mrs Matthews, you're to tell me right away. Can't have anyone threatening nice young ladies like that."

Sally blushed. "Thank you." As she walked out the door, she turned to Maggie, "Ask Rachel to drop the children home for me, will you please, Maggie?"

"I'll call to check on you later, Sally," Maggie said. Sally heard her tell the constable to get Dalton on a short leash as she wouldn't be held accountable if he touched a hair on Sally's head.

Good old Maggie, she was always there when she needed her. Sally strolled to her own house, trying to get her emotions in check before she went inside. She had to be strong for the child waiting for her. Despite his sixteen years and his conviction he was old enough to look after himself, she sensed he was terrified. Who wouldn't be, given his experiences?

CHAPTER 20

*S*he opened her front door, calling out to let Harry know she was home. She didn't want to scare him.

She found him in the sitting room. One glimpse at his face told her he'd been crying, but she sensed he'd rather she ignored that. She headed straight into the kitchen.

"Would you like a sandwich while I heat the water for your bath? Dinner won't be ready for a while."

"I can wait. Thank you, Aunt Sally." He gave her a hesitant smile.

"You can call me Sally. You're a man, after all."

He smiled again, completely transforming his face. She could see he'd be handsome once he got regular good food and lost the haunted look from his eyes. How could anyone hurt this young man and others like him? She pushed those thoughts aside. She had to concentrate on the tasks at hand; dissolving into a puddle of tears wouldn't help either of them.

"The bath is upstairs." She pinched herself as she said it. Rose Cottage was the first home she'd had with an indoor bathroom. Shivering, she thought of the old days, in her grandmother's house, when she'd have to fill a tin bath with water, bathe and then empty it out again. Now, thanks to Derek's talents as a handyman, and his savings, she enjoyed all the luxuries. "But it will take a while to get enough hot water. Sit down and I'll make you a drink."

He smiled as he took a seat at the table. "You are kind. Tomas has grown very big. The baby too."

"They are wonderful children." She turned to face him. "Both of them."

He nodded. "I will keep my word but I think you should change Liesel's name to something more English. Tomas is easy for people to say, but Liesel…"

She wasn't prepared for his remark. She took her time, trying to think of an answer.

"What about Lisa? People here often assume that's her name anyway."

"Lisa, Lisa." He repeated the name a couple of times before nodding. "Ja, gut." He blushed. "I mean, yes, it is good name."

Relaxing slightly, she started preparing the dinner.

Although he'd said no to a sandwich, she gave him one anyway. It disappeared in seconds.

"When was the last time you ate?" she asked.

"Yesterday. Lunchtime. Farmer said we didn't do enough work so we couldn't eat."

The rage inside her built up again. She chopped the vegetables fiercely, struggling to focus through her tears. He stood up and took the knife from her. "You will chop fingers off. That will not help anyone." He grinned as he took over preparing the vegetables.

She made them a cup of tea. When the water for the bath was hot enough, she led him to the bathroom, giving him a towel and showing him where the soap was. She pointed to Derek's shaving kit. "You can borrow those if you want."

He nodded, glancing around.

She pointed to the bedroom opposite. "That's a small room filled with bits and pieces but I can clear it out for you, or you can share that one with Tomas. It's up to you."

"I will share."

She nodded. "Put your clothes in the corner. I can wash them, although I doubt they can be saved. Do you have something else to wear?"

"My Sunday clothes."

His tone told her everything. The Daltons couldn't

have let the boys attend church wearing the rags she had seen. She looked Harry in the eyes.

"Did you want to attend church?"

He shook his head. "We not have any choice."

"You do here. If you want to come to church, you can. If not, you don't have to. Tomas used to go to see you, but he has decided not to now. He stays with Rachel and Ruth. They also mind Liesel, I mean, Lisa." She smiled as she corrected herself.

"You don't mind?"

"Harry, you are free here. Free to make your own choices."

She couldn't say anything else but turned and walked down the stairs.

CHAPTER 21

*T*he next few weeks passed by in a blur of preparation. The air raid warden called to see Sally to explain what she needed to do to secure her house in case of a bomb attack. The arrival of refugee children from London had brought home to everyone that Abbeydale needed to be ready for war, even if the anticipated German attacks had yet to start.

Harry filled up some bags with sand that Derek had stored in the garden shed to build the extension on Rose Cottage. He placed them near the stirrup pump and water bucket.

"That air raid man said we needed to be careful in case of incendiary devices."

Sally shuddered, sending up a quick prayer for

Derek's safety and wishing for what must be the thousandth time that he was home with her.

Harry continued as if not noticing he was scaring Sally. "I have digged – I mean dug – the hole for the Anderson shelter. I hope we do not have to use it, as it will be cold and – what do you call it – wet?"

"Wet is when the water can be seen, damp is when you can feel it." Sally liked to explain the words to Harry, and his English was improving daily, though he was not yet quite at the same level as Tom, who had lost his shyness. "You build the shelter and I'll worry about it being cold. I have some old curtains I can use to make some cushions and we'll have blankets too." She glanced over at Lisa; the child was up to her ears in mud, trying to eat wriggling worms. "We'll have to think of some toys to keep Tomas and Lisa amused."

Harry moved to pick up his sister, not caring she was dirty. "Lies– I mean Lisa will be happy with the worms. She doesn't need fancy dolls or things like that."

Lisa patted Harry's face, leaving a streak of mud behind. She said, "Lisa want walk. Down, down."

Sally itched to grab the almost two-year-old Lisa and take her inside for a bath, but she kept her hands by her side. Harry's relationship with Lisa was developing, slowly but surely, and she didn't want to do anything to stop that.

She picked up yet another soap box. "Thank goodness Mr Callaghan gave us these old boxes. Although why we need to fill them with earth and stack them around the door is beyond me. How can they stop a bomb?"

"They don't, but they protect the doors from the debris." Harry answered as he put Lisa back down on the rug spread out on the small piece of grass remaining in the garden. The rest had been turned over for planting. "When do you plant the garden?"

Sally rubbed her muddy hands on her apron. "Not til the spring, I think. I'm not very green-fingered."

Harry looked confused, glancing at her fingers, which made Sally smile. "It means I'm not very good at gardening. My husband," her voice trembled slightly, "Derek, he looked after things like this."

Harry moved forward and took the soap box out of her hands. "Why don't you go inside and rest for a while, play with Lisa. I will finish here."

She smiled her gratitude before whisking Lisa up into a hug, tickling her to make her laugh. "I better give this young lady a bath before Tom gets home from school. He'll be full of chatter and will want my attention."

"He speaks English very good."

"Very well," Sally automatically corrected. "Sorry, Harry, I do it without thinking. Your English is coming on well too. Do you enjoy your lessons with the reverend?"

Harry's ears turned pink as he started filling the soap box with mud, like his life depended on it. "Sometimes," he muttered.

She was tempted to ask him whether it had anything to do with when Rachel joined the class, but didn't. The young couple had little enough to be happy, both worried about family and friends back in Germany. They deserved some privacy to see how their relationship developed.

WHEN HARRY HAD FINISHED OUTSIDE, he and Sally blacked out all the windows in Rose Cottage. On the inside, they covered the windows with tape in a criss-cross fashion.

"This way, if the glass breaks it won't fly all over us," Sally explained. Harry helped her hang the black-out curtains.

"They have to be closed carefully every evening or the air raid warden will come and fine me. We have to be extra careful." She could have cut out her tongue as she realised what she'd said.

Harry's expression was solemn. "Because you have Germans living with you."

Sally didn't know quite how to respond to him.

He wasn't stupid, he had seen the dirty looks they got from some of the townspeople when they walked through Abbeydale to do the shopping. Harry was always polite and helpful but no matter what he did, not everyone was charmed by him.

LATER, Sally was sitting at the table planning the next week's meals. She looked up at Derek's picture, seeing him in her mind as he was that day in July when he left for training with the Territorials. She sorted through some recipes Maggie had given her, trying to decide what the children might like, when the door burst open, announcing Tom's return from school. Harry had Lisa on his lap, feeding her the leftovers of lunch. Lisa was protesting, trying her best to feed herself.

Tom's hat was in his hand, his shirt hanging out of his trousers and his coat covered in mud.

"Tom, your coat?"

Tom glanced at it. "Sorry, we needed goalposts for football." He grabbed an apple from the table, munching it without washing his hands. "Aunt Sally, we got more children in our school today. They arrived on trains and have brown paper bags with them. They are so lucky. They have biscuits and chocolate, tins of meat, and milk. They said it was called iron-rations. I don't understand that. Is iron not a metal? And, why do they look so sad, when they have such nice food?"

Sally exchanged a smile with Harry. Tom was always the same, talking so fast and not waiting for an answer to his questions.

"Tom, those children are sad because they had to leave their families and their homes. The iron-rations are the name given to the food parcels they were given to last forty-eight hours until they find new homes."

"Are they Jewish too?" Tom looked so puzzled that Sally couldn't hide her smile. She put down the recipe cards and held out her arms to give him a hug. He must have been anxious as he didn't protest he was too old for cuddles.

"No, darling, although some of them might be. They have been sent here as the government doesn't think they are safe living in London. They live in areas near the docks, which could be bombed. So, they have to live in safer areas."

Tom looked into her face, his eyes holding hers.

"Tom, it's alright for you to miss your family. You can talk about them if you like."

Tom held her gaze. "I miss home sometimes. Don't tell Heinz, I mean Harry, as he'd get annoyed. I love it here but sometimes I wish we hadn't come. That things hadn't changed."

She reached for his hands but he kept them by his side. "Darling, it's normal to miss your home, your friends and your mum."

Tom's face scrunched up. "Mother is dead and I don't miss her. Trudi wanted to send us away and keep her baby but then Papa died..." His voice quivered with suppressed tears.

Sally didn't know what to say to that remark. She didn't want to alienate Tom yet it was clear he misunderstood his stepmother's actions. But now wasn't the time to explain.

"Those children miss their parents and homes too."

"I should be friendly to them."

"Yes, darling. You should. They'll be placed with different families in the village." She ruffled his hair but he hadn't finished with his questions.

"Will some come here to live with us?" Now he looked anxious. Surely he couldn't be worried she would take in more children, or worse, would give up Tom and his family to take in an English family.

"No, we don't have room. This is your home. Now, what are we going to do this afternoon?" Sally wanted to get off the reason for the evacuees leaving their families.

Tom nicked another apple. He was always hungry, despite having had sandwiches at school.

"Harry wanted to take some pictures with the

camera. You said he could. It's a sunny day. Could we go to Brooklands?"

"Brooklands?" Surprised, she looked at him. "What do you know about Brooklands?"

Tomas stared at her as if she had two heads. "Every German boy knows Brooklands. It's where the car drivers used to race their cars. Can we go see it? Please?"

"Not now. It's not a racetrack anymore. It's been turned into a factory and we wouldn't be allowed near there. Why don't we go to Virginia Water instead? To the lake? Would you like that?"

Tom considered for a few seconds. "Can we bring a picnic?"

"Yes, a small one, as we will only have an hour or so before it gets dark. Tom, go and get ready." Sally exchanged a smile with Harry.

"He loves living with you. He is so happy here." Harry reached over to hand Lisa to Sally. "Lisa loves you too."

"You don't mind that she calls me Mum? It was the first word she said to me."

"No, you are like her mother. You protect her, feed her, keep her warm. You are a good parent."

Embarrassed, Sally looked away. "Do you think Tom minds? He's sleeping a little better, I think. He's lost that haunted look he had when we first met at Liverpool Street station. But I think you building the Anderson shelter made him a little scared."

Harry grimaced. "I will turn it into a game. He has to know if the siren goes, he must go to the shelter. Tom is right. All Germans know about Brooklands. The Luftwaffe will know it is near London and could use it as a target."

Sally didn't want to think about bombing raids. It was frightening enough to have to carry gas masks everywhere.

"Thank you, Harry. I don't know what I would do without your help – not just around the house but with the children."

She could see he was pleased, even if he found it hard to show it. Sally had an idea. "I'll take everyone out for a treat on Saturday. We shall go and see a Laurel and Hardy picture."

"But it will be in English. You shouldn't waste your money."

"No, Harry, don't think that way. You will laugh so much your tummy will hurt. I promise. We'll ask Rachel, Ruth and Maggie to join us. You'd like that, wouldn't you?"

She didn't know if he understood her teasing or just decided not to answer. She'd seen how he looked at Rachel when he thought nobody was watching. His admiration wasn't one-sided either, with Rachel casting glances under her eyelashes too. Sally could have clapped her hands with glee when he nodded shyly, but settled for a smile.

HER PREDICTION TURNED out to be correct. Rachel and Harry, seated together, both laughed so much they cried. Maggie and Sally enjoyed seeing the young couple act their age for once – not having to behave like adults.

CHAPTER 22

*S*ally's heart missed a beat as she heard the postman cycling up the lane. Would he have a letter from Derek?

She put Lisa back in her cot, kissed her on the forehead and ran down the stairs just in time to see the envelope drop on the mat. Picking it up, she saw it was addressed to her but didn't recognise the handwriting.

Breathing heavily, she sat on the stairs and tore the envelope open. She read the first few lines, tears of relief blurring her eyes.

Darling,

Please don't worry. I'm fine but I hurt my right hand so the lovely nurse said she'd write the letter for me. I had to promise not to make her blush.

I miss you so much.

Sally read the letter rapidly until the end, before reading it slowly once more. He was somewhere in France. Not that he said so, but they had devised a code before he left to get past the censors. The mention of the red-and-white cloth he'd picked for their dining room table seemed an obvious odd sentence to her now. At the time of choosing, they'd thought it was funny.

Lisa's cries of protest at being left alone made her return upstairs. She picked up the baby, sat her on her knee and read the letter to her.

"This is from your uncle Derek, Lisa. He's in France, fighting. He got hurt but it's not bad enough for him to come home so we won't see him for a while. He won't make it home for Christmas."

Christmas. That was only a month away. She had to send him a parcel, show him how much she loved him. He hadn't mentioned the children. She bit her lip, looking at the letter again. Was he annoyed? Not her Derek.

"Come on, little one, let's get you dressed, and we'll go to the shops. Maybe see Auntie Maggie. Would you like that?"

Lisa smiled.

MAGGIE SPOTTED SALLY on her way back from the town. "What's up, love?"

Although Maggie was smiling, Sally's restraint fled and she burst into tears.

"Aw, Sally love, come in and sit down. I'll put the kettle on. You go on, I'll take the pram."

Maggie pushed the pram in after Sally and kicked the door shut behind her. She took Lisa out of the pram and put her on the floor to play on the mat, away from the stove. She handed the child a couple of spoons before turning her attention back to Sally. "Is it Derek?"

Sally nodded her head. "It's good news; I got a letter. He didn't write it – a nurse did. He's injured, in a hospital in France. I don't think he got any of my letters as he didn't mention the children."

Maggie put her arms around Sally and hugged her, effectively stopping her mid-sentence. "Thank God, he's fine and being looked after. Sit down and get a cup of tea into you. It's good for the shock."

Maggie busied herself making the tea and slicing a fruit loaf. Lisa stood up and made her way over to Sally, putting her arms up. "Mum, up." She half-crawled up onto Sally's lap. Maggie persuaded her to sit on the floor again by handing Lisa a piece of loaf with butter on top. The child flopped back down on the ground.

"Lisa, say thank you to Maggie."

"Thank you, Aggie," Lisa said with her mouth full.

Maggie laughed before pouring out the tea and then taking a seat opposite Sally.

"The girls are at school and himself is out and about so nobody but Lisa will hear us. Start at the beginning and speak slowly."

Sally made an attempt to smile. It was ironic for Maggie to tell others to talk slowly when she was the fastest talker for miles.

"I don't know where he is but he says he's involved in training men. He was supposed to get leave but landed in hospital for a bit. He says the injury isn't bad enough to send him home."

Maggie patted Sally's arm.

"I never thought I'd wish my husband ill, Maggie, but if he had been worse, I could have seen him. It's so hard not seeing him. I miss him so much." Sally turned away, not wanting her friend to see her tears.

"Of course you miss him. You being newlyweds and all. It's not natural to be apart like this." Maggie entertained Lisa by blowing bubbles and making faces at her. "Now dry those tears and let's put a package together for Derek and the other men with him in that hospital. Can't be fun staying in a place where they don't speak English or drink decent tea. Heard it's awful cold over there too. You need to send some tea and biscuits. I'll make you one of my special fruit cakes and give you some of my cigarettes. I should have given up long ago."

Lisa held her hands out, so Sally pushed her tea back from the edge of the table and picked Lisa up to sit on her knee. Lisa put her arm around Sally's neck, using her other hand to wipe the tears on Sally's face. "Mum no cry."

Feeling guilty at worrying the child, Sally gave her a quick hug and resolved to pull herself together. Her husband was alive and safe. For the moment.

"HARRY, soon it will be Christmas. I always have a Christmas tree, will that upset you?"

"Me? No. Why?"

"I know Jews don't celebrate Christmas."

"No, but you're not Jewish, Sally, unless you want to convert. I would say it is not the best time."

Sally laughed at his black humour. "I would like to have a tree. It's not Christmas without it."

"I shall go and find you the best tree there is. It will be my thank you for looking after my family."

CHAPTER 23

CHRISTMAS DAY 1939

*O*n Christmas morning, Sally woke to the sound of animated discussion coming from downstairs between Tom and Harry over whether it was time to wake her. She turned over to check on Lisa, but the child was still asleep in her cot. She stretched out in the bed, not wanting to put her feet on the cold floor. It was freezing, even for this time of year.

Christmas Day. Dinner! She pushed the covers back and ran down to the kitchen to stoke up the range. She'd never cooked a turkey before. Why on earth had she not agreed to Maggie doing it again this year…

"Happy Christmas, Aunt Sally, can I open my presents now?"

"Tom!" Harry exclaimed but Sally only laughed.

She hugged Tom and was going to shake Harry's hand but he gave her an awkward hug instead.

"Happy Christmas, Sally. What do I do to help?"

"Open presents?" Tom asked, his eyes lit up with excitement.

Sally pinched his cheek. "Harry, will you bring Lisa downstairs, and then Tom, you can open a small present. We said we would keep the larger ones until later. At dinner."

"Do we have to go to church first?" Tom whined.

She was about to tell him he could stay home with Harry but Harry answered. "We're all going together to hear the reverend speak. Now, put some dishes on the table for breakfast while I see to Lisa. Sally has enough to do."

Sally didn't breathe a word. Harry never went to church. It was lovely of him to make the effort today. She looked out the window at the grey clouds. Would it snow or hold off until later?

They had a light breakfast of scones with butter and jam. The children didn't like porridge so she didn't make that today. Tom almost swallowed his scone whole before picking out a present. He rattled the box, trying to figure out what it was.

"Go on, open it before you break it," Sally admonished gently as she picked Lisa up. Harry handed Sally a small present before taking the child.

"This is for you, Sally, from all of us. Thank you for bringing us to your home."

Choked up, she couldn't answer, but took the present from him. She opened it carefully, her tears spilling over as she saw what was inside. A Max Factor lipstick in her favourite colour red, some face powder, a brow pencil and a packet of nylons.

Harry blushed when she unwrapped the last item. "Maggie brought them; she said they were from Lisa."

"Thank you so much, boys, for such lovely gifts and, Lisa, for the stockings. I'll wear them when Derek comes home and takes me dancing." Her voice wobbled on her husband's name but she didn't cry. She didn't want to ask where Harry had got the money; she knew he did odd jobs for the reverend, the constable and others, but he must have used all his earnings on her.

She dressed in her best, protecting her clothes with a pinny as she peeled and prepared the potatoes. She had prepared the rest of the vegetables the day before. Then she gave Lisa a quick wash and dressed her in a new dress, woollen stockings and a beautiful red coat. Maggie had knitted her a hat and scarf to match.

Both boys had new shirts and trousers too and looked very smart, but Harry didn't have a coat that fit him.

"Try this on," she said, taking a coat from the rack by the front door. "Derek won't mind."

A lump formed in her throat as Harry put the coat on. It fit him perfectly. "That will keep you warm in church."

"Can I bring my plane to church with me, Aunt Sally? Please?" Tom put on his best smile, but she couldn't give in.

"Darling, it's too big for church but you can play with it when you come home. You can show Ruth."

"Girls don't like planes." Tom's lip curled.

"They like pilots who fly them," Harry replied, before taking the plane and laying it on the table. "It will be here when we get back. At church, you must make Aunt Sally proud."

"Like Papa would want?" Tom asked, his voice trembling as he gazed up at his brother.

Sally had to turn away for fear she would cry too. Christmas was a time for families. "Come on, boys, we don't want to be late and have to stand."

* * *

MAGGIE PRODUCED a Christmas pudding and a cake. Sally rooted around in the cupboard for a bottle of whisky. She wanted the children to see the pudding lighting to see their reactions. She'd been mystified when she first saw Maggie do it.

"I made a couple of puddings and three cakes. One for the reverend to take over to the old people's home, and a larger one to go over to Botley's Park. Those poor nurses and doctors away from their homes over Christmas. Thought it might give them a little bit of cheer."

Maggie was cut off by Reverend Collins taking a seat at the head of the table. "Have you seen the state of the place? God help us all. The Ministry of Defence have built fifteen more huts in addition to the work done by the emergency medical services, they are expecting—"

"Maggie, you are amazing. So thoughtful of you." Sally cut off whatever the reverend was about to say next. She didn't want any talk of the casualties of war at the table.

"Here, Rachel, Ruth, take those seats next to Harry and Tom. Lisa will sit in her high chair, won't you, darling?"

Lisa grinned, her mouth smeared with butter and jam.

"Does our butter queen know butter and bacon are being rationed from early next year?" Maggie wiped the child's mouth with a napkin.

"Lisa doesn't eat bacon. None of us eat pork." Tom's screwed-up face suggested what he thought of anyone who did.

"I made two sets of Brussels sprouts, one flavoured with bacon the way you showed me, Maggie. The second just has butter on it."

"Yuck. I don't like sprouts. You could have made them all with bacon." Tom's reaction earned him a laugh from the adults but a stern reprimand from Rachel. "You are being rude. That is not nice when Aunt Sally made such an effort."

"Say sorry, Tom," Harry said.

Sally turned to hide her smile. Harry had been laughing until Rachel reprimanded his brother. He'd changed course, hoping to be in her good books. She wondered when he'd give Rachel the book he'd bought her. He'd asked Sally to help him pick one out.

She turned the radio to the BBC, leaving it playing low in the background. They didn't want to miss the King's speech. After the King told them the poem Princess Elizabeth had written and said goodbye, they all sat in silence, each caught up in their own memories. Sally sniffed, her eyes drawn to Derek's photo.

Maggie took her aside and said quietly, "Sally, go upstairs and let the tears come. You'll feel better. Come back in a while. The children won't even notice."

Sally nodded, and escaped while she could. After

a good cry, she felt much better and tidied her face, ready to re-join the celebrations. When she came back downstairs, she found Harry alone in the front room.

"Harry, it's freezing in here. Why aren't you in the dining room with the others?" She'd lit the fire in the dining room due to the larger table. The sitting room was too small for everyone to sit in at the same time.

"I needed to think."

She edged closer but didn't touch him. "You miss your family?"

"Always, but it is not what I think about. I wonder what will happen to me. I can't stay here without going to school or working. I feel useless."

"Never say that, Harry. I don't know what I would do without you."

"You are very kind but not everyone is like you. At some point, people will wonder why I do not contribute to the war effort. I should be fighting the Nazis, not sitting here while my people are being murdered."

Sally didn't want to hear anymore. "Wait until you are older, Harry, please."

He didn't answer but stayed sitting in the dark, while she returned to the others. Maggie glanced at her, concern in her eyes, but she smiled to reassure her friend. She had to put on a brave face for the children; she could cry for Derek when she went to bed.

She pulled out Derek's camera. "Come on, everyone, let's take a photograph so we can remember this moment." *And share these precious memories with our loved ones when they come back.*

CHAPTER 24

JANUARY 1940

Sally pushed open the door to the vicarage on her way to the shop. "Maggie, did you hear the news?"

"I didn't need to. I saw the queues in Callaghan's shop." A cigarette hung out of the side of Maggie's mouth and waggled as she talked. "Everyone was buying up all the tea, bacon and butter they could afford. Mr Callaghan almost had a riot on his hands. He sold out of everything."

Sally looked at her empty basket. "I was just going down there now. I guess you saved me a trip."

"I did more than that. I got some for you. I didn't bother with bacon as I know you don't cook that for the boys. But I got you butter and sugar. I know how you like your tea."

Sally smiled gratefully as she took a seat at the

table, settling Lisa on her lap with a couple of teaspoons to play with. "When do you think tea will go on ration? The newspapers haven't said when but they said it will happen."

"Margarine, cooking fats and tea will be next, according to the reverend." Maggie put out her cigarette and set the teacups and saucers on the table with a plate of home-made biscuits. "Don't know where he hears things but I've learned to listen. I know we shouldn't hoard, Sally, but I can't live without my cup of tea. It's the Irish in me. I have a good excuse."

Sally burst out laughing, taking Maggie by surprise, until she laughed too.

"Mum," Lisa said, clearly trying to feed Sally with the empty spoon. "Want Mummy."

Sally met Maggie's eyes over Lisa's head. "What will I do when she asks about her real mother?"

"Cross that bridge when you come to it." Maggie lifted her cup to her mouth but said, "Did you see Constable Cooper? He mentioned he was going to call on you."

"Me, why? Please say it's not because of Harry." Sally tried to suppress the flicker of fear she felt that Beryl Dalton might still do something bad to make her pay for taking Harry home.

The puzzled expression on Maggie's face made her feel better. "No, it's to do with pigs."

"What? I don't know anything about pigs."

"They're going to raise two pigs at the police station. Constable Cooper read about it somewhere. Seems the idea is the whole community contributes food for the pigs until they're ready to be slaughtered. When that time comes, everyone who fed the pig gets a share."

"Eww, I don't fancy that, do you? I think if I raised a pig, I would think of it as a pet." She wasn't sure she could face the smell or, worse, the cleaning of the sty either.

Maggie spurted her tea out over the table. "Sally Matthews, you'd never make a farmer. Where do you think your meat comes from?"

Sally wrinkled her nose. "I try never to think about it."

Maggie chortled. "I'll remind you of this conversation later in the war when Germany has starved us."

Sally mimicked Mrs Shackleton-Driver's posh accent as she said, "Maggie Ardle, you should be ashamed of yourself. You can't let people hear you say something like that. You'll be accused of defeatism." Although joking, Sally didn't want to think about the government warnings that food supplies would run short if they weren't careful. "We have to obey the posters. 'Grow your own food' – or the one Enid should read – 'Rationing means enough for everyone'."

Maggie pushed away her cup and lit up another cigarette. "Ah, will you go on with you. I'll keep your shopping for myself if you say things like that."

Sally stood and buttoned up Lisa's coat, sticking her hat on her head. She kissed her friend on the cheek. "I'll send Harry over to collect it. It will give him a chance to see Rachel."

"Are you still trying to match make between those two?"

Sally grinned. "I think they're in love, and it's very sweet. We need something to make us smile in times like this."

She left Maggie giggling behind her.

CHAPTER 25

pril 1940

MAGGIE'S COMMENTS at Christmas about the staff at the hospital and the recent news about the failed landings in Norway, made Sally realise she could do something to help the war effort.

The next time her friend came round for a cup of tea and a catch-up, Sally said, "Maggie, would you look after the children if I volunteered up at the hospital? They're bound to need more staff and if they had domestics like me, the nurses would be free to look after patients." Sally glanced up from her ironing to see her friend's reaction.

Maggie nodded. "Course I'll look after the little

beggars. But are you sure you want to do that? You know you won't be pouring cups of tea or reading passages from some book of poetry."

Sally smiled at Maggie mimicking some of the ladies of the parish. When the reverend had asked for volunteers to visit the sick or those injured in the blackout, at the local hospital, he wasn't ready for the line the women had taken. Instead of getting stuck into the chores, they took to reading to the patients, often leaving the nurses with even more work to do.

"I looked after Mum and Nan so I've got a bit of experience. I'm young too, so I can do more than some I see getting on the bus every day. Poor Mrs Dobbs has such puffy ankles, she should be a patient not a charlady."

"Don't you go telling Minnie Dobbs that, or she's likely to hit you. That hospital has been her life ever since her boy Joe ended up in the looney bin."

Sally held the iron up. "Maggie, don't call it that. It's a mental hospital." She put the iron down to rest as she picked up the next bedsheet. "I thought Joe died years ago."

"He did but his mam keeps working there. Says she's got nothing else to do to keep her busy. She needs the money, is my guess." Maggie leaned back in her chair, her eyes fixed on Sally, though she looked like her mind was far away.

"What?"

"I was just thinking. Would you take Rachel with you? I know she's too young to become a charwoman but perhaps they might take her on as a student nurse. Her English is good and she wants to be a doctor. This could be her chance."

Sally would have been delighted as the girl was great company – but Rachel was German, and with the loss of HMS Courageous and the HMS Royal Oak before that, followed by the recent failed attempt to land in Narvik, Norway, the anti-German sentiment was getting worse.

As if Maggie could read her mind, she said, "She's a German and she's staying here. She might as well try to do something useful. People might be more accepting of her then." Maggie blew a thin stream of smoke into the air. "Plus, she wants to volunteer but is afraid to go on her own."

Sally coughed a little, wishing her friend wouldn't smoke, at least not in her house. She hated the smell.

"She has nothing to be afraid of. Tell her I'll collect her in the morning and we will go up together. I know one of the matrons up there. She's a good one if a little strict."

THAT EVENING, Sally told Harry what she'd decided.

"I will do the shopping for you and Mrs Ardle.

That way, you don't have to find time to queue and the basket won't be too heavy for Maggie."

Sally grinned. "Don't tell Maggie you're worried about her age. She's likely to thump you."

He looked puzzled for a second. "Thump? Oh – you mean hit me?" He sniffed the air, his nose wrinkling with distaste. "Papa said smoking was bad for people. Maggie needs to stop smoking. It makes her cough."

"Try telling her that." Sally went upstairs to look for something suitable to wear to the hospital. She wanted to look smart but not posh. She had no interest in sitting around reading to inmates. She wanted to make a difference and she needed to keep busy. She gazed out the window at the sunset wondering where Derek was. *Keep safe, my darling.*

THE NEXT MORNING, she escorted the children to Maggie's, where Lisa would be spoilt while Tom and Ruth were at school. Harry came too, to tell Maggie he was going to do the shopping. He would also help her with any chores around the house. They'd found out quite quickly that the reverend couldn't hang a nail for a painting correctly.

Rachel appeared nervous, her gaze darting around the room.

"Rachel, you look perfect, doesn't she, Maggie? The matron is a bit of a dragon but she knows a hard worker when she sees her."

"A dragon?" Rachel looked mystified, making Maggie and Sally laugh. It broke the tension in the room.

Maggie explained, "It means she's very strict."

"Like Mama. She wouldn't like this." Rachel bit the nail on her finger.

Maggie pulled the finger out of her mouth. "Your mam would be dead proud of you, love. You are going to do your bit to end this war. Now shoulders back, chest out and watch the girl in front."

Sally pushed the confused-looking girl out the door before she had to explain another of Maggie's sayings. "Rachel, please don't worry. We won't start work today. You'll be fine. I'll be there."

Rachel didn't look convinced. They walked to the bus stop where Enid stood waiting. Sally almost groaned aloud. Curiosity lit up Enid's face, turning her plain complexion a rather becoming shade of pink. "Where are you two off to, all dressed up? You look like you are going to church or court."

Enid was practically salivating at the thought. What was wrong with the woman?

"Good morning, Enid. We're going to Botley Park to volunteer. Want to join us?" Sally smiled sweetly, knowing Enid hated the sight of blood.

Enid paled as she pushed her glasses onto the bridge of her nose. "I don't have time to be volunteering, what with Arthur somewhere in France and me left with four little ones. I have to go into Woking to find some material for new clothes. Can't keep them dressed, they're growing so fast. Alright for those who have live-in babysitters or friends with nothing better to do all day. I suppose Maggie is minding the baby."

"She is, among other things. Not sure the reverend would consider Maggie's contribution to the war effort so lightly."

Enid flushed slightly at the mention of Reverend Collins. "Yes, well, of course … What are you taking her with you for?" Enid shredded Rachel with a look.

Sally pushed her fingernails into the palms of her hands so she wouldn't respond in kind. "Rachel has offered to help. She's going to train to become a doctor. Oh, there's our bus. Look after yourself, Enid."

Sally paid their fares. The driver greeted them with a smile, helping Rachel to lose some of her pinched expression.

When they arrived at the hospital and walked up to the gates, Rachel said, "This is so big. Is it all the same hospital?"

"Yes, but it wasn't always a medical hospital. Until the war, this was a mental hospital."

"In Germany, we have no need for such hospitals. The Nazis got rid of anyone who wasn't perfect. In their eyes."

Horrified, Sally lost the ability to speak for a few seconds, and then the moment passed as they met some other ladies also walking up to the main entrance. One, of a similar age to Sally, dropped back to speak to them. She seemed nervous, wiping her hands down an ill-fitting coat, her legs bare of stockings but wearing rather high shoes.

"You are volunteering too? Do you think they'll take me on? I ain't got much experience in a hospital, although plenty of scrubbing and charring. Only I can't stand the countryside. I miss me 'ome but the nippers need to be here. I could leave 'em I suppose but what type of mum would that make me?"

Rachel stared at the woman, obviously not understanding much of what she said, given her London accent and fast speech. Sally held out her hand and introduced both of them.

"The name's Belle – me ma, she weren't too clever. By the time the tenth one came along, she named me after the bells of London. I guess it's better than Bow." The young woman laughed at herself before turning to Rachel. "You're rather quiet. Lost yer tongue?"

"Lost my…?" Confused, Rachel looked to Sally but Belle interjected.

"You a Jerry? Gawd, they must be desperate to have Jerries working in the 'ospital."

Sally was about to defend Rachel but the young girl spoke softly, "I am Jewish. I hate the Nazis."

"Jewish?" Belle looked her up and down before smiling. "Bet you don't find many of your lot down 'ere. Back 'ome I had me some Jewish neighbours. Salt of de earth, they was. You get the job, and anyone gives you trouble you send them my way. You 'ear?"

Rachel smiled for the first time that morning. Sally wanted to hug Belle but restrained herself. They'd reached the main entrance, and a porter sent them towards a waiting room. He seemed used to women just turning up to volunteer.

Sally breathed a sigh of relief when she spotted the matron she knew coming towards her.

"Sally Matthews? Is it really you? The sun has shined on my day. You're just the sort of woman I need around here. We're rushed off our feet getting things ready for our new patients. Can you still sew as well as you did at school?"

Bemused, Sally nodded, wondering why her sewing skills were needed.

"Good. We have a shortage of shrouds. You will sort that out in no time."

Sally gulped but the matron had moved onto Rachel. "Who is this young lady?"

"This is Rachel Bernstein, Matron," Sally injected quickly when it seemed Rachel wasn't going to speak up. "She wants to become a doctor. She's a wonderful young woman, intelligent and hard-working. I wondered – I mean, we – if you had space on a nursing training course for her."

Matron held Rachel's gaze. "So you want to be a doctor?"

"Yes, Ma'am. When the war is over."

Matron's eyes widened at her accent but Rachel didn't give her a chance to ask.

"Yes, I'm German. At least I was born there. I'm a Jew. I want to help Britain win the war so I can go home to my family." Rachel's voice trembled over the word *family* but otherwise you couldn't guess at the tragedy she'd been through.

"Ah, a refugee. I can't place you on a nursing course." Rachel frowned before the matron continued, "I will give you a chance as a VAD. Do well and we'll see."

"A VAD?" Rachel repeated.

Belle piped up, "She means a general skivvy. You'll do the jobs the nurses don't want to do." She would have kept talking but for the glare from Matron.

"Who are you?"

Belle withered slightly before recovering. "Name's Belle. Belle Clark."

"What sort of name is Belle? What's it short for."

"It ain't short for nuthin'. Mum ran out of names by the time she had me. I think I'm lucky. Me sisters got called Siobhan, Grainne and…"

"Enough. Do you ever stop talking?"

Belle blushed a little but smiled back. "Me old man says I don't."

Sally held her breath as Matron continued to frown. She willed Belle to paint herself in a better light or she wouldn't end up working here. Sally wanted Belle to be at the hospital, not just because she'd look out for Rachel but she seemed a good laugh.

Belle coughed as the silence continued. "Look, I ain't got any fancy education or nothin'. Never lived out in the country either. But my nippers are 'ere for the duration and I got to find a job. I ain't afraid to get my hands dirty. Living within the sound of the Bow Bells you can't afford to be choosy. I'm a hard worker, missus."

Sally couldn't restrain herself any longer, especially as she sensed Matron was about to explode.

"Matron, give her a chance. She's a worker, you can tell by her hands. She won't sit around reading all day."

At the reference to Mrs Shackleton-Driver and her committee members, Matron exhaled loudly.

"We're short-staffed so I'll give you a trial. But

you best learn to keep quiet. This is a hospital not a theatre."

Within an hour of arriving, all three of them were in an empty ward scrubbing and polishing. Everything had to sparkle, including the sluices and bathrooms. As they worked, Belle kept them amused with stories of London, but her talking never interfered with her work. The sister in charge seemed surprised they were finished so quickly although she didn't mention it.

Next, they were sent to make dressings. Under the watchful eye of a sister, they made different types of bandages, swabs, eye pads and some padded splints. Sally was directed to a sewing machine and shown how to make shrouds. She didn't want to think about why they needed so many.

After six hours of continuous labour, Matron arrived back.

"Mrs Matthews, what are you still doing here? You were only supposed to be shown what to do and then given your schedule."

Sally stretched her aching muscles but it was Rachel who responded. "You needed help. We did what was needed."

Her words earned her a beam of approval. "We'll make a nurse of you, Miss Bernstein. Now I insist you all go home after Sister outlines your rota. Thank you for your time and efforts today."

Sally and Rachel didn't have the energy to speak as they caught the bus home. Belle was heading back to Woking and gave them a cheery wave as she walked to her bus stop.

When they got back to Maggie's, Lisa clambered all over Sally, hugging her and refusing to be put down.

"That's charming. You'd think I'd been mistreating her all day with the way she's behaving," Maggie huffed, but Sally was secretly thrilled. She'd missed Lisa too but she bent her head in closer to Lisa's neck to avoid Maggie seeing her blissful expression.

"Did you see any dead bodies?" Tom asked a little too gleefully.

Ruth said, "Yuck!"

Sally ignored Tom's question. "Come on, you lot, let's get off home. I've dinner to make."

Maggie handed her a casserole. "I figured you'd be tired so I made extra. Now go on home and have a bath. You look like you're about to drop. You can tell me all about it later."

Sally leaned in and kissed the older woman's cheek gratefully. "You're one in a million, Maggie."

SALLY SOON SETTLED into working at the hospital and enjoyed her time there, although to begin with there weren't many war patients. She liked chatting to other women volunteers and then going home to the children after her shifts. She had the best of both worlds.

CHAPTER 26

*T*he siren wailed, causing a number of nurses to jump.

"What is it now?" Belle shouted above the siren. Sally shrugged, trying to concentrate on the patient she was tending to. "I'm sorry, Nurse. I didn't mean to mess up the bed. I just…"

Sally reassured him as best she could. It must be so embarrassing for a young strapping lad to be confined to bed, never mind having to use a bedpan.

"Relax, soldier, you've done your bit for the war. Now let us do ours."

The soldier stared at something over her head, and she guessed he was back on the beaches of France. From the little they'd heard from similar patients, Dunkirk had been hell on earth. The Nazis had continued to shell the beaches, even the hospital ships. Thousands died on the beach or in the water waiting to get on a ship.

"You should have seen it over there, Nurse. Bodies flying all over the place or bits of them. The things I could tell you…" The man fell silent; he was a boy really. He couldn't be much more than eighteen. She pushed his fringe out of his eyes.

"Look at me. You got through. You're home. Try to think of that, or think of when your mum and dad get word you're back home."

"Home." The boy smiled as he drifted off to sleep, the morphine finally working its magic.

The ward sister came by seconds later. "How's he doing?"

"He's seen too much for a young lad." Sally muttered a prayer for Derek. Where was her husband? Was he on a beach waiting for a ship to rescue him?

"You'd make a great nurse, Matthews. You have a way with the patients. Pity you're married."

Sally stared at the sister as she walked off, but Belle burst out laughing. "Shame on you, Matthews, for getting a ring on your finger!"

Grateful to her new friend for trying to lighten the mood, Sally asked, "Did you find out what the siren was for?"

Belle looked uncomfortable.

"What? Tell me."

"Someone said it was a Jerry firing his guns at the

Red Cross train in Chertsey station. He put a load of bullet holes in the four coaches but thankfully they had already been unloaded. Minutes earlier, they would have been full of patients. The platform isn't long enough to unload the whole train; they have to take it four coaches at a time."

Jerries shouting at Chertsey station. They normally targeted the bigger cities.

"Surely he saw the Red Cross markings?" Sally stuttered, horrified at such depravity.

"He couldn't miss them, could he? Anyway, one of our lot shot him down."

Sally crossed herself. She wasn't sure why but it seemed the right thing to do. Maggie's influence on her. Although her friend didn't practise now, she had been born Catholic and hadn't lost some of the characteristics.

Belle patted Sally's arm. "Our kids will be in a shelter. The schools would have seen to that. Don't be worrying. We'll be home soon."

* * *

IT WAS hours later when Sally almost crawled home from her shift at the hospital. The newspapers and the radio might be heralding Dunkirk as a magnificent feat, and she knew it was, in many ways. The little ships had rescued so many men, but the wounded kept on coming. The sheer numbers of injured men arriving from the trains overwhelmed the small hospital. The shrouds she'd made had been used; she could have made three times as many and still they'd have run out. She brushed a tear of frustration from her eye. All those young men. Battered and broken in ways she would never had dreamed possible.

She'd tried her best to help the harassed nurses, but rolling bandages, cleaning bedpans and making beds were as much as she could do. She admired the nurses' skills, as much as their ability to remain calm, even cheerful, in the light of so much suffering.

As always, she'd checked the face of every new patient, looking for Derek, thankful when it wasn't him.

As she got closer to Rose Cottage, she noticed a small crowd standing outside. What was going on?

"Sally! About time you showed your face, we've been waiting for ages." Enid Brown stepped forward.

Sally's stomach churned at the sour look on Enid's face. She glanced around to see many of the women from the Women's Institute meetings sporting similar expressions. Only one or two failed to meet her gaze and looked slightly uncomfortable. She spoke directly to Enid, "I was working at the hospital. Did I forget a meeting?" She turned and addressed Mrs Shackleton-Driver directly, purposefully calling her by her first name, "Jane, what are you doing here?"

The woman, all done up like a dog's dinner, her ridiculous hat with the peacock feather on sideways, frowned and looked down her nose at Sally, before drawing herself up to her full height. "We insist you release the Germans to us. We are going to take them to the army."

"What?" Sally couldn't have heard correctly. She looked around again, noticing the women had edged forward, the tension increasing. She stretched, rubbing her lower spine to ease the ache in her back.

Enid pointed to the upstairs window of Rose Cottage. "They showed that plane where to fire his bullets. It had to be them."

Sally glanced at her bedroom window, surprised to see the curtains pulled during the day. Fear twisted her stomach; were the boys alright? What about Lisa? The plane … The one that had shot at the Red Cross train. They were blaming the children. That was just ludicrous. But Belle's face flashed before her eyes. Her friend had looked uncomfortable when telling Sally about it. Surely they couldn't really believe anyone had told the pilot to shoot at a train full of injured soldiers?

"Ladies, I don't know what you're talking about and, to be honest, I've just done a double-shift and I'm shattered. Can we talk about this in the morning?" She took a step but Enid moved to bar her way. Mrs Shackleton-Driver pointed a gloved finger at Sally's chest.

"No. We'll talk about it now. You know the Red Cross train carrying our heroes from Dunkirk was strafed by an enemy plane when it stopped at Chertsey station. If it were not for one of our brave RAF boys tackling him in a dogfight, there could have been dozens killed. How did the Germans know that station was being used for our wounded?"

"The coaches they hit were empty, the Dunkirk wounded had already been moved to the hospital. I know as I've been at the hospital nursing the casualties." Sally let her words hang in the air for a moment, looking at a few of the women to see if the implication had hit home. They were staging a protest while she had been up to her tonsils in blood and guts. Mrs Shackleton-Driver didn't seem fazed. Sally adopted her best impression of Matron, speaking firmly, "Mrs Shackleton-Driver, I can assure you it had nothing to do with my family. Now, please, excuse me and let me get into my home."

The woman took a step to stand in front of her. Others in the crowd muttered, moving forward.

Sally turned to Enid. "Enid, you've known me for years. Can you please tell this … this woman, I'd have nothing to do with traitors? For goodness sake, my Derek is over there with your Arthur."

"My Arthur's dead. I got the telegram yesterday, but you weren't around, were you? I hate you, and your German brats. I told you before, nobody wants them here. They should all be sent back to Germany – in boxes."

Sally couldn't believe it. Poor Arthur dead. What about Derek? Was he dead too? She swayed slightly before processing the rest of what Enid had said. *How dare she?* Incensed with rage, Sally pushed forward, coming face to face with Enid. She saw Enid's eyes widen as she took a step back.

"Enid! How could you say a thing like that?" Sally grappled for something to use to appeal to Enid's senses. "You have children. Lisa, Tom and Harry are as innocent as you and me. They couldn't help being born in Germany."

Enid wasn't listening. Sally glanced up and caught Tom's face peeking through the curtains. No wonder the curtains were pulled. The poor children must be terrified.

She turned back to the crowd. "You ladies listen to me. This is my house and you are trespassing. Leave, or I shall go for Constable Cooper. He has no time for vigilantes, as you all know. Go and pick on somebody your own size instead of a group of defenceless children."

She shoved past Enid and Jane Shackleton-Driver

and stood at her front door, key in hand. She wasn't going to open it until they left.

It took a few minutes, but gradually the women dispersed, still muttering to one another. Sally heard one of them say the word "traitors". She took a second to compose herself; crying in front of the children would scare them. They wouldn't believe these were tears of frustration and tiredness. But she didn't get to turn the key, as the door opened and she was pulled inside, and Maggie banged the door shut behind her.

"Maggie, oh thank God you were here with the children."

"I sneaked in the back way, over the wall. Look at the state of me." Maggie glanced down and Sally saw a giant rip in her dress. "Been a long time since I flashed my drawers at anyone and everyone."

Sally gave her friend a hug. "Thank you for being here."

Maggie hugged her back and whispered, "The children are terrified. They keep talking about *Kristallnacht*. They are all set to run away."

Sally ran up the stairs, two at a time. She knocked on the bedroom door, trying the handle, but it didn't work.

"Harry, let me in. Tom, it's Sally and I'm alone. Maggie is the only other adult in the house, I swear."

The lock turned and the door opened slowly. She

pushed into the room to find all five children staring at her, their eyes huge in their pale faces. She could see straightaway that Tom had wet himself. Ruth wouldn't look at her.

"Come here, oh my goodness, come here." She gathered the younger ones in her arms. "I promise I'm back and I won't leave you. You are safe. You don't have to run away. This is your home."

"Those people ... They sounded like the people on our street at home," Rachel stuttered, as she stood, back straight, knuckles white, at Lisa's bed.

Sally couldn't believe Lisa had slept through all the noise. She struggled to keep her temper. "I can't imagine what you have been through today. I'm sorry I wasn't here. But it won't happen again. I promise."

Harry frowned. "Don't make promises you can't keep. They hate us. You heard them." He turned his back.

"Harry, don't let a few people change how you feel about living here. Maggie and I love you. The reverend, the doctor, Constable Cooper, the shop owners, they have all been kind to us. Enid lost her husband, she found out yesterday he died in France. Arthur was a lovely man and the sadness she feels is making her angry. She needs someone to blame."

Sally cuddled Tom and Ruth. "How about I make you both some cocoa and we can listen to Children's Hour on the wireless. It's just coming up to five."

They didn't answer but kept hold of her. If she could get her hands on Enid Brown and those other ladies, she'd strangle them.

"Children, I promise those ladies have left. Maggie's gone for Constable Cooper. He will tell those women off for scaring you. Now, why don't I go and make the cocoa and you come down when you're ready?" She looked to Rachel who gave her a nod. She hoped the older girl would reassure the little ones and tell them to believe her.

She ran into her room and quickly changed, hating the hospital smell on her clothes. The children were still in Tom's room when she went downstairs to put the cocoa on. She tuned in the wireless too. As soon as the sounds of Children's Hour filtered up the stairs, Tom and Ruth came down, racing each other to be the one sitting nearest the wireless.

Rachel followed, carrying Lisa in her arms. The poor child was sobbing on Rachel's shoulders. "Harry will be down in a few minutes. He is very angry."

"I don't blame him, I wanted to kill those ladies too."

Rachel didn't smile. Sally could see the worried look in her eyes. Rachel said, "Harry feels he cannot protect his family. He thinks it is time he did something. I don't know what he plans but he has a short temper. I worry he may get into trouble."

Sally took Lisa into her arms, dried her tears,

loving the way she snuggled into her. Lisa had become more independent since turning two and was less inclined to give cuddles. How dare those women frighten *her* baby. She saw Rachel's troubled expression and immediately felt guilty. The girl might be older than Lisa but she was still an innocent and she needed reassurance too.

"I'll speak to Harry. Rachel, I hope you know how much you are wanted here. I heard glowing reports today about your work. Matron is very impressed with you. Says she wishes other fifteen-year-olds were as mature as you."

Sally kissed Lisa's head once more before setting her in her seat at the table.

Rachel, looking at Lisa, sighed. "I had to grow up fast. Maybe it is best, other girls do not."

Sally couldn't think of an answer to that and was glad when the milk started frothing in the pan.

CHAPTER 27

The next morning, Sally went into the dining room and telephoned the hospital to speak to Matron.

"I'm sorry, Matron, but I have to take the rest of this week off. I know it's a horrible inconvenience, but I have to protect the children."

"Sally, I've known you for years. It must be something serious for you to ask for time off. Can I do anything to help?"

Sally gave Matron a brief description of what had happened, conscious the operator would come back on if they took longer than five minutes.

Matron tutted down the line while Sally explained, then said, "I find it despicable how supposedly rational people can turn so quickly on children. Of course you must stay at home, Sally. I'll ask one of the other women to cover and perhaps when everything settles down, you can cover for her."

"Yes, Matron. Rachel will still be coming in to help out. Please look after her. I told her how happy you were with her but she feels Britain is becoming like it was in Germany. She thinks we hate the Jews."

"I'll speak to her. If I had ten girls who worked as hard as she does, I'd be a happier woman. Look after yourself, Sally."

Sally thanked her and hung up. Deep in thought, she jumped when Tom came up behind her, a racket and ball in his hands.

"I'm glad you will be at home with us. You make nicer meals."

"Tom Beck, Maggie is a wonderful cook!" Sally admonished her charge, but she was pleased he appreciated her efforts.

"I still prefer you being here. I'm going to teach Ruth how to play tennis." He put the racket and ball down, came over and gave her a hug before picking them up again and running off to play with Ruth.

Sally stared after him, amazed at the resilience of children.

Harry's voice came from the stairs. "Where did Tom go? I told him to stay close to the house but I just saw him running off."

Sally whirled around. "You gave me a fright, Harry. I didn't hear you come downstairs. He's gone to play with Ruth. He'll be fine. Maggie will watch him."

She saw the mutinous look on his face. "It is my job to watch over my brother."

"Harry, you share that job with me. I'm happy Maggie will look after him. I know you got a fright yesterday."

He glared at her, his hands curling into fists. "I am not scared. It is time I fought back. I won't be a victim again."

Sally put her hand on his arm, gently pushing him to sit down at the table. She took a seat opposite him. When he moved to stand, she said, "Sit and talk to me, Harry. What happened yesterday was wrong, but there is nothing you can do to make it right. Try to forget about it."

He sat on the edge of the chair. "But they said they hated us."

"Yes, they did, but they didn't mean it. Enid is speaking from hurt and the others the same. People say horrible things when they're angry and upset. Try to forgive them. Now what are you going to do with your day?"

Harry's eyes flitted from object to object in the room, although she doubted he saw anything.

"Harry?"

"I thought I might try to find a job like Rachel has. Not at the hospital, but maybe somewhere in town."

"Excellent idea." Sally hid her concern about the reaction he might get. "I think you should talk to Reverend Collins and see if he knows of anything you could do. He's been tutoring you and I'm sure will give you a reference. But don't forget you have to keep your English studies up even if you get a job. It's important you do well in your exams if you are going to live in England."

"Yes, Sally." His words didn't match his tone, which suggested studying was the last thing he needed to be doing.

Sally turned away to hide her smile. He may think he was a grown-up, but sometimes he sounded and acted just like Tom.

* * *

It took Maggie a little longer to calm down. She was still raging over the way they had treated the children when Sally caught up with her later that week.

"I swear to you, if I had my hands on that Enid or Jane, I could rip their hair out."

"Maggie! What would Reverend Collins say?"

"I don't care about turning the other cheek. A slapped cheek would be good enough for them," Maggie muttered. "Rachel doesn't go for a walk anymore. She comes home from her shift at the hospital and sits in her room."

"She's just processing what happened. She'll go back to normal in time, Maggie. She has you and me and Matron at the hospital who thinks she's a gift from heaven."

Maggie didn't look convinced, but she wasn't as angry-looking either when she left.

* * *

A FEW DAYS LATER, Sally hummed one of Vera Lynn's tunes as she took advantage of the beautiful summer day. She took the wash basket to the garden, hanging the clothes on the line. She listened to the birds singing, watched as the bees flew from one flower to another. It was such a pretty scene and so different from that playing out over in France. She could only imagine what a battlefield was like; the wounded men at the hospital had tried to describe it but couldn't find the words.

Once the clothes were all on the line, she picked up Lisa from her blanket on the grass where she was giving her dolly a tea party. Maggie had found a second-hand tea set for Lisa's second birthday back in March. That, and the doll Sally had given her, were her favourite possessions. Snuggling her close, Sally said, "Why don't we go visit Maggie and have some tea?"

Lisa giggled and tried to pull Sally's hair before pushing her arms against Sally's shoulders to get down. "Lisa walk. Not a baby."

Sally smothered her smile at the child's insistence on being older.

"Tom, I'm going to Maggie's for a cuppa. Do you want to come?"

"No thank you. I'm playing with my marbles."

Sally rolled her eyes at Lisa, making her laugh again. "Boys and their toys."

"MAGGIE, how are we going to make cakes for the children, with butter and margarine being on ration? Powdered egg is horrible."

Maggie filled her cup with watery-looking tea. "Sorry, third time I've used these leaves. Why don't you get a few chickens from one of the farmers? You have plenty of space and they don't cost much to feed. Then you will have fresh."

Tom's shout interrupted Maggie mid-sentence. "Aunt Sally, come quick. They've arrested Harry."

"What?" Sally jumped to her feet, rattling the table in the process. Lisa burst out crying.

Maggie attempted to reassure her. "Sally, calm

down. The children must have it wrong. Why would anyone arrest Harry?"

Sally grabbed Lisa and gave her a quick kiss. "I'll be back soon, darling." She put her back down. "I don't know, Maggie – mind Lisa for me, will you?"

Sally didn't wait for an answer but ran outside. She stopped; two members of the Home Guard were outside her house, one with a gun fixed with a bayonet. They wouldn't look at her. She pushed past them into the house, where to her horror a member of the Home Guard she didn't recognise had a gun pointed at Harry. She walked in front of Harry and pushed the man's gun away.

"What do you mean by coming into my house and pointing that gun at a child?"

"He's no child. He's a German spy and he's coming with us."

Sally couldn't believe her ears. "A spy? He's a Jewish refugee."

"He didn't register with the police though, did he? And what's he doing taking photographs? He's an enemy alien, shouldn't even have a camera."

Sally groaned. The camera. She shouldn't have lent it to the children but they'd wanted to take photographs to show their families. "It's my camera, or at least my husband's. I lent it to the children so they could take a picture for their mother. She, a

Jewish woman, is stuck in Nazi Germany. Harry is innocent. You just have to ask Constable Cooper."

"I don't have to ask anyone. If you are that keen on the lad, do him a favour and pack him a case. We're leaving in five minutes. I'll take the camera too."

"You can't. It's my husband's, and he's in France fighting for his country."

The man's face flushed at her response. He stepped closer but this time Harry pushed her behind his back.

"Aunt Sally, please don't argue. I will go. You can sort it out, and then they will let me come back." He stepped towards the stairs.

"Where are you going?" she asked, still determined to keep him with her.

"To pack my case. I will be right back."

The man shouted at the men outside to watch the windows. He posted a sentry on both the front and back doors as if Harry was a common criminal eager to escape.

Sally begged the men to reconsider but to no avail.

"Don't you have anything better to do than terrorise Jewish survivors of Hitler? That lad has already been in a camp, back in Germany. He isn't a dangerous anything, never mind a threat to Britain."

"Your neighbours don't agree. They said he was taking photographs of sensitive targets."

"Sensitive targets, out here in Abbeydale? There isn't anything of interest to the Germans in this small town. I could maybe understand if Harry had been taking pictures of the palace or government buildings. Who could have claimed otherwise?"

"We have our sources."

Beryl Dalton or Enid Brown. She knew whichever woman was behind this, if she caught her this second, she'd likely kill her.

She heard Tom's voice coming from outside. "Get off me. Let me in. Aunt Sally!"

The guard tried to stop her, but Sally ignored the man and opened the back door, the child falling into her arms.

He looked up at her, distraught. "Is it true, have they come for us?"

"Not you, darling."

"But Harry? You can't take him! Not again. The last time soldiers took my brother and father, Papa didn't come home. I won't let you have my brother. I won't!"

The child kicked at the guard's legs. Sally didn't restrain him; she felt like kicking the guard too. But when the man raised his hand to give the child a clout, she grabbed Tom.

"Calm down, darling, you aren't helping. We will

bring him home, I promise. But for now, we have to be brave."

Tom gazed up at her with tear-filled eyes. "Why? Is it because he's Jewish?"

"He's German," the man spat, losing his temper as he shouted up the stairs. "Come on, you. Downstairs and out into the truck. Got others just like you to pick up."

Harry walked down the stairs, a resigned look on his face, which scared Sally more than tears. She pulled him into a hug. "It won't be like last time. This is Britain. I'll find you and bring you home."

For a second, he held her and then released her. He picked Tom up and threw him into the air but the child didn't squeal in laughter as he usually did. "I will be back, little brother. But for now, you must be the man of the house. Mind Lisa and Aunt Sally."

Tom nodded, tears running down his face.

"Can I say goodbye to my baby sister?" Harry asked the guard.

Sally's heart soared. He did love Lisa. She piped up, "I left her at the vicarage. It won't take a moment for me to get her."

"We don't have time for that. Say goodbye for him. Now come on, you."

The man prodded Harry in the back, pushing him none too gently out of the house.

Sally couldn't bear it. Why wouldn't they let him

say goodbye to a baby? It was so unfair. But she'd forgotten the force that was Maggie Ardle.

She saw her friend, carrying Lisa in her arms, Ruth running along beside them.

"Just you wait a minute," Maggie shouted, getting the attention of all the soldiers. "That lad is going nowhere without this parcel of food and a hug from his friends. You men should be ashamed of yourselves, picking on decent young boys like this one. Harry, come here."

Harry glanced at the corporal, who didn't make a move to stop him. Maggie thrust Lisa into his arms. The young girl wrapped her arms around her big brother and sighed. Sally saw the first hint of tears in Harry's eyes.

He cuddled the child, kissed her forehead and then gave her to Sally. "Look after both of them for me."

"I will." Sally held his gaze for a couple of seconds. "I will find you, Harry. Don't forget that."

He held her gaze but she didn't see any hope, only resignation. He shook hands with Maggie, who apologised for the reverend being away. "Rachel went to the station in case he came back early. If he was here, he'd stop this, I know he would."

As though she heard Maggie say her name, Rachel came running at that moment, and flung herself into Harry's arms, almost knocking him off his feet. She kissed his cheek. Then she turned on the guards and gave them a piece of her mind in her native German. They wouldn't understand the words but there was no mistaking the meaning. Sally saw a couple of the men wouldn't look at Rachel or Harry but seemed intent on studying their boots. At least they had the grace to look ashamed.

Ruth burst into noisy tears as Harry bent down to pick her up. He whispered something to her, and the child gulped noisily before nodding. He put her gently back on the ground. She walked over to Tom and took hold of his hand.

Then Harry pulled Rachel back into his arms and kissed her on the mouth before walking away. Sally watched, her heart breaking for the girl, as Rachel, looking stunned, stared at Harry walking away towards the army truck.

CHAPTER 28

*a*s the truck pulled away, Harry looked back at the group of people he'd come to care for until they disappeared from sight. He kept his feet pinned to the floor of the truck to stop his legs from shaking. He refused to show these men how terrified he was. What would they do to him? Would it be like Dachau? He knew he couldn't survive another camp like that.

Two more young men were picked up, one Jewish but the other was German. He didn't say a word, but sat as far away from the other two as possible, as if they were tainting the air he breathed just by their presence.

Harry spoke a few words to the Jewish boy in Yiddish.

"Talk English or shut up," the guard with the gun snarled.

* * *

THEY SPENT the night sleeping on straw mattresses on the floor of one of the stables at Ascot racecourse. The atmosphere was very tense. The Jewish boy, Joseph, kept close to Harry. Without saying anything, they picked the opposite side of the hall to where their other companion had chosen.

"What do you think they will do with us?" Harry whispered.

"Not sure. Maybe they'll realise their mistake and send us back." Joseph glanced around him as he spoke. "I liked where I was living. My mother's old employer got us out of Germany and gave her a job and us a place to stay. She will go out of her mind when she gets home and finds me gone. They wouldn't let me leave a note."

An older man of about fifty was sitting on a mattress near them. He reminded Harry of a younger version of the rabbi who led the services back in Berlin. His beard wasn't white but flecked with grey. "Take the weight off your feet, boys." He gestured to his side.

They sat beside him.

"You speak like an English man," Harry said.

"I've been living in England since the end of the first world war. When Hitler came to power, I changed my name, Hirschman, to Hillman, to make it sound more English. Did it for the children. They were getting picked on at school. Never thought much about it. Certainly didn't think they would use it as an excuse to arrest me one day." Mr Hillman sighed. "This is my home. I couldn't believe it when Bob – he's our local policeman – came to arrest me. Not that he could look me in the face. Didn't we used to play football every Saturday and Sunday? Went to see Arsenal matches together too."

Mr Hillman took another breath. Harry wondered if he had breathing problems or was just emotional.

"But he was only doing his job. Said something about Churchill telling them to collar the lot." Mr Hillman glanced down.

Harry looked at Joseph but his eyes were closed.

Harry found himself feeling sorrier for the man than he did for himself. At least he and Joseph had only recently come to live in the country. "You will find yourself at home soon, Mr Hillman." He gave the man a few seconds to compose himself. "How long have you been in this hall? What's it like, and where are they planning to take us?"

"Only been here a few days. It was alright at first but last night someone got trigger-happy and shot an internee. I think it was an accident. Still, it didn't help the mood." Mr Hillman looked him in the face. "It's my own fault I'm here. I should have paid for my naturalisation papers but I never got round to it. They say they are sending us away. To Canada or Australia or something."

Stunned, Harry could only gape at him. He couldn't go to Canada. How would Sally find him and reunite him with his siblings? "I can't leave the country. I've a younger brother and sister back in Abbeydale. They need me. Papa died in Dachau. They've nobody else."

"Your mother?"

"Dead," Harry answered, deciding not to elaborate about Trudi.

"Do the children have someone to look after them?" Joseph asked Harry.

"Yes, Sally Matthews. An English lady, she's very kind. But she's not blood, not family. She isn't even Jewish."

Joseph said, "Do you think that matters? Even now? Look around you. Most everyone in here is Jewish. They lock us up in Germany and now here in Britain. Everyone hates the Jews."

Harry knew Joseph was stating the truth. He glanced around too, spotting the man who'd travelled with them in the truck. The man glared at him before saying something to the man beside him. They looked straight back at Harry before spitting. The insult was clear.

Mr Hillman shook his head, stroking his beard. "Not everyone in here is Jewish or anti-Nazi. I guess Churchill had to be careful. There are bound to be enemy agents operating here. What better disguise than to pretend to be on the run from Hitler?"

The boys didn't respond, knowing the boy that had been picked up with them – Weiss – would fit in with Hitler's pack.

"They'll be pretending to be Jewish next. Did you hear that joke about Himmler and God?" Mr Hillman asked.

Harry and Joseph shook their heads.

"Himmler dies and goes to Heaven. He tries to confess his sins but St Peter won't let him in. But finally he convinces Peter he is genuinely sorry and wants to atone for his sins. God appears and asks if he is serious. Himmler thinking this is great, says he would do anything."

"And?" Harry prompted when Mr Hillman looked as if he was waiting for a reaction.

"God tells him he needs proof of his remorse. He sends him back to earth as a Jew living in Nazi Germany." Mr Hillman laughed heartily but the boys simply exchanged a look. Being Jewish in Germany wasn't something to joke about.

"You must never forget to laugh or live for the future, boys. If you do, the Nazis have won, even if they don't kill you. There will always be murderous fanatics but the majority of people you meet have a good heart regardless of their race, creed or nationality."

Harry didn't want to hear a lecture. Especially as it reminded him of Papa. That had been his attitude too. It hadn't protected him. He lay back and pretended to sleep while Joseph asked Mr Hillman about the routine and day-to-day activities.

TIME PASSED SLOWLY, tensions rising among the inmates. Harry came out of the toilet one day to find himself facing Weiss and a friend.

Weiss sneered. "This is the Jew boy who was picked up with me. Had to share the cart with him."

Harry glanced around but there was nobody. At least no one he recognised to call to for help. He clenched and unclenched his hands. He could take on Weiss alone but two of them would be tough.

Speaking German, Weiss threw a barrage of insults at him, making his friend laugh.

"Shut up, Weiss. You're so full of it, you can't even think of something original," Harry responded in English. He went to walk away, Rachel's words rattling in his mind. He could fight but it was time to use his brain.

But Weiss had other ideas. He put his hand out, placing it on Harry's shoulder, and forced him to turn around, punching him in the stomach. Despite being winded, Harry punched him in the face, knocking him to the ground. Out of the corner of his eye he saw the friend pick up a metal pipe, raising it into the air. Harry instinctively ducked, unable to run away due to the building behind him. Just then, he heard a roar, and saw Mr Hillman running towards them. The roar was loud enough to attract the attention of the soldiers on guard. A shot was fired into the air, and the two Nazis took off, leaving Harry shaking and Mr Hillman furious.

Harry refused to tell the guards who the boys were, claiming he didn't recognise them. He'd deal with them in his own time. He expected Hillman to disagree, but the older man claimed his eyesight wasn't what it had once been.

CHAPTER 29

*I*n the Ascot camp there was a sort of routine, with roll calls every morning and evening. Harry didn't know why they bothered as the numbers never tallied. There were rumours about post arriving but it failed to materialise. They got hot food twice a day, rather lumpy porridge in the morning and hard brown bread and cocoa each evening.

Boredom was their biggest enemy.

Harry and the younger boys played football with an improvised straw-filled ball. They ran and exercised to keep fit. Harry joined in, taking every opportunity to increase his physical fitness. He ran around the race track more times than he could count, training in all weathers, all with a view to escaping. But the chance never materialised.

One morning at roll call, they were told to wait in line, rather than being dismissed as usual.

"Something's up," Joseph muttered. "Someone saw some officers drive in, and empty trucks are outside."

A chill ran down Harry's neck. "Where are we being taken?" He scrutinised the faces of the guards they had come to know, the ones who were pleasant to them. A few saw him staring but looked away. That didn't help the feeling something bad was happening.

An officer stepped forward and started calling out names.

"Beck, Harry. Hillman, David. Stein, Joseph." Harry felt Joseph tremble at his side.

The officer continued to call out names. Weiss and Horstman were also called.

Joseph and Harry stood beside Mr Hillman. They had no idea what they had been singled out for.

Mr Hillman whispered, "Boys, wait here. Cover for me. If they ask, I have gone to the bathroom."

Instead, he walked up to their cook, a veteran from World War One who came from the same area as Mr Hillman. They had a quick conversation with some gesturing. Harry saw Mr Hillman's face pale as his friend gripped his hands. The friend was trying to get Mr Hillman to listen to something but Mr Hillman just shook his head. He seemed to have aged ten years when he came back.

"They are sending us to Canada. Boys, you have to get out of this line. You are too young to go."

Before the boys could say anything, Mr Hillman addressed the officer in charge, telling him the boys were only sixteen. He said something about them needing parental permission to take children abroad. The officer looked uncomfortable, checking his lists and glaring at Harry and Joseph as if it was their responsibility they were young.

"Mr Hillman, we'd like to stay with you," Joseph pleaded. Harry felt the same.

Mr Hillman put one hand on each boy's shoulder. "Boys, you must act like the gentlemen your parents brought you up to be. German U-boats patrol the Atlantic. Now is not the time to go travelling by sea."

The officer conferred with other uniformed men before briskly telling Harry and Joseph to stand down from the line. Two other men took their place.

* * *

About a hundred or so men gathered together by the time the officer finished his list. They were told to gather their things and report back. A bus would take them to the train station for onward transfer to Liverpool. Harry and Joseph helped Mr Hillman pack his few belongings.

"Don't forget, boys. This is a great country

offering religious freedom. This…" Mr Hillman spread his arms wide to take in the camp "…is the fault of the Nazis. Churchill is acting to protect his country. You will be back living with your brother and sister soon, Harry, and you with your mother, Joseph."

Harry gulped, trying to keep his voice steady. "What of your wife, Mr Hillman? Will they tell her where you are?"

"My wife died in a motor accident caused by the blackout. I'm thankful she didn't live to see this."

The order came for the men to leave. Harry and Joseph watched the bus until it disappeared from sight.

* * *

A FEW DAYS LATER, a guard threw away his paper. Harry grabbed it, hiding it under his jacket. Later, he and Joseph sat down to read it. Harry used the cast-away papers to improve his English reading skills with Joseph correcting him.

The headline of one article jumped out at Harry: "Shipload of Internees Torpedoed".

He turned to Joseph. "This story is about a ship being bombed. The Arandora Star. Isn't that the ship Mr Hillman and the others were loaded onto?"

Joseph took the paper from Harry's shaking

hands, reading the article for himself in silence. When he finished, he looked up, his eyes suspiciously bright, his voice trembling. "Mr Hillman's prophecy of the U-boats came true. A torpedo struck and sank the ship off the coast of Ireland with the loss of most of the people on board. He saved us."

"He could have survived. Do they list the names?"

Joseph shook his head, before turning over in his bunk to face the wall. Harry saw his shoulders shake but Joseph didn't make a sound. They had learnt to cry in silence.

CHAPTER 30

JULY 1940

"Sally, are you in?" Maggie shouted from the lane.

Sally dropped the clothes she was hanging on the clothes line and ran to the garden gate to greet her. "What's wrong?"

"Come in and sit down." Maggie tried to lead her indoors to the kitchen. "I'll make the tea."

"Is it news of Harry? Reverend Collins promised me he would find him but that the government would keep him safe. Was he wrong?"

Maggie didn't say anything.

Sally couldn't move, her feet rooted to the spot. "Tell me what's going on, you're scaring me." She put her arms around herself, knowing that look on Maggie's face. It was the same one Maggie had worn when she'd come to find Sally at school to tell her about her mum.

"Who?" Sally demanded. As Maggie stayed silent, Sally heard the bell on a pushbike. Ian, the telegram boy. *Ride on past*, she shouted in her head. She and Maggie stared at one another in silence as they heard the boy put the bike against the wall, the squeak of the gate as he pushed it open. She'd asked Derek to mend the gate but he'd run out of time before he'd gone away. *Derek, please God, no!* It couldn't be. Not her Derek.

Her knees weakened as she heard the knock on the door.

"Round the back, Ian," Maggie shouted.

Ian poked his head around the side of the cottage. "Mrs Ardle, you know I have to give it ... oh hello, Mrs Matthews, I didn't see you. I..." Ian's voice was drowned out by Sally's scream.

She shouted, "No! I don't want it. Take it away. Go away, do you hear me? Scram. Get on your bike and leave. Take that with you. I won't open it. I won't."

A gentle slap across her face brought her back to her senses. For a split second, she held her hand to her face before Maggie pulled her into her arms.

She heard Maggie say over her shoulder, "Go on, Ian, lad. Leave it on the table in the kitchen."

"But Mrs Ardle..."

"Leave it, lad. Nobody will know that you didn't put it into her hand. Now go on. Find Reverend Collins and let him know."

Sally heard all this from a distance. She couldn't move, couldn't feel anything, even though she knew Maggie had her arms wound tightly around her. She was glad of that, as she might topple over otherwise. She looked up. The sky was bright blue, birds were singing, the sun was shining. It shouldn't be like that. The sky should be black, the sun hiding behind the dark clouds, with rain teeming down. That's how it happened in films, all the time.

She could hear the boy leaving, the scrape of the bike against the wall, the sound of tyres on the pebbles.

Maggie led her into the house and forced her to sit down. She heard her put the kettle on.

Sally glanced at the table, the brown envelope sitting where Ian had left it. She put her hand out towards it, surprised to see her hand shaking. She held one hand with the other before she could pick up the envelope. She didn't want to open it, didn't want to know what was inside.

"He may not be ... he could just be hurt." Maggie's voice broke through her thoughts.

Sally grabbed the envelope and tore it open, reading it over and over, but the words wouldn't register. She held it out to Maggie. "What does it say? I can't make it out…"

Maggie took the telegram from her gently and read it. She looked up. "He's missing, presumed…"

Sally stood up to stop Maggie from saying the last word. She didn't want to hear it. She started laying the table with plates and cutlery.

Maggie watched her for a moment and then said firmly, "Sally, sit down and have some tea. Put a teaspoon of sugar in it. It's good for shock."

"The children will be hungry. You know what they are like. Lisa will be awake soon. She doesn't sleep long these days. Into everything, she is, the little rascal. She's changed so much from the baby she was when she first arrived. She tried to run off the other day. Did you know that?"

"Sally, sit down now or I'm going for the doctor. Dunkirk was a mess. There're thousands missing. He's probably a prisoner of war or something. You need to contact the Red Cross. I think they are the ones who find out where the soldiers are, what camp they are in."

Sally knew Maggie was trying to be helpful but she didn't want her there. She didn't want anyone in her home. In Derek's home.

"Maggie, can you take Lisa to your house and wait there for Tom? He has to walk past your house from school. Can you keep the children there for a while? I have to think. I need to be alone."

Maggie frowned. "Alone is the last thing you need."

"Don't tell me what I need. I want my Derek right here beside me, that's what I need. But that's not going to happen now, is it?"

"Sally, I—"

"Please, just go. I don't want to hurt you but I have to be alone. I just have to be."

Maggie didn't say another word but went upstairs to collect Lisa. When she came back downstairs, carrying the child, Lisa was squirming to get down. She hated to be carried anywhere. She called for Sally but Sally couldn't look at her, she felt numb.

Maggie said, soothingly, "Come on, Lisa pet, we are going to see Rachel, Ruth and Tom. You'll enjoy that, won't you?"

"No! Want Mum. Not Tom."

Sally heard the child complaining as Maggie led her outside, closing the garden gate behind them. Then there was silence, apart from the ticking clock on the mantlepiece. A wedding present from some relative of Derek's. Sally couldn't remember the old man's name. Her gaze landed on Derek's photo. She picked it up and headed upstairs to their bedroom.

Lying on the bed, she held his photograph close. He couldn't be dead, not Derek. He just couldn't be.

She'd have felt something if he'd died. She'd have known.

REVEREND COLLINS CAME BY LATER. She heard him call her name when he knocked, but she didn't answer or open the door. She'd pulled the blackout blinds shut so had no idea what time it was. Later, she heard Maggie come, but as her friend let herself in and climbed the stairs, calling her name, she pretended to be asleep. She didn't react when Maggie told her she'd got some of Tom and Lisa's things and would keep them overnight at her house. She closed her eyes and pretended the whole world didn't exist. There was no war, nobody was dying, children weren't being arrested by soldiers with guns. It was just her and Derek. Only, he wasn't there. She was alone.

SHE DIDN'T KNOW how long she lay in bed. The hours rolled into each other. She didn't eat, bathe or change her clothes. She didn't leave the bed unless she absolutely had to. It was safer in her blackened-out corner of the world.

THE SOUND of crying woke her up. In her dream, a little boy had screamed her name. But now she was awake, she realised it wasn't a dream. It was Tom, and he was calling for her. He kept banging at the door, screaming for her to come out.

She almost fell out of the bed and down the stairs, before opening the door to allow Tom to fling himself into her arms.

Tom cried, "You're not dead. You haven't gone away. You're still here. Promise you won't go away. You won't leave us. I love you. Lisa loves you. We need you..." The boy continued repeating himself, over and over.

Sally couldn't say anything, just held him tight.

He put his arms around her neck, his tears wetting her skin. "Maggie said you were very sad, as you had a broken heart. People die when their hearts stop working. I thought you were dead."

"Tom, darling Tom. I'm not dead."

"Why didn't you come and get us? You left us with Maggie. Rachel is being really bossy. She hurts my hair when she brushes it and makes me take a bath every night."

Sally couldn't stop the smile at those words. Nobody hated bath time more than Tom.

"How's Lisa?"

"She's sad too. She was crying over and over but she doesn't cry now. She says you're gone. Mum's gone, Mum's gone. That's what she says. Over and over."

What had she done? These little children depended on her and she'd let them down. She wasn't fit to be looking after them. A real mother wouldn't have put her children aside and wallowed in misery, as she had.

"Can we come home, please? I promise to be good. I won't get into trouble at school. Please?"

"Tom, this is your home. I'm sorry. For the last few days, for everything. Just give me a few minutes to get changed and I'll come with you to Maggie's and get Lisa."

Tom wrinkled his nose. "You need a bath. You smell horrid."

Sally burst out laughing and gave him another cuddle. This time he struggled to get away.

She said, "Go and see what you can find to eat. I think Maggie may have dropped off some food. I won't be long."

"I'm starving." Tom walked into the kitchen and whistled. "Maggie must have thought you needed to eat a lot."

Sally put her head around the door and saw her table was loaded with provisions and small dishes of her favourite foods. Or at least those available on ration.

Maggie had done everything to make her feel

better, and she'd pushed her friend away without a second thought. It was a good job Derek wasn't here to see how selfish she'd become. She ran upstairs and shivered through a cold bath.

Dressed in clean clothes, she opened the blinds in the bedroom and pushed the windows out as far as they would go. Tom was right, the smell was horrid.

She came downstairs to find him munching his way through second or third helpings, by the looks of the dishes.

"Come on, Tom, let's get your sister and bring her home."

His look grazed her from head to toe before he smiled. "You look like Aunt Sally again."

"I feel like her too. Just one minute, there's something I forgot to do."

She ran back upstairs and retrieved the photograph of Derek from her bed. Kissing it, she brought it back downstairs and put it back, in pride of place, on the mantlepiece.

"Love you always," she whispered, before turning to take Tom's hand. Together, they walked up the short lane to Maggie's house.

CHAPTER 31

*S*ally pushed the door open, feeling shy, which was silly given how long she had known Maggie.

"Maggie, it's only me."

"Hi, stranger. Feeling better?"

Sally saw the concern in her friend's eyes, despite the light-hearted greeting.

"I'm sorry, Maggie. I behaved like a spoilt child. Forgive me?"

"Don't be daft. You did what you had to do. The sun went out of my life for a long time after I lost my Reg. Now, what you got there, young man?"

Tom held up half a slice of cake. "Aunt Sally told me to help myself. I cut a big bit."

The adults smiled as Tom stuffed the cake into his mouth, probably in fear of getting it taken away. He glanced around and tried to speak with his mouth full, resulting in a coughing fit and crumbs flying everywhere.

Maggie frowned as she looked up from the kitchen table, which was covered in an array of vegetables. From the looks of it, Sally guessed she was making a vegetable pie for dinner. Maggie picked up some carrots and started chopping them, the knife hitting the chopping board a little too sharply. Sally knew she was finding cutting back on cigarettes difficult.

Tom asked, "Where are the girls? I have to tell Lisa we are going home."

"The girls had a letter, Tom, and it's upset them, so I need you to be really kind to them."

Tom looked into her face. "Like I was kind to Aunt Sally?"

"Yes. Just like that." Maggie ruffled his hair but Tom squirmed and moved closer to the door. Before he left the room, he turned. "Who was the letter from?"

"Their mother."

"Oh!" Looking thoughtful, Tom paused before asking, "Do they have to go back to Berlin? I don't, do I? I want to stay here with Aunt Sally."

"Nobody is going back to Berlin," Maggie reassured him quickly, as Sally moved close and gave him a cuddle. "Be nice to them, Tom."

Tom ran to find the girls while Sally took a seat in front of the china cups Maggie always used for her table.

"How did Rachel's mother get a letter out of Germany? What did it say?" Sally asked, tempted to take the knife from Maggie's hands.

"It was written in a type of code from what I can work out. For one thing, she used the term *Liesel's mother*, instead of Trudi, as you would normally." Maggie stopped cutting and held Sally's gaze. "I think Mrs Bernstein knows her days are numbered but she was trying to reassure her girls she will be fine."

Sally held her cup and saucer but her shaking hands made them rattle, so she put them back down on the table. "Why do you say that?"

"She says a friend of Trudi's, is keeping them supplied with food and they have to all stay in the one place. I think she is hiding somewhere. Reverend Collins says that the Nazis have a policy to clear the large cities of Jews. The letter has a Swedish post-mark. Mrs Bernstein doesn't give an address. Rachel noticed that but she didn't tell Ruth."

Sally stared at the ceiling, her heart aching for the young girls. Since she and Rachel had started working at the hospital, she'd come to love her almost as much as Tom and Lisa. "So, they can't write back. The poor girls. I think the letter might have been worse than hearing nothing, don't you?"

"I don't know. At least they know their mother was alive as recently as last month. Hope is a wonderful thing. Maybe a miracle will happen and she will live through to the end of the war and be reunited with her family. She did say one of Rachel's brothers, Izsak, had made it to Palestine. The girls were happy about that."

"That's good news. What about the other one? Where is he?"

Maggie shrugged.

"I wonder where Harry is, Maggie. Reverend Collins can't locate him. I wrote to the Red Cross but they didn't answer. I promised him I would find him. I don't want him to think I've forgotten him. I wish he'd write to us."

"I guess he will when he's settled, if he can."

Sally stirred her tea, trying to find the right words.

"You'll wear a hole in my cup. Take the spoon out and drink the tea, love."

"I'm sorry. For being rude and—"

"Be quiet. We're family, and that means we stick together through good and bad. You needed some time alone. Now you need your family, and those children need you."

Sally smiled, her eyes full of tears. Maggie's tears glistened, making her Irish eyes bluer than normal.

"I'm so lucky to have you, Maggie. I don't know

if I could ever live without you. I wonder if his mother knows or whether I should write to her."

"That woman doesn't deserve your kindness."

Sally reached for Maggie's hand. "You're always protecting me, Maggie. Thank you." Sally knew she had to tell Derek's mother, that was only right. Maggie squeezed Sally's hand. Neither of them spoke for quite a while.

LATER, Rachel translated the letter for Sally and Maggie.

My darling Rachel and Ruth,

How are you, my dear daughters? I hope you have found a happy home together in England. I wish I could give you my address but it is not safe. Should this letter fall into the wrong hands, we would pay a high price.

I am living with Liesel's mother and some other friends. It was easier for us to keep one apartment. Liesel's mother knows someone who gives us food and other things. I don't know who he is; it is safer that way. I think he may be one of them.

I had word of your brother. Izsak made it to Palestine. I pray Gavriel is with him.

Things are difficult here in Berlin but they are not as bad as they could be. We are still here and not shipped off East. They sent some people, including your father's friend, Mr Stanislaus, to Poland. They say he is Polish, as he arrived in Germany when he was six months old. It doesn't matter that he has been living here and running a successful company for forty years. His manager took over the factory without paying a single pfennig for it. So many families you know from school have left. Some to England, some to Palestine, some to America and other places. Your uncle is in Holland. He tries to help me. Maybe there will be time for me to move there.

I know you tried to find me a job in England but it wasn't possible. The war came too quickly. I don't know if you will get this letter but I pray you do. Liesel's mother's friend may have a way to reach you.

I have to go now.

Rachel, look after your sister and Ruth, be good.

I love you both and I will see you again when the war is over.

Mama.

Rachel folded the letter carefully, placing it in her pocket. "Ruth kissed Mama's signature before running upstairs. I followed her but she wanted to be alone."

"I'm sorry things are hard for your mother, Rachel. What can Maggie and I do?"

"Nothing, but thank you for asking. There was a

note from Trudi too. I don't know if you want to tell Tom. I didn't say anything."

"What did she say?" Maggie asked.

"'Dear Rachel, I hope you get this letter. I pray you are near my darling baby and her brothers. Please give them a kiss from me. I hope to see them again.'"

Sally waited for Rachel to say more. When she didn't, she asked, "That was it? No signature or anything."

Rachel handed over the note but it was written in German.

"It is odd, isn't it? Almost as if Trudi is hiding more than Mama. Maybe she is better known? Dr Beck had many wealthy, Gentile patients."

Maggie sniffed and blew her nose in her hanky before saying, "Let's hope some of those patients are helping his wife survive."

CHAPTER 32

S itting with her thoughts for a minute in the sun while the children played in the garden, Sally was surprised to hear a car pull up outside the cottage. Nobody drove these days, not unless it was an emergency.

"Tom, watch Lisa. I need to see who is at the front door."

Lisa toddled over. "Me coming."

Sally smiled as the determined two-year-old held onto her hand and together they walked through the side gate. Sally stopped at the vision before her. An older woman of about Maggie's age stood at the front door. But that was the only similarity between the two women. This woman had no laughter lines on her face, her eyes pierced Sally to the spot with a venomous expression. Lisa must have noticed as she squeezed Sally's hand, moving closer to her leg.

The woman stood waiting as if expecting Sally to curtsey or something. Sally caught herself. This was her home. She stood her ground, taking in the woman's well-cut summer coat, the shapely dress underneath, the silk stockings and fabulous shoes. Her whole outfit screamed money.

"Can I help you?" Sally said, her tone wary but not unfriendly.

"This is my house. I'd like to come inside."

Sally's mouth fell open. Who did this woman think she was?

Sally said, "Excuse me, I'm Mrs Matthews, and I—"

"No, my dear, I am Mrs Matthews. You, on the other hand, are some … girl who seduced my son and trapped him into marriage. I heard the child calling you 'Mum'. I didn't think you'd known Derek that long."

Derek! This was his mother. She bristled at the insult, and then tried to keep calm, telling herself the woman was grieving for her son; that's why she was behaving like this.

"I'm so sorry, Mrs Matthews. Do please come inside. Perhaps you could come around the back as the front door is locked. Lisa can reach up and open it now and has a tendency to run down the road to Maggie's." Why was she babbling? Sally tried to pull herself together.

The woman looked as if she had been asked to cross a field full of cow dung. "My dear girl, I never use the back door. Run along."

Sally turned and almost ran all the way to Maggie's house. Instead, she whisked Lisa off her feet and walked around the back, while Lisa asked who the woman was and said, "Not nice lady."

"Shush, darling. Go play with Tom for me now. There's a good girl."

Sally closed the garden gate behind her, and watched Lisa toddle back to Tom's side before wiping her hands on her apron. Dear Lord above, she had greeted Derek's mother in her gardening pinny. She tore it off, throwing it onto the laundry heap before running a hand through her hair, praying she didn't have mud on her face and opening the front door. The woman sailed past her into the house without a word of thanks.

Mrs Matthews looked around her with disdain. "Oh, this is simply awful. What have you done to my house? It was never much more than a little bolthole outside of London, but now, with the threat of bombing, I had thought to … What are you doing, standing there gawping at me? Couldn't you offer me a cup of tea or perhaps something stronger?"

Sally couldn't move.

"Are you simple?"

How dare she.

Sally turned her back on her visitor and walked purposefully out the front door to the car outside. The chauffeur put out his cigarette and stood up straight.

"Can I help you, madam?"

The man's tone was formal but his eyes were kind. She immediately liked him. She held out her hand. "My name is Sally Matthews. I'm Derek's wife." Her voice hitched on his name.

"I know who you are, Missus. Name's Sam. If I may say so, Master Derek picked himself a nice lass."

Sally nearly dissolved in tears at his kindness. "Won't you come inside? You must be dying for a cup of tea after the journey down from London."

"My throat is as dry as sandpaper but I couldn't do that, Miss Sally. Mind if I call you that? Master Derek told me about you. Perhaps I could have a drink of water in the garden. While I wait."

"This is my house, and I say who can come in."

Sam looked at her approvingly. "That's the spirit. You stick to your guns. Don't let that one ride all over you. If the master were here, he would put a stop to her gallop. But I'll stay out here all the same. Won't do you any good if I poke my nose in. You best get back. Patience isn't her virtue."

Sally smiled tightly before turning to look at her

house. She pictured the day Derek had carried her over the threshold, telling her the cottage was hers and nobody would ever look down on her again.

She marched into the house. As she entered the hallway, her mother-in-law came down the stairs, not looking the least bit ashamed at having been caught snooping. "Did you forget something?"

"Mrs Matthews, I will be polite for the sake of my husband. You have no right to waltz into my house and act like you own it. I will happily make you a cup of tea but I insist S…" she caught herself in time, "your driver comes inside too. It's far too hot for a man of his age to be standing outside."

The woman bristled but Sally ignored her, sweeping past and walking into the kitchen to fill the kettle. The back door opened, admitting the children, Tom leading the way.

"We're hungry. Is that woman gone? Lisa said she wasn't nice." Tom's words carried through to the dining room where the woman had taken a seat.

Sally whispered, "Tom, mind your manners. Take your sister upstairs to wash her hands and then you can come down for some milk and a piece of cake."

A voice behind her startled her. "I will not be treated like this. You expect me to take tea with your brat and a German child? I will give you a week to pack up and leave. I owe my son that much, though why he had to die is beyond me. He never should have joined up. It was bad enough when Roland went but I suppose it was to be expected of a man in his position. At least he had the grace to join the Royal Air Force like a gentlemen."

Sally gripped the back of the chair, her knuckles turning white as she listened.

"Have you finished? Derek joined up because he believed Hitler and his like needed to be stopped. My husband is … is a fine man. Now get out before I throw you out."

"You wouldn't dare!"

"She would and what's more, Maggie will help her." Tom aimed a kick at Mrs Matthew's ankles before racing out the back door screaming for Maggie to come.

Sally watched him go, then turned to Mrs Matthews and straightened her shoulders. "This isn't your home any longer. Derek owns it."

"My son is dead!"

"No, he's not. He's missing. I'd know if my husband wasn't coming home," Sally replied through clenched teeth. "And I won't let you insult my children. Two refugees who arrived with barely more than they stood up in. They have suffered more than you can imagine and I won't have you scaring them. This is my home. Now get out before I throw you out. I will call Constable Cooper if I have to."

"You'd create a scene."

"From where I'm standing, it isn't our Sally that's creating a scene, Imelda Matthews. Remember me? Maggie Ardle. My Reg and your Richard were good pals. They went off to the trenches together." Maggie was standing in the doorway, with Tom behind her.

"Your husband was his batman. Hardly his best friend."

"My husband died saving your husband's life." Maggie drew herself up to her full five-foot-two inches and pushed her shoulders back. "You always were a stuck-up witch. Get out of here now, before I shove you out so fast you will land on that well-fashioned behind of yours."

Sally could only stare at Maggie, never having seen her so fired up before. She hadn't known about Reg saving Derek's father either. That was typical of Maggie, not to boast about her husband's heroic actions.

Derek's mother gave them a look that could have felled them. "I will leave now because I am a lady, and I will not entertain such common behaviour. I will return with our family lawyer. You have been warned. Pack your bags and leave. Or I shall have you thrown out."

The woman turned on her heel and marched out the front door.

Maggie let out a long breath and then gently

pushed Sally down into a chair, allowing Lisa to climb up on her lap and throw her arms around her.

"We won't leave you," Tom said, as he put his hand on Sally's shoulder. She knew she should reprimand him for kicking out at the woman, but she didn't have the energy right at that moment.

Maggie said, "Tom, take this and go see what Mr Callaghan has to give you. Tell him I sent you." She put the kettle on the range to boil. "Thank goodness they haven't put sweets on ration yet. That will keep them occupied for a while. You need something stronger than tea – where's your brandy?"

Sally shook her head, noticing for the first time that her hands were trembling. "Tea is fine. I can't believe that woman. How dare she be so horrible to the children? How can she be Derek's mother? Do you think she could really have us thrown out?'

"Never. You're legally wed, despite what she thinks. Derek will have left everything to you."

Sally looked up in time to meet Maggie's gaze. "You think he's dead, don't you?'

"Ah, child, sure I don't know, do I? All we have is that telegram. Nobody knows anything until they find … until the war is over." Maggie busied herself making tea, and added a large quantity of sugar to the pot. "I'll replace the tea and sugar from my own rations later but for now we need a cup of decent, strong tea, not dishwater."

Sally sipped the tea for Maggie's sake. She knew Derek was alive – he was out there somewhere and he'd come home to her one day. Until then, nobody was taking her house away from her and the children. Over her dead body.

CHAPTER 33

Orders came for Harry and the rest of the people in the camp to move once more. They also left by train for Liverpool. Harry tried to memorise the route – if he escaped, he might be able to find his way back to Abbeydale.

The soldiers from Ascot didn't come with them. This time, their guards were those who had survived Dunkirk. They didn't distinguish between Nazis or Jews, it was enough they were Germans. The guards spat in their water and threw food out the window. Harry and Joseph tried not to let it get to them. They were more concerned about where they were going. Was it Canada, or had Mr Hillman been right about the government needing permission to send them away?

The train pulled into another unnamed station. "Where are we?" Joseph asked.

"Liverpool, I think. Someone said they removed all the station names to stop Germans knowing how to travel around but anyone can tell this is a port. Smell that?"

Joseph sniffed the air, looking confused.

Harry clapped him on the back. "That's the sea, and you can hear the seagulls. It has to be a large port; listen to the sounds of the different boats, the smell of the motor oil." Harry kept talking, trying to hide his fear. Where were they taking them?

They were marched off the train and held on the station platform until they formed orderly lines. Once the guards were satisfied all was in order, they marched them the short way to the port.

The wind pulled at Harry's clothing, the salt biting into his skin. Or was that sweat from fear? There were so many ships, some built for battle, some looking like converted passenger cruise liners. The sheer number of ships ahead of them startled him.

When they were ordered to stop, they saw groups of other internees waiting. Harry guessed there were over eight hundred internees gathered together. Joseph saw one of the men talking to a soldier and sidled up to them. When he returned to Harry's side, he pointed at a boat in the busy port.

"That's our ship, right there, Harry. Hans asked that soldier, the nicer one."

"It's not a ship, it's tiny. That can't be going to Canada or Australia, can it?"

Joseph shook his head but he didn't seem convinced. Anxiety gnawed at Harry's stomach, making him feel queasy. He shuffled from one foot to the other as they stood waiting to board. When would someone tell them where they were going?

* * *

THE BOAT SWAYED under his feet, making him want to return to land via the ladder he had just climbed down. A glance at Joseph told him he was just as scared. Neither would admit to fear, of course. Harry looked around and spotted a crew member not much older than he was. He smiled in Harry's direction, so he got the courage to speak out.

"Are we going to Canada?"

The lad laughed but stopped when he saw Harry was serious. "No, mate, wouldn't get too far in this old girl. You lot are off to the Isle of Man." At Harry's blank stare, he added, "It's an island. The capital is Douglas, I grew up there. It's a nice place, and they are used to you lot."

Joseph slipped on some oil and would have fallen flat on his face but for Harry grabbing him. The crew member and some of his mates laughed, telling them they would soon find their sea legs. Their friendliness helped Harry's anxiety to dissipate slightly. Maybe this Isle of Man place would be alright.

THE JOURNEY PASSED RELATIVELY QUICKLY, both boys gazing at the sea until the island came into view. Someone said they were docking at the capital, Douglas. Armed guards with fixed bayonets escorted them from the boats.

They marched at a quick pace down the streets. Some had been closed off with barbed wire yet it didn't instil fear in the boys. Crowds of inhabitants of the Isle of Man stared at the new arrivals but they weren't unfriendly. They didn't shout words of hate or look threatening.

Harry saw some of them smiling. He marched on, wondering where they would end up. Joseph stuck to Harry's side, not wanting to be separated. As they marched, Harry looked around at the Edwardian houses, streets and streets of them. He guessed they would have housed summer visitors in the pre-war years, given their close proximity to the sea. Were they going to live there?

His chest felt light. This was so much better than the camp they had come from. Ordering them into a group of thirty, the soldier came to a stop at a large building, which looked like a hotel from the outside.

Harry walked in the door, following the men in front of him. Excited shouts came from upstairs; the building had indoor plumbing, including a bath. All rooms had double beds, and Joseph and Harry elected to share. Joseph turned on the electric light, which for some reason had an orange painted lightbulb. It gave off a weird glow, which together with the dark blue painted window frames was a bit creepy.

"Turn it off, Joseph," Harry instructed from the bed – he was testing it for comfort. Despite having to share, it was much better than their accommodation at Ascot.

They left their bags on the bed and ran downstairs to explore the rest of the house and the gardens. There was next to no furniture in the rooms downstairs but given the number of men joining the boys, they would soon be converted to bedrooms. The kitchen had basic utensils, such as a cooker and a sink, and there was a table and chairs in the back room.

Harry dragged Joseph outside. They could see the sea from the garden. "Maybe they will let us go swimming?" he said. Joseph didn't look too enamoured.

LATER THAT EVENING, they sat on the wall outside the house enjoying the sea breeze.

"It's a pity Mr Hillman wasn't able to come here, isn't it?" Joseph said after a while. "I think he would have enjoyed it. Look how many older men there are. Someone started a school. I think we should go."

Harry half-listened to Joseph, his mind occupied with plans to escape.

"We could learn English and other stuff. Someone is teaching Chinese. Can you imagine that?"

Harry let Joseph talk. It kept the boy calm.

"Did you know some of the old boys haven't seen each other since the last war when they were interned here? Back then, they said, it wasn't as strict. Families were allowed to come and visit. I wish Mother could come. I guess you'd like to see your brother and sister too. Do you have a girl?"

Harry closed his eyes and pictured Rachel's face. He thought of kissing her as they said goodbye. She'd been surprised by the kiss but not offended. Maybe he had a chance with her. But not until he escaped and got back home.

"Did anyone talk about escaping?" Harry asked.

Joseph shook his head, his face white. "They said they'd shoot anyone who tried to escape. Where would you go? They'd just pick you up again and maybe send you to Canada or Australia next time. I think you should wait it out here. Like everyone else."

Harry didn't argue. It was pointless telling Joseph he wasn't going to sit on his backside. He had to avenge his father, and that meant getting back to Germany.

Joseph was chatting again. "I think I'll take up martial arts. That way, I can defend myself if someone like the Nazi Weiss or his friends turn up. What about you?"

"Good idea. Sign me up for that and any physical education activities you can find. I'm going for a walk. Catch you later."

He dismissed Joseph's pleading look from his mind. He knew his friend didn't like being alone but Harry needed time to think and plan. He took a walk along the stretch of road, walking the distance from one piece of barbed wire to the next. How was he going to get back to Germany?

CHAPTER 34

ABBEYDALE, AUGUST 1940

*S*ally pushed the hair from her eyes, her back aching. She missed Derek every day. Harry too. Especially on days like today when she had work to do in the garden.

The front lawn didn't exist anymore. Harry had started to dig it up before he was taken away, and she'd finished what was left. They had to plant vegetables. "Dig for Victory", the government called it. Given the pain in her back, victory couldn't come fast enough.

The children enjoyed playing in the newly turned turf, as the birds flocked down to grab worms and bugs. She loved listening to Tom and Ruth's giggles as they ran, sending the birds flying away.

"We should stop them scaring the birds, it isn't kind," Rachel said.

Maggie sitting on the blanket under the big apple tree, gave them a tender glance. "Let them be children. They haven't had much chance over the last few years. The birds will be just fine." She had tried to help dig the garden but Rachel and Sally refused to let her.

"You keep Lisa out of trouble. That's enough of a job for anyone." Sally smiled at the toddler she considered hers. She couldn't help it. Lisa, sensing she was being talked about, looked up from the hole she was digging with her hands and giggled.

Sally laughed. "Look at her, you can't see any pink on her skin anymore, it's all mud."

Maggie said, "She'll wash."

"Aunt Sally, can we collect the eggs now?" Tom stood in front of her, his shadow, Ruth, standing behind him.

"Later, Tom, it's a little too early."

"Aww, please. I want to show Ruth I can get them without Mrs Hitler pecking me." The children loved calling animals the names of the main Nazi figures.

Sally threw her eyes up to heaven. "Go on then, but don't break them. Maggie and I have to bake cakes tomorrow. For the cake sale."

Tom and Ruth ran off towards the chicken shed.

"Wish they were as keen on cleaning the shed as they are on collecting eggs. Maggie Ardle, you never told me how much dirt chickens make."

"If I had, you wouldn't have got them, now would you?" Maggie replied.

Rachel laughed. "You two are like little children sometimes, always teasing each other."

"How're Goebbels and Goering doing?" Maggie asked Rachel.

Rachel wrinkled her nose. "They smell so bad. Constable Cooper is sorry he decided to keep the pigs near the station. Said he should have set them up in the wild, especially when the wind blows a certain way."

Maggie rubbed her stomach. "I can't wait for a decent fry up. Fresh eggs and bacon."

Rachel pretended to be ill.

Maggie said, "I know you don't want to eat the pigs when they are slaughtered but you will be glad of the chocolate I get."

Puzzled, Rachel asked, "How can you turn Goebbels and Goering into chocolate?"

"We can trade your share with Mr Callaghan at the shop."

"My share? I don't own those pigs."

"You do. I took out a share in your name. You deserve it. Aren't you the one who takes the scraps down there every day?"

"Oh." Rachel didn't look too certain.

"Maggie's teasing you, love. Not about the chocolate but about the pigs. All the families who feed them will get an equal share."

"That's better. I don't think Mama would like me to be involved with pigs. She was very strict about keeping kosher while we were growing up. But then things changed, and it wasn't possible anymore. One of her uncles starved to death as he wouldn't eat non-kosher food."

Sally looked at Maggie. What could you say to that?

"Rachel, try to think of happier times," Maggie said, squeezing the girl's hand. "Speaking of which, do you want to help us bake cakes tomorrow?"

"Me? I would but I am up at the hospital tomor-row, working the early shift."

"Silly me. I forgot about that. I bet your pretty face makes our boys feel better."

"Maggie!" Rachel blushed, her pink cheeks making her look prettier. "I best get home and do some reading for my English class. Reverend Collins likes to check my progress."

The girl almost ran out of the garden, leaving Maggie and Sally laughing behind her.

"I love days like this when the children are around us," Sally said, realising to her surprise that she felt happier than she had in a long time since the telegram had arrived.

Maggie replied, "Me too, Sally love, me too."

* * *

SALLY CUT OPEN THE ENVELOPE, not recognising the handwriting on the front. She gasped as she saw the signature.

"What's wrong?" Maggie and Doris asked in unison. They'd gathered in Sally's kitchen to bake some cakes for the Women's Institute meeting.

"News of Derek?" Maggie asked, as Sally remained quiet.

Sally shook her head and turned to Maggie, beaming. "It's Harry, he's finally written and he's safe. Living on the Isle of Man." She quickly scanned the letter.

Mrs David Duncan
10 Merryfield Terrace
Douglas, Isle of Man.

DEAR SALLY,

I'm sorry for not writing. This is the first time I have had paper. I met a lady in the village, she is very nice and has promised to send this for me. If you write back to the above address, she will keep the letter for me.

How are Tom and Lisa? Please tell them I am fine and looking forward to seeing you all again soon.

I have a new friend, Joseph. The same men who arrested me picked him up sometime later. He worries about his mother who wasn't home when the army came to pick him up and the army refused to let him write a note to explain. An old employer of Joseph's mother moved to England and rescued Joseph and his mother from Frankfurt, Germany. The old man got her a job here. But he has written to her now, so hopefully, she is happy.

Can you please help me find out what happened to another friend, a Mr Stephen Hillman? He's lived in England since the last World War when he met and married his wife. He never got his papers. He was very kind to us, protected us from the worst of the camp. Not from the guards. They were alright. It was the Nazis they arrested who hate us Jews. Even in the camp where everyone was locked up and subjected to the same rules about food and such, they make our lives miserable. Things could have got bad for me and Joseph, if not for Mr Hillman. The guards respected and liked him, as he could speak good English.

I think he was lonely, as his wife died in an accident. Mr Hillman stopped them sending me and Joseph on the Arandora Star, a ship to Canada. He had to go and we wanted to leave with him but we heard the boat sank. We hope he survived. Can you find out?

After they took Mr Hillman and the others away,

they rounded us up but wouldn't tell us where we were going. The guards who looked after us were worse than those who arrested us. The new ones had been to somewhere called Dunkirk and they hated us. They didn't care we were Jews, not Nazis. They spat in our water, beat us and everything. But it still wasn't as bad as Dachau and as you can see, I lived through it.

When they put us on a small ship, I thought we were going to Canada or Australia but one sailor laughed when I said that. He said we would be lucky to stay afloat until we got to the Isle of Man. Have you ever been to Douglas? It is a nice place, with plenty of fresh air from the sea. I like it.

I hope to see you soon. Please write back and if you can, please send me cigarettes. No, I don't smoke now but they are useful for other purposes.

Harry

PS: My friend helps me with my English. I know it is not yet so good but I am working on it. Being an internee gives me time to study.

PPS: Please address your letter to Mrs Duncan. I don't think I should get letters with my name on it.

TAKING A SEAT, she read it out to her friends.

"Oh my goodness, he was lucky," Maggie said, as she beat the eggs into the flour vigorously.

Sally gave her friend a curious look. "Maggie, you'll ruin the cakes. Here, give that to me." Sally took the bowl out of the older woman's hands, realising that they were shaking. "Maggie, what's the matter?"

"They had all sorts on that boat. Italian families who'd lived here since before the last war. Maybe some of them were fascists, I don't know, but they didn't send Mosley and that wife of his, Diana Mitford, away on a boat, did they? They had Hitler and Goebbels as guests at their wedding. If anyone should have been sent off across a U-boat-filled Atlantic, it should have been them."

Maggie blew her nose into her hanky.

"Did you know my Reg was from Wales? Every year, we went there for a week or so. He had a huge family, miners most of them. When he died, his family wrote to me and invited me to come on my own. After a few years, I was brave enough to go.

"Some of my friends were on that ship. I had a favourite shop where I went for ice cream. My friend Luigi and his two brothers were all arrested, they'd been living here since the 1920s. Their kids and my Reg's nieces and nephews played together. They hated Mussolini and all he represented. But they still came, with guns, for Luigi in the middle of the night. All three of the brothers were sent on that ship. Luigi escaped but one of the brothers, either Franco or

Giuseppe, went back to the ship for his teeth." Maggie let out a big sob.

Both Sally and Doris were crying now too.

They could barely make out what Maggie said next. "Those lovely men died because of a pair of false teeth."

Sally rubbed her eyes with her hanky. "Maggie, don't cry. Please don't. I can't bear to see you so sad. I didn't know anything about your friends, why didn't you tell us?" She put the bowl to one side. They all needed a cup of tea. Hot tea always helped in a crisis.

Maggie snuffled into her large hanky as she pulled herself together. "I couldn't burden you. Not with you getting the news about Derek and worrying about Harry."

Sally put her arm around Maggie's shoulders. "I am always here for you despite what I have going on in my life. We're family, you and I."

Maggie gripped Sally's arm, a couple of stray tears making their way down her cheeks.

Doris coughed to clear her throat. "Do you think you will be able to trace Harry's friend? Will the government release that information?"

Sally glanced at Maggie but the older woman was miles away.

"I've no idea, Doris, but I can ask. I'm not sure about writing to this lady though. Why should I keep my letters to Harry a secret, surely that makes him look guilty of something?"

"Best ask Constable Cooper, as he'll know the rules," Maggie answered. "We don't want Harry getting into more trouble. Reverend Collins is working on trying to get him released but he says Churchill's view is that all enemy aliens should be interned for the duration of the war."

Irritated, Sally snapped, "Churchill is wrong. Harry is no more an enemy alien than I am." She picked up the bowl, looking at the contents with dismay. "I don't think our sponge will win any awards. We've beaten it so hard it will be as flat as a pancake."

"Turn it into some buns for the kiddies. They won't be fussy. I'm sure I have some dried fruit at home. Let me run and see." Doris was gone before they could argue. Sally sensed her friend and neighbour needed a weep in private. Doris hated anyone seeing her lose control.

Sally poured Maggie another cup of tea.

Maggie looked up at her, appalled. "Sally, the rations."

"The rations and the people who decide on such things can get stuffed. I'm having another cup of tea and so are you. So there."

CHAPTER 35

*T*om walked in the back door with his head glued to the comic he was reading.

"Aunt Sally, have you finished baking yet? Only, I met Mrs Shackleton-Driver in the village and she said to remind you the stall was open at two this afternoon." Tom didn't look up from his comic as he spoke.

Sally said, "Tom, put down your comic and have some manners in front of guests."

Tom quickly scanned the page before reluctantly putting the comic on the table. He looked at Maggie. "You aren't really a guest. You're always here."

"Tom Beck, don't be rude," Sally admonished.

But Maggie pulled him into her arms and gave him a hug. He pushed her away, wiping his face on his sleeve.

"Yuck, what did you do that for?"

"Nothing wrong with a hug now and then, child. Sally has a surprise for you."

"A piece of cake? I'm starving."

"You're always hungry, lad," Sally said. "I got a letter. From Harry."

"Harry. Really? Where is he and when is he coming home? Can I read it?" Tom paused for a second. "Is it in German because my English reading isn't too good."

"I'll read it for you if you like." Sally tussled his hair, making him smile.

"Yeah. Can I go find Rachel, Ruth and Lisa? They'll want to hear the letter too."

"Go on then. We'll have lunch here. Mrs Shackleton-Driver can just wait for her cakes.

"Can I tell her that? She's really mean and says nasty things, especially to Rachel."

Sally and Maggie exchanged a look over his head.

"No, Tom, you leave Mrs Shackleton-Driver to Maggie to deal with. Now, go find the girls."

Tom ran, screaming the girls' names at the top of his voice.

Maggie said, "The whole village will know you've had a letter. I'd suggest you speak to Constable Cooper as soon as you can."

"I will, Maggie, but first, what will we do about

Rachel? What do you think that horrible woman has been saying?"

"I don't know but I'll handle her. It'll give me an outlet for some of this anger growing inside of me."

Sally nodded, feeling just the tiniest twinge of sympathy for Mrs Shackleton-Driver. Maggie rarely let her temper go but when she did, you stood back and thanked God you weren't the target.

SALLY GAVE the letter to Rachel to read to the children while she finished the cakes. The buns turned out very well, even if she did say so herself. The children happily ate two each and would have had more if she hadn't rescued the plate.

Staring at the four children around the table, she wondered how she would make them cakes, buns or anything nice now that everything seemed to be going on ration. From bacon, butter and sugar at first, to meat being rationed in March, and now they were rationing tea, cooking fats, jam and cheese. She agreed with rationing in principle; it was unfair for some to horde tins of fruit, sugar and whatnot. An egg per person a fortnight, and needing points for break-fast cereals, canned fish, fruit or biscuits if you could find them made for a very confusing system. She and Maggie often combined their rations to make them stretch further. A picture of the Daltons flashed into her mind. She doubted they and other farmers were in the same position.

"Sally, stop it," she told herself. She was luckier than most, thanks to Maggie's idea about the chickens. The children could have an egg every day if they wanted, in addition to the milk, cod liver oil and orange juice the Ministry of Health insisted on providing.

Spotting the time, she tore off her apron and ran upstairs to put on a dash of lipstick and a spray of perfume that Derek had brought her on his last trip home. She closed her eyes and prayed for her husband, as she had every day since she'd got that horrible telegram. Despite having no news of Derek since, she refused to believe he was dead. She'd know inside if he was.

"Aunt Sally, you're going to be very late," Rachel called up the stairs, a worried edge to her voice. Rachel fretted a lot, particularly over upsetting the villagers. After Tom's comment earlier, Sally could guess why.

"Coming. Are you sure you don't mind keeping the children here?"

"I love it here," Rachel said quietly. "We are going to write back to Harry and tell him about Mother's letters."

Sally impulsively kissed the top of the girl's head.

She was so young, yet she was carrying the weight of adult worries.

"I won't be long, I promise." Sally picked up her cakes and stalked out the door, ready to do battle if she had to. There was no way on this planet Constable Cooper was going to stop her from sending parcels to Harry, now she knew where he was.

When she got to the village hall, Doris caught up with her. "Did you hear Maggie and Mrs Shackleton-Driver went at it hammer and tongs?"

"They did?"

"Maggie gave her a slap, right across her face. Left a red mark but the Constable refused to arrest Maggie. Said Mrs Shackleton-Driver should be happy she wasn't the one being arrested."

"Why? What did she do?" Sally asked.

"Seems she was spreading horrible rumours about Rachel being a German spy. How she was in bed, literally and figuratively, with the Nazis. Said she'd heard Rachel got regular letters from her mother in Germany, and as no letters get through the regular post, it must mean she was a spy."

Sally's hands itched to slap Mrs Shackleton-Driver herself. What a horrid, mean old woman.

"Rachel got one letter from Sweden, not Germany. Anyway, it's none of that woman's business."

"The loss of her sons is making her worse."

Sally's anger cooled a little. Jane Shackleton-Driver had lost her twin sons in the Battle of Britain. She had always been a tyrant but the news had pushed her over the edge.

"I should go and speak to her."

"Who? Maggie? Reverend Collins took her home. He didn't seem a bit pleased."

"I'll see Maggie later. I meant Jane. I never sympathised with her over the loss of her children. Whatever else she is, she was a loving mother and adored those two lads of hers. No wonder she's lashing out."

Doris stared at her for a few seconds before she smiled. "Your heart is way too soft, Sally. Your mum was the same. Always looking out for other people."

Sally couldn't talk about her mum. She missed her all the time, but since the telegram had arrived, she really wished she was here to give her a cuddle and tell her the world was going to get better. Things would go back to normal. To a time when men of Derek's age and even younger, in the case of the Shackleton-Driver boys, weren't killed, and young girls like Rachel didn't have to run for their lives.

She handed Doris the cakes, asked her to take over her slot on the stall and went in search of Mrs Shackleton-Driver. Her trip was in vain as the woman refused to see anyone. Her housekeeper dismissed

Sally with a look that could have frozen the River Thames. Sally took the hint.

Her next visit went much better, with Constable Cooper agreeing she should send Harry a parcel, care of the detention centre on the Isle of Man.

"Better being honest about things like this, Sally. Well-meaning gestures such as the lady sending on Harry's letter could have landed both of them in a lot of hot water."

"You won't turn the lady in, now will you, Constable?"

"How could I?" Constable Cooper winked at her. "You haven't told me anything other than you found out where Harry was."

Sally vowed to bake a cake, if she could find the ingredients, for the lovely constable. His wife had died years back and she guessed he didn't get around to home-cooking.

"Will you come for dinner one evening, Constable? When you're free? I'd like Tom and Lisa to see that not all men in uniform are like the ones that put them on the train."

"I would be honoured. Thank you kindly."

Sally hesitated, hoping she wasn't asking too much but Harry had specifically asked her to find out. "I have another question. Harry asked about a friend of his who might have been on the Arandora Star."

The constable's facial expression changed so fast

that Sally faltered and then started speaking way too quickly.

"This man, he was very kind to Harry. In fact, he stopped Harry being put on the ship. It would mean a lot to Harry if he knew he'd survived."

"And what if he didn't? Isn't the lad safer not knowing."

Sally considered her answer. "In times like this, I think honesty is the best policy. We can't protect Harry, Rachel and all the other children who will suffer in this war."

The constable stared down at the pile of papers on the desk in front of him. She took up a pen and wrote Mr Hillman's name on a piece of paper and left it beside Cooper's hand. She looked him in the eyes, before adding, "I'm glad we have people like you to look after us, Constable Cooper."

She walked away without waiting for him to speak, having guessed he was finding it difficult to find any words.

CHAPTER 36

*H*arry felt that he was having a good time in the camp, if he forgot he was a prisoner. He caught up on his education and discovered a taste for music. He could listen to the symphony orchestra all day long if it was allowed.

He studied hard, having heard it was easier to get into the army if you passed English exams.

His teacher said, "Well done, Harry, soon you will write and speak English better than the English themselves. What do you want to do when you get out of here?"

He was only curious but Harry seized his chance. "I want to join up. I want to fight the Nazis."

The teacher looked up from his papers. "Are you serious?"

Harry held his gaze and spoke firmly, "Yes, sir. They killed my father, destroyed my home and separated my family."

"But Germany is your home. You would be fighting your own countrymen."

"Germany hasn't been my home since the early 1930s when they decided to make us Jews stateless. I have no allegiance to anyone."

The teacher's eyes widened as he rubbed his chin. "You would swear allegiance to our king?"

"Your king, Mr Churchill and anyone else you like. I'm not a boy but a man."

The teacher stared for a few minutes and then went back to marking papers. Harry bit on his pencil, wondering if he had taken him seriously.

* * *

FOUR MONTHS LATER, Harry was called out from class by the school secretary. An older woman with small glasses and a permanent frown on her face. The boys were always in the wrong, even if the evidence suggested otherwise.

"Officer wants to see you. Headmaster's office. What have you done, Beck?" Her expression was almost gleeful.

Harry shrugged his shoulders. He hadn't done

anything. He'd written his one letter a week, and stuck to the 24-line limit. He expressed concern for his siblings and Aunt Sally, given the Battle of Britain was in progress. Nobody could have found fault with that. He walked the corridor in silence, sensing this would annoy the secretary even more.

She sat down at her desk. When she wasn't looking, he wiped his palms on his trousers. He didn't want anyone thinking he was nervous. He knocked at the door. The head teacher opened it, his eyes lit up with curiosity. Harry entered and came face to face with a uniformed officer, wearing a khaki great coat, who dismissed the head teacher. Only when the door was firmly closed behind the man did the officer speak.

"Morning, Beck. I've heard good things about you. Seems you want to join up and fight for Britain. Is that right?"

"Yes, sir." He wanted revenge on the Nazis but guessed admitting that wouldn't get him very far.

"Your English is excellent, and obviously you speak fluent German. You score highly in maths and science too. We have a number of opportunities for you. Always in need of translators and whatnot."

Harry didn't want a job in an office. "Excuse me, sir, but I was thinking more on the front line."

"You want to go to war, son? There's nothing

glorious about getting shot at, let me tell you. You boys are all the same. Think it's all a big game."

That was too much.

"With all due respect, sir, I don't believe it's a game. I watched the Nazis kick my Papa to death, starve and torment my friends. They tore my sister from her mother's arms and threatened my kid brother with death if he didn't hand over his teddy bear. Then I came here to find myself arrested and imprisoned for exactly the same crime. My being Jewish."

"Now hold on a minute, lad, you weren't interned because you are Jewish. You are a dangerous alien."

"To who? I obviously don't support the Nazis, do I? Who of my people would support that group of murdering swine?"

The officer coloured but didn't argue.

"So again, I request, respectfully, not to be assigned to an office."

The officer scrutinised him for several minutes in silence. Just as he thought he'd be arrested and thrown into solitary or some other punishment, the officer spoke.

"What about the feelings of those you serve with? Not many are going to stop to ask questions once they hear your accent, they may use their fists first."

"I can handle myself."

"Yes, I can see that." The officer indicated the report on his desk. "Seems you've prepared yourself for this role for some time, Mr Beck."

Harry stood straighter. "Yes, sir. It's all I've thought about since I was fifteen in Dachau concentration camp."

The officer's widened eyes showed he recognised the name. He put down the papers in his hand.

"I'm sorry, son. I had no idea. I must have sounded like a patronising old git. If you want to join up and get revenge, I won't stop you."

"Thank you, sir. I have another request."

"Go on."

Harry took a deep breath. He didn't want to ruin his chances of joining up but he had promised to keep in touch with his family. "I'd like to check on my brother and sister before I leave. They are living—"

"In Abbeydale, Surrey, with a lady called Sally Matthews. Her husband is missing presumed dead. He was at Dunkirk."

Harry flinched.

The officer looked concerned. "Sorry, son, did you know him?"

"No, sir. He'd joined up before we arrived. But Aunt Sally, I mean Mrs Matthews, she was only married a short while. She must be devastated."

The officer nodded. "My son was there too. He's a POW now. We got notification yesterday."

"He'll be fine, sir. The Nazis won't hurt the British. They like them. It's the Jews, Roma, Poles and those on the eastern front they have issues with."

"We'll see. Now let's get your papers in order, shall we?"

CHAPTER 37

"*A*unt Sally, there's a man at the door wearing a uniform. He's a pilot. He won't come in but said you had to come down."

Sally grabbed a towel, wrapping her wet hair up in a turban style. She hadn't heard the front door. She took off the pinny she'd worn to protect her dress from getting wet and walked downstairs, butterflies turning over in her stomach. Was it about Derek?

No, they wouldn't send a pilot to see you, silly.

Taking a deep breath and forcing a smile, she opened the door to find herself staring into a face much like Derek's but older. She held onto the door for support as her legs trembled.

"Gosh, I'm sorry. I shouldn't have surprised you like that. I'm Roland, Derek's older brother. Perhaps you should sit down?"

Wordlessly, she held the door open and motioned for him to come in. He stood inside but waited for her to lead the way.

Tom ran down the stairs. "Are you a real pilot? What type of planes do you fly? Spitfires?"

"Pleased to meet you, young man, but it seems your mum could do with a drink. Do you think you could find one for her?"

"Aunt Sally likes tea. She drinks a lot of it." Tom screwed up his face. Sally saw and heard all this play out but from a distance, as if she was miles away rather than standing in her hall.

"Come into the kitchen, it's warmer in there." Tom led the man to the kitchen, leaving Sally to follow, thankful Lisa was up at Maggie's, playing dolls with Ruth. Sally was due on shift later so Maggie was keeping Lisa for the night.

"Sally, do you mind if I call you that? I'm sorry for just turning up like this but I only have a short leave. Sam only told me about Mother's visit to you when I got back to London yesterday. I came as fast as I could. I've been on continuous ops, you know how it is."

Sally examined him more closely. Yes, he did resemble Derek but his eyes were grey, not blue like her husband's. He looked exhausted, and there was an air of tension around him. Touches of grey peppered his hair, particularly at his temples. He had Derek's smile though.

"Forgive me, Roland, seeing you standing there like that. For a second I thought…"

"I was Derek? I wish I was."

She saw the sincerity in his eyes, along with the sadness. So he believed his brother to be dead too.

"I've searched everywhere I can think of, spoken to people in all branches of the service but I can't find out a thing. We know for certain he was on the beach at Dunkirk but after that he seems to have disappeared. He isn't on the list of prisoners of war in any camp. The Red Cross do their best but there is always a chance someone has been missed but…" Roland, still standing, looked down at his hands.

"Please sit down. Would you like some tea? I could make you breakfast if you want? I have some eggs and a few slices of bacon?" She didn't tell him that was her meal for later.

"No, thank you. I'm not hungry but I will have some tea. I have some things in the car for you but I will give you them later. I hope I'm not keeping you from somewhere." He indicated the turban.

She flushed – she'd forgotten all about the towel.

"I'm sorry. I'm on shift later, and I was washing my hair. Oh, listen to me babble. No, please don't stand up. Tom, can you run and ask Rachel if she could cover the start of my shift and I'll work hers tomorrow. I'll write a note to Matron to explain. Thank you, darling."

"Sure but can I talk to the pilot when I come back?"

"You better, young man, as I have some things for you. Sam gave them to me."

"Oh boy!" Tom ran off with a grin as wide as his face.

* * *

SALLY MADE THE TEA, finding Roland incredibly easy to speak to.

"I wasn't always like this. Being in the services brings you down to earth with a bang. I was rather like Mother, if truth be known, before I joined up. A right snob, as Derek no doubt told you."

"He didn't say a lot about his family. He was upset none of you managed to come to the wedding but—"

"Sally, I apologise. For missing your wedding. It's true I was away training but I should have made an effort to get back. If I knew then what I know now … but there isn't time for regrets. Can we put that behind us? I should like to get to know you better. If there is time."

A chill ran through her at his words. He seemed to notice as he rolled his eyes. "Forgive me for sounding like a bad film actor from a cheesy film. Now tell me about young Tom."

Sally twirled the teaspoon in her cup, curiosity getting the better of her. "Your mother must have mentioned him."

"She did. At length. But I'd rather hear his story from you. I know about the Kindertransport, of course, but I never met anyone who travelled on it. I take it he has an older brother?"

Sally stood and got Harry's picture from the wall dresser before passing it to Roland. "This is Harry. He was taken away by the home guard, they said he was an enemy alien. Can you believe that? A boy on the run for his life. Tom took it badly but he seems to be bouncing back now we've heard from Harry. He's on the Isle of Man." She paused.

"And your daughter?"

"My what?" She laughed at his confusion. "Lisa, or Liesel to give her German name, is Harry and Tom's half-sister. She arrived as an eight-month-old. I'm afraid your mother jumped to conclusions." She blushed.

"My mother? You do surprise me." But he gentled his sarcasm with a smile. Then the smile vanished. "I can only imagine what my mother said to you when she visited. I know she gave you some nonsense about this place being hers. It never was. It was Dad's hideaway. He used to come here when things got too much for him at home. Then he gave it to Derek. He and Mother, well, let's just say they never saw eye to eye. Her fault entirely, not that she will ever admit that." He took a second and then continued. "Did you know she met a neighbour of yours that day. Mrs Shackleton something or other.""

Sally groaned.

"She's that bad." He grinned. "That makes sense, listening to the total rot she fed mother. Anyway, forget about both of them. My brother adored you." Roland held her gaze. "I can see why, and after hearing from Sam about how you handled Mother, I understand how he fell in love with you so fast."

"Thank you, Roland."

"He wrote to me and asked me to look after you, should anything happen to him."

Sally's eyes filled with tears as his voice trembled a little. He coughed. "Look at me, I'm doing a brutal job, aren't I? I won't be around much, too busy with all that's going on."

"You were in the Battle of Britain?"

He nodded. "Lucky to come out of it. I was shot down but thankfully the kite landed the right side up." He turned serious again. "I have written to the family solicitor. If anything should happen to me, Sally, you will be looked after. Just in case."

"He never comes home." Sally filled in the gap.

She bit her lip, taking a second to recover. "He will. I know he's alive. I can't prove it but I can feel it."

She knew he didn't agree but was too kind to say so. The moment passed as the children arrived back, dragging Maggie in their wake. Not that she looked put out.

Sally was surprised to see her greet Roland frostily though.

"Afternoon, Master Roland. Sally, you alright?"

"Just fine, Maggie."

"Mrs Ardle, or can I call you Maggie now I am out of short pants?" Roland smiled, with a smile that would weaken most women but was lost on Maggie. She just stared. "I heard what you said to Mother, and it was bloody marvellous if you pardon my language. Just what she needed to hear."

"She best not darken the doorstep down here again. She'll feel my boot in the back of her…"

"Maggie!" Sally interjected quickly, looking pointedly at the three children. Tom, Ruth and Lisa stood watching.

"Message received and understood, Mrs Ardle." He turned to Tom. "Would you help me carry some things from the car while your Aunt Sally speaks to Maggie about me. I'm hoping she'll put a good word in for me."

Sally burst out laughing at the look on Maggie's face as Roland took Tom and Ruth by the hand and led them outside. "Lisa come too," Lisa demanded. He bent down to pick her up, and the child didn't show any resistance. Together, the four of them headed outside.

"Maggie, why are you being so harsh? He's lovely. So pleasant. He told me not to worry about anything. He's spoken to his mother."

"Least he could do."

'Maggie, that's not like you. He's spoken to the solicitor as well. Said I'm to be looked after if he doesn't come back. He flew through the Battle of Britain. Maggie, we owe our freedom to young men like him."

"Did he explain why he snubbed your wedding?'

'Yes. And he apologised for it. He also said he was a snob before but he's been cured by mixing with others in the services. I like him, Maggie. Give him a chance. You only knew the child, not the man."

"Aye. That's true."

Maggie was marginally warmer when Roland returned. By the time he had showered the children with games and footballs and other goodies, had a dozen cups of weak tea and insisted on washing the potatoes for dinner, Maggie was convinced. While her friend and her brother-in-law stayed in the kitchen chatting, Sally went outside and collected some eggs, vegetables and fruit. There were fresh apples and blackberries from their recent foraging trips. She packed them together with a pound of butter that a kind farmer had given her for Lisa and put them in a basket. Coming back into the kitchen, she put it on the counter. "When you go back to London, could you give that to Sam for me? Tell him thank you."

"He'll be right chuffed." Roland sniffed appreciatively. "He's a principled man and won't touch a piece of black market food. Eggs, real butter and fresh fruit are novelties in lots of homes now. Thank you for your kindness. Cook, Sam's Sarah, may even make an apple pie."

"You come to my house and I'll give you apple pie. Stay the night and go back to London on the train tomorrow. I know the reverend would love some male company. He finds the three of us girls rather overpowering at times, doesn't he, Ruth?"

"I wonder why?" Roland asked with an innocent expression.

Everyone laughed, and Sally was sad to leave but she had to get to the hospital. Rachel had already covered two hours of her shift and she had studies to be getting on with.

PART II

CHAPTER 38

"When's Mummy coming?"

Sally took a deep breath as she gathered the seven-year-old girl up in her arms. With one hand, she pushed the child's blonde hair from her eyes.

"Lisa, we've spoken about this. They have only just announced the war is over."

"But she said. She wrote in her letter that Tom used to read to me. She said she would come as soon as the war was over. Then we would go home." Lisa bit her lip, her brown, tear-filled eyes staring into Sally's face.

Sally's heart ached. How could she tell this poor child the chances of her mother being able to keep her word were all but nil? Lisa wrapped her arms around Sally's neck, dampening her skin with tears. Sally tried to find the words as she felt the child's heart fluttering against her chest.

Lisa whispered, "Do I have to go with her? I want to stay with you. I love you."

Shock made Sally's voice shake. "Oh, you poor darling." Sally buried the guilt that fought for dominance over the warmth the child's words gave her. "I love you too."

She loved Lisa desperately and couldn't bear to think of the day when they might be separated. Although the chances of the child's mother reappearing were small, she did have other close family. Her half-brothers Harry and Tom – and there could be cousins, aunts and uncles too. Who knew what members of the family had survived the Nazis' hatred?

Lisa held tight to Sally. "Is Harry coming back soon? Now the war is over?"

"I think Harry might be busy for a while. He has his new job now, do you remember? He's helping the people in Germany. He's done very well, your brother, hasn't he?"

Lisa nodded her head but the worried expression hadn't left her face. Then the front door banged and they heard eleven-year-old Tom shouting, "Aunt Sally, where are you? Can we go to London? Please say yes, all my friends are going. Oh, what's wrong with Lisa?" Tom came to a standstill at the entrance to the kitchen.

"Lisa was upset and asking about your mother."

Tom rolled his eyes. "My mother's dead. She died before the war started."

Sally took a breath; now was not the time to scold the boy. "Tom! Lisa's talking about her mother, your stepmother."

"Oh, her." Tom's cheeks grew red, and he refused to look Sally in the face.

Sally looked pointedly at Lisa. "Tom."

For all his dislike of Trudi, Tom idolised his baby sister and would do anything for her. At least he would until his friends were around, when he was far too grown-up to play with a six-year-old girl.

Tom took the hint, pulling Lisa into his arms and tickling her until she begged for mercy.

"Lisa, we're going to have a party. A big one with jelly and cream and everything. We're going to have so much to eat, we will all be sick."

Lisa giggled, the noise making Sally's heart sing. Tom, like many growing boys, was always hungry and found rationing difficult. Sally gave Lisa a hug before standing up and patting down her apron.

"I have baking to do. I promised Maggie I'd make some carrot cake for the street party. It's the best we can do, seeing everything's still on ration."

"Wait," Tom said, catching his breath. "Before

you start making cakes, can we go to London? Please. Everyone is going. Please say yes, Aunt Sally. It's a historic day. Mr Churchill himself is going to speak and we might even see the king and queen."

Sally hid her smile. Tom knew she loved the royal family. Amused to see him using this as a means of getting her to say yes, she clapped her hands, surprising both children.

"Why not? It's a special day, as you so rightly say. Let me go and change my dress. You both should change too, you look like right little horrors."

Tom glanced down at his clothes; his shorts were muddy but not as bad as his socks and shoes.

"Aww, do we have to? We'll miss the train."

Sally put her hands on her hips. "Tom Beck, do you want to go, or don't you?"

"Yes, Aunt Sally. Come on, Lisa. Race you."

Tears forgotten, Lisa ran after her brother up the stairs. The sound of laughter floated downstairs as they raced to get into their Sunday best. Sally glanced around her kitchen, her gaze flickering over the picture of her husband, Derek. It had been so long now since he had been declared missing, it was impossible to keep hoping. *If only you were coming back*, she thought.

Shaking those thoughts away, she picked up the dishcloth and quickly dried and put away the dishes.

Only when her kitchen was spick and span did she head to her room to change her clothes.

* * *

AT THE TRAIN STATION, they found that many of their friends and neighbours had had the same thought. Enid, looking worse than usual in her black widow clothes, stared at Sally. When Sally refused to greet the woman – having not forgiven her for her part in Harry's arrest and the vicious things she'd said about the children – Enid was compelled to speak first.

"Wouldn't be the same to miss it, would it, Sally? After all these years. Especially with your Derek and my Arthur giving their lives for freedom. Imagine their faces if they could see us now."

Sally forced a smile in greeting.

Belle came up behind her and whispered, "Keep smiling like that and your face is going to turn funny."

"Belle!" Sally burst out laughing at her friend's comment before linking arms with her. "I'm so glad you're coming too. Pity Maggie didn't want to, but she says she's too old. At least she has Doris to fuss over. Imagine breaking your leg just as the war is finished."

"Mark would never 'ave forgiven me if I 'adn't agreed to go. He and Tom said you were goin', so I thought it was a good idea. Poor little tyke has little to look forward to."

Sally chuckled. "We've been taken for fools. That's what Tom told me. You were going and could we please go too."

They looked at the boys, who both adopted a totally innocent expression.

"Aunt Sally, Mrs Clark's family are heading to Parliament Square. Can we go with them and sit by the Houses of Parliament? That's the best spot, we reckon."

Sally and Belle rolled their eyes; they were at it again. "Can Ruth stay with you? Us boys want to explore."

"Tom, what have I told you before? You and the Bernstein girls arrived here from Germany together. That bond is unbreakable, and I won't have you ignoring Ruth. Is that clear?"

"Yes, Aunt Sally."

Sally ignored his fed-up expression.

"Aunt Sally, they say Mr Churchill will speak at three this afternoon. We won't be able to see him but we can hear him on the loudspeakers outside. Just think, he will be a few feet away from us, yet people all over the world will be listening to him. Won't they?"

"Yes, Tom."

"After that, we could wander through St James's

Park and round by Trafalgar Square to the Health Ministry. I heard Mr Churchill is going to speak again at five – he must have a lot to say." Tom squinted his eyes at the thought, making Sally exchange an amused glance with Belle.

"What about my visit to the royal family, Tom?" Sally couldn't resist teasing the youngster. She loved him almost as much as Lisa, although she'd never admit to having a favourite. She could still see Tom's tear-stained face as he told her, via an interpreter, that the Germans had stolen his teddy. Her heart raged at the memory, even after all these years, and despite the countless atrocities reported in the paper, she simply couldn't understand how any man could have torn a teddy bear from a child.

"Aww, do you have to go and see them? You could see them any day."

"But Tom, you said yourself this is a special day, and me being English, I have to see my king and queen."

As his face fell, she couldn't stop herself from laughing. "I'm teasing you, sweetheart. I would love to see them, of course, but it might not be possible. The whole country will be looking to be near them. Our brave royal family who stayed by our side through thick and thin. No running away for them."

Tom rolled his eyes, having heard more than once about the virtues of dear Queen Elizabeth who refused to take the princesses to live in safety in Canada. Instead, she had insisted on staying by her husband's side and facing whatever the Germans wished to throw at them.

The train arrived at Waterloo, and everywhere they looked people were dressed in all sorts of gay colours. Women wore flowery dresses with garlands of red, white and blue around their necks or in their hair. Even the men had buttonholes. Sally gave Tom a couple of coins to buy some flags and was touched when he came back with a hair ornament for Lisa and a matching one for her.

"You aren't going to wear it, are you?" Enid said, her face all pinched into a sour expression.

"Of course I am! Why would I disappoint the child? Anyway, it's a special day and we're going to have some fun. Come on, Enid, the war is over. Loosen up and live a little bit, will you?"

Before Enid could argue, Belle said, "I want one too. Lead the way, Sally. Let's make this a day to remember. Children, if you get lost, ask a policeman to direct you to the main gate at the Houses of Parliament. We'll find you there."

Sally said, "Let's get one for Maggie too. She'd like a reminder of the occasion, since she couldn't make it."

The children cheered and then they were off, surrounded by people smiling and clapping. Sally knew everyone was happy that the war, at least in Europe, was finally over. But what would the next few weeks, months and years bring? She gripped Lisa's hand tighter, telling herself she didn't want the child getting lost in the crowd – but the reality was, she never wanted to let her go. Of course, she hoped Trudi had survived the war, but she really didn't want her to claim her daughter. Sally loved Lisa like her own, and had done so since that first day she'd picked up the eight-month-old in her arms and cuddled her close. She'd promised Harry she'd protect the child with her life and love her like her own. And it was a promise she still intended to keep.

CHAPTER 39

8 MAY 1945

Sally stood at the bedroom door, watching Lisa sleep. The street party was still going on when she had taken the children home, Lisa almost sleepwalking. Sally had her arm wrapped around the child, while Tom protested he wasn't tired, despite his big yawns. She ushered the children upstairs and straight into bed, not minding about their teeth. One night not washing wouldn't hurt.

She moved to the bed as Lisa moaned in her sleep. Pulling the sheet back over the sleeping child, she kissed her on the head. Lisa snuggled into her teddy. "Sleep well and have lovely dreams."

As she left the bedroom, Tom called her.

"Aunt Sally, is that you?"

"Yes, darling, sorry, did I wake you?" She walked into his room, and over to his bedside.

"No, I had a nightmare. Someone came to take us away. You won't let that happen, will you?"

Sally's chest tightened. "I don't want anyone to separate us, Tom. I love you."

At some point she knew she might have to explain to him that eventually he would have to leave, but this wasn't the time. Children's fears magnified at night, and he needed his sleep.

"I had a fabulous day, Aunt Sally. I can't remember ever eating so much."

Sally laughed. "You did eat a lot. Do you have a pain in your tummy?"

"Not anymore. I did earlier, but it's gone now." He sat up in the bed and offered his arms for a hug. She tried to hide her surprise. In the last couple of months, Tom had stopped giving anyone hugs, claiming he was far too old.

Sally hugged him before ruffling his hair. "You should go back to sleep. It will be morning soon."

"Aunt Sally, I'm glad I'm not leaving. I'm the man of the house now, and my job is to protect you and Lisa. At least until Harry comes back." Tom stared into her eyes. "He will come back, won't he?"

"He will, darling, but not for a while yet. The war may be over, but there will be lots for our soldiers to do. Why don't you write to him tomorrow? He'd love a letter from you. You can tell him all about your antics."

At his troubled expression, her heart twisted. "What is it?"

"I don't think I should tell him about going to London to see a flying bomb. He will be angry. I can't tell him about going to the crashed plane and trying to get a souvenir. He wouldn't understand. He's a grown-up."

Sally bit back her smile, trying to be serious. "Tom, he'd be as worried as I was. The flying bombs killed lots of people, and you running away to London caused a lot of worry." She saw his eyes glistening. "But you had the sense to go to the police and tell them you couldn't get home. That was very sensible and mature. Harry would be proud of you. Just like I am. Now go to sleep, darling." She bent and kissed his head, pulling the sheet and blankets around his shoulders, just as he liked.

He yawned and whispered goodnight. She sat on his bed until she heard his breathing deepen into sleep.

She could smile now at his antics over the last few years. He was a typical boy and wanted to see the bomb sites in London and get souvenirs of shrapnel and bombs. At least he hadn't brought a live grenade into school like some children up in London. It wasn't their fault. They'd only known what it was like to live in wartime. She and other parents had aged twenty years in the last five, worrying about their loved ones fighting abroad, fretting over trying to put food on the table, find time for queuing for meat, butter and all the other rationed items and everything else.

Still, there had been some good points. She was a different woman from the one who had kissed Derek goodbye. If she had told her younger self she'd hold down a job, raise two children, run a house and volunteer in the war effort, she'd have rolled her eyes. She'd managed, just like thousands of women throughout Britain. Now their struggle was over. The men would come home, rationing would disappear and life would return to normal. She walked into her bedroom, her eyes going as always to the photo by her bed.

Not everyone would come home. She picked up the photo, kissing Derek's image. "I miss you so much, Derek. How envious I feel towards the women waiting for their husbands to come home. I know it's not a nice reaction and I wouldn't want them to go through the heartbreak of losing their husband. But, I admit, I can't help feeling jealous. I wish with all my heart you'd come home. I can't believe you're dead despite the silence. We had so many dreams … I guess Maggie would tell me to count my blessings. I have two wonderful children and Harry in my life now. So many young widows have lost not only their husbands but their chance for children. I'm lucky compared to some." She kissed him again, feeling a little stupid for talking to his photo.

Lying in their bed, the photo didn't provide much comfort. Life went on and she prayed for strength to deal with whatever was coming but begged God not to let them take her children. She muffled her tears with her pillow – she didn't want to wake them. They didn't need to know how worried she was about losing them. The war had taken part of their childhood already; she wouldn't let it take anymore.

CHAPTER 40

END OF AUGUST 1945

"*M*um! Mum! Where are you?"

Sally ran at the sound of terror in Lisa's voice. The washing she had been taking in from the clothes line fell onto the grass.

She ran into the kitchen but skidded to a stop, unable to believe the vision in front of her. Lisa was crying openly but Sally couldn't look away from the man standing in front of her, dressed in an ill-fitting suit, his body stick-thin, and yet…

"Derek! Oh, my goodness, Derek! It *is* you!"

She flung herself at her husband, only to be pushed back.

He crossed his arms, his legs spread wide. "Who owns the brat?" His jaw was tight, a harsh look in his eyes. "I heard her call you *Mum*."

Sally glanced at Lisa and then back at her

husband, the gentle giant she adored. The man who loved children and had spoken often of his plans for a large family. What had the war done to him?

She pulled Lisa to her side. "Lisa, this is Derek, my husband. You know. You've seen him in the pictures on my bedside table and out in the hall."

"Pleased to meet you," Lisa said, her vivid-blue eyes wide open.

Silence reigned for a second or two, only to be shattered by Tom running in the back gate. "Lisa, what's wrong? I heard you screaming. Oh, who are you?"

"I'm Derek Matthews," Derek roared, causing Lisa and Sally to flinch. Derek pointed at Sally, accusation written all over his face. She couldn't bear the look in his eyes. This was her dream come true, she had prayed for it over and over. But this man in front of her wasn't her Derek. The man she loved, the man she married, would never have scared a child. Not on purpose.

Tom was glaring at him. "Something wrong with your ears, or do you always shout?" Tom asked curiously. He was used to men shouting at him, teachers normally, when he didn't behave as they thought he should.

Derek looked fit to explode.

Sally hastily intervened. "Derek, love. These lovely children are the ones I wrote to you about, do you remember? Lisa was less than a year old and Tom was almost five. They were part of the Kindertransport." At no sign of recognition on her husband's face, she tried to prompt his memory.

"You must remember? I sent you pictures of the children, with my letters. I couldn't wait for you to meet them. You were due home on leave but you got hurt; the nurse had to write me a letter from France. We had made a cake and everyone was so excited you were coming home on leave."

"Only I didn't come home, did I? And it looks like you didn't care a bit. This nice little family you have … a younger lad too by the looks of it." Before she could stop him, he sent the pictures of Harry flying to the floor, shattering the frames and covering their feet in glass.

Sally couldn't keep quiet. "Derek Matthews, you should be ashamed of yourself. The picture is of Tom and Lisa's brother, Harry Beck. He's with the British Army, stationed somewhere in Germany."

"A German in our army," Derek scoffed. "I'll believe that when I see it. Some welcome home this is!"

"We aren't Germans, and why are you shouting, you big bully? You made my sister cry, and Aunt Sally. She never cries. Go back to where you came from and don't come back. We don't need you here." Tom stood, his arms wide, as he held her husband's gaze. She was both proud of him and terrified of how Derek would react.

Her husband took a step towards Tom but she intervened, moving between them, his hand catching her on her cheek. The force of the blow knocked her to the floor onto the glass. Lisa screamed and Tom shouted at Derek to leave, then began shouting for help. Sally grabbed a cloth to staunch the blood running from the gash just under her eye.

Derek stood looking at her in silence, his eyes wide, but she couldn't read the expression in them. He seemed horrified – but whether at having hit her or the fact that Tom had stood up to him, she wasn't sure.

Her back gate banged, and the next thing she knew, Enid Brown was standing in front of her. "Sally, what's wrong? Oh my goodness, you're bleeding. What did you do to her?" Enid turned on the soldier, then her expression changed from fury to amazement. "Derek! Derek Matthews, you're home. As I live and breathe, I never thought I would see the day. We thought you were dead. Have you seen Arthur? Is he with you?" Enid looked behind Derek as if expecting her husband to materialise.

Derek seemed to soften briefly. "Enid, Arthur is dead. I'm sorry. It was quick. He didn't feel anything though. He was lucky."

"Lucky?" Enid repeated in disbelief.

Horrified, Sally stared at her husband. How could he tell a woman that her dead husband was a lucky man?

"Yes, lucky. He didn't spend the next five years at the mercy of the Krauts. Can't bear to be near them. Get those kids out of here and leave me alone with my missus."

Enid stood, her facial expression telling everyone how she felt about being ordered about. Derek must have sensed he'd gone too far. He turned on the charm Sally remembered from old, but there was a harsh edge to him now.

"Enid, please. I'll call in to you later and tell you about Arthur. Just for the moment, leave me and Sally be. Can you do that?"

Enid melted, just as Sally knew she would. She had always carried a torch for Derek, always flirting with him despite being married to Arthur. Arthur was a decent man. But then Derek had never behaved like this before. She couldn't remember Derek ever being cruel to anything or anyone, let alone backhanding a woman or a child.

She caught Lisa's terrified look, and saw behind Tom's façade to the scared little boy he'd been when he first arrived in Liverpool Street. She gathered her wits to her.

"Enid, be a dear and take the children to your house. Take this with you. I baked two of them."

Sally pressed the mince tart into her neighbour's hands. Not that there was much meat in it, mainly vegetables these days, but still. Her thoughts danced around; anything to avoid thinking of her husband and how he was alive. Well, the man in front of her was a living, breathing copy of Derek but he was nothing like the man she had fallen in love with. Though they had only really known each other a few short months before he had shipped off to training, one of the first to sign up. They might have been married almost seven years but all together they had spent about a month as a married couple, if that.

Tom moved to protest but Sally silenced him with a glance. "Please, Tom, take Lisa with you. I'll come to Enid's in a while to talk to you."

Tom glowered in Derek's direction but thankfully kept his mouth closed. He took Lisa's hand, keeping clear of the mess of glass, and together they followed Enid out the front door. Sally closed the door behind them, wishing it had been Maggie who'd happened to come to her aid. She didn't like leaving the children with Enid; still, there was nothing that could be done about that now.

Derek sat down heavily in a chair, his head in his hands, not speaking. She walked over to the sink, where she wet a clean dishcloth and rubbed it over her face. The cold had the desired effect on the blood flow, which was only a trickle now. She looked around at her once-sparkling floor, now covered in glass, blood and goodness knows what else. Picking up the brush, she attempted to clean up.

Derek looked up, his face riddled with guilt. "Leave it, woman, for God's sake."

Shaking, Sally reacted, saying sharply, "Don't take the Lord's name in vain, Derek. Nothing calls for that." She quickly cleaned up the broken glass, and got a sheet of newspaper to wrap around it before putting it in the bin.

He laughed but it wasn't a nice sound. She stared at him, not recognising him at all. He looked shattered. Despite what had just happened, he was her husband and he had come back from the dead.

She gestured towards the table. "Would you like a cup of tea and a piece of that tart? Are you hungry?"

"Sally, just stop and sit down, will you. I won't hurt you. That was an accident and I'm sorry. You will have to make other arrangements for those kids now I'm back."

Sally stayed silent. She knew she wouldn't send them away. She needed time to convince him to let them stay.

She couldn't sit at the table doing nothing. She filled the kettle and made a cup of tea using fresh leaves, more than usual. If there was one time that called for a strong cup of tea, it was now.

She placed a cup in front of him, putting the

milk jug on the side. She couldn't give him any sugar. He didn't say a word but his eyes never left her face.

Only after taking a long sip of tea and savouring the strength, did she ask, "What happened? I was told you were missing assumed dead."

The look of despair on his face took her breath away.

He pushed his fingers over his hair, which was cropped close to his scalp. She'd read somewhere that they shaved prisoners in the camps to keep the lice at bay. "I wish I had died."

"Derek. You can't say that." She itched to go to him, put her arms around his wretched, thin body and tell him everything would be okay. But she couldn't. She didn't know this man.

"Why not? It's true. It would have been better than stuck in Germany for the past five years, while my family, friends and neighbours forgot about me."

Why had no one told her, he was alive in a camp?

"We didn't forget. I kept feeling I would know if you were dead. I told your mother how I felt but she just laughed." She didn't think it would improve the atmosphere by telling him about how badly his mother behaved. "She'll be delighted you're home. Have you seen her yet?"

She didn't add that the only time she had seen his mother was on the day she called to Rose Cottage.

Derek tapped the table, the noise bringing Sally back to the present.

"Derek, did you contact her?"

He shook his head.

She asked, "Do you know about Roland?"

"Did he go west?"

"Derek, that's a horrible thing to say. Roland died in the service of his country. Your mother thinks both her sons are dead." Sally stood up. "I should send her a telegram or something."

"Leave it. I'll do it later. Sit down, woman."

She glared at him. But he put his head in his arms and started to cry. Surprised, she stood looking at him for a few seconds before she flung her arms around him. He gathered her to him and pulled her onto his knee.

"I can't believe I hurt you. I'm so sorry. I'd never hit you. You don't deserve that. You're what's kept me alive. The thought of coming back to you, to this house. That's what kept me sane or at least as sane as you can be when you are a prisoner."

Sally held onto him, his painfully-thin skeletal form making her wonder just what he had experienced. They had seen pictures of the concentration camps in Germany and the mountains of bodies on *Pathé News* but she couldn't remember seeing anything about English prisoners of war.

Sally said, "Why didn't they tell me you were

alive? When I got that telegram, I thought I would die too." But for the children, she might have; she had to behave like normal for their sake. They had been through so much already.

Derek wiped his face and looked at her. Sally waited for him to speak but he just stared.

She put a hand up to his face, whispering, "What happened to you? Why didn't someone tell me you were alive?"

He pushed her away, gently directing her to her own seat while he stood up and lit another cigarette.

"Were you at Dunkirk?" She tried to keep her tone neutral, despite wanting to scream at him to hurry up and tell her. Didn't he know how upset and worried she'd been?

"I was but I wasn't. I mean, I never got to the beach. Arthur and I got separated from our regiment. You have no idea what it was like, the confusion, the guns, the smoke, the bombs. The senseless killings, all of it." He looked at her, but it was as if he was back there. "We wandered around for a bit, trying to find any regiment, other soldiers, when there was a loud bang and a whoosh sound. I couldn't see, I couldn't hear. I was propelled forward and hit the ground with a thud. Arthur was killed instantly by a bomb or grenade. I'm not sure what hit us." He took a deep drag of the cigarette before continuing, "I don't know how, but I lost my dog tags."

She wanted to take him in her arms, to comfort him, but his monotone voice and the look of horror in his eyes fixed her to her seat. She'd never been scared being around Derek before but this man, despite looking like her husband, didn't sound like the one she knew.

"I heard German voices, laughing and the odd shot. I knew I had to get away, so under cover of darkness, I crept along some hedges, keeping out of sight. I had no idea where I was going. I heard some voices, English this time." He sat down again, his eyes focused on her now. "Sally, I was so relieved. I wasn't alone anymore. The men, they were from the Worcester Yeomanry, the anti-tank regiment. They'd been ordered to protect the rear guard. There wasn't a chance of any of them getting to the beaches, never mind a boat."

How could anyone be ordered to stay behind? Weren't their lives worth the same as the men picked up from the beaches? But she didn't voice her thoughts. Instead she waited. He finished his cigarette, stubbing it out on a plate on the table.

After a few seconds, she whispered, "So what happened then?"

"When we knew there was no point in fighting any longer, we surrendered. We'd run out of ammunition. Anyway, it was like David against Goliath, only this time Goliath had won. Jerries surrounded us, behind, in front and above us. The officers said we'd be protected under the Geneva Convention. They didn't know."

He lit another cigarette, this time his hand was shaking so much he had difficulty lighting it.

"Know what, Derek?" Curiosity won over fear.

"We might have been alright if we'd been taken prisoner by the normal army or, better yet, the Luftwaffe. We were handed over to the SS; we knew almost immediately we were in trouble."

"Why?" she whispered.

"They shot the injured, those that couldn't keep up."

"No! Don't tell me anymore. I can't listen to this." Sally put her hands over her ears. How could anyone shoot defenseless men?

But he continued as if he hadn't heard her. She reluctantly lowered her hands, squeezing them together on her lap.

"They took us to a barn. Just an ordinary barn, much like you would see on any farm around here. The most senior officer, James Lynn-Allen, he protested at the treatment of the injured, only to get rebuked by their senior officer for his troubles. They shoved us all inside. The men, you should have seen them, Sally. They were terrified, we all were, but they didn't show it. They were real soldiers right to the end. The French as well as the British."

349

What did he mean by the end? She folded her arms across her chest, trying to breath slowly to stop her heart racing.

"They threw grenades into that crowded space."

Sally swallowed hard, bile rising to her mouth.

"Two men threw themselves on the grenades to save the rest of us. Can you imagine being that brave?" Tears were running down his face now. She wanted him to stop, she wanted to put her hands over her ears, she wanted to run away but she couldn't. He needed to tell her.

"But that wasn't enough for them German bas…." He checked his language. "They called out men in groups of fives. We heard the shots."

Sally put her hand to her mouth, afraid she was going to be sick.

"Lynn-Allen told us it was every man for himself. We had to make a dash for escape. So we did. Of the hundred or so of us in that barn, only about ten of us made it, Sally. Ten? How did I end up one of them? Lynn-Allen died, as did over fifteen who had escaped but were so badly wounded they were dead in hours. Yet I lived."

"Oh Derek." She moved forward to embrace him but he leaned away from her.

"I was lucky. Private Evans, another barn survivor, found me lying face down by a stream. He, a nineteen-year-old, stayed with me, making me drink until the regular German army found us. They took me to the hospital despite the lack of dog tags. The SS would have shot us." Sally let out a cry but he didn't stop talking. "In the hospital, they treated us as if we were one of their own men. I couldn't believe it. But their *charity* didn't last long. Evans disappeared one day, I found out later he'd been sent to a POW camp."

Derek took a deep breath, before continuing, "When Evans found me, I was unconscious and when I came around; I remembered nothing about who I was, where I was from. The hospital disposed of my uniform – it was in tatters. It took longer to transfer me due to my injuries but they eventually shipped me off to a camp too. "

"I didn't know who I was for a couple of years until I met someone I used to go to school with. He recognised me and over time, my memory came back in bits and pieces. Still don't remember everything, but I remembered you, even when I didn't know your name. Every time I closed my eyes, I saw my brown-eyed girl smiling at me. You, Sally, you are the reason I lived."

"Derek, I'm so sorry." She hesitated but the words flew out of her mouth, before she could stop them. "Couldn't you have got word back to me, when you remembered I mean?"

He glanced up, his eyes blazing with resentment and anger, "Why are you pretending? I wrote to you.

As soon as I found out who I was, I told the commanding officer. He told me a telegram was sent."

Her hands flew to her face, her stomach churning. "I never got anything but that first telegram. I swear, Derek."

He didn't answer but at least he didn't pull away when she took his hand. "I'm so sorry what happened to you. I can't believe you're here."

"I wouldn't be but for the bravery of others. They rescued me. Arthur must have pushed me out of the way, then Evans. He might have got to the French resistance but instead he stayed by my side. But for their bravery…"

Tears choked her throat as she cuddled him as he cried and cried. She lost track of time; their tea went stone-cold but neither of them moved. Only when his sobs subsided and he wiped his nose with his sleeve much like Tom did, did she remember the children.

"Oh my, is that the time. I have to go to Enid's. She will be wondering where I am."

"Let her wonder. She will probably be telling all the neighbours what a savage I am. And she'd be right. Look at what I did to your beautiful face."

She held her hand up to the tender area. "It was an accident. You didn't mean to hit me." *No, you meant to hit a defenceless child* … but those words were left unsaid.

CHAPTER 41

"*L*et me help you." He took the brush and swept up the broken glass, not commenting when she retrieved the picture of Harry. Lisa loved looking at her brother dressed up in his uniform but Sally preferred the second photo, the one of the four of them together. Her, Lisa, Harry and Tom. They looked like a family. A real one.

Only now her real family was standing in front of her and he didn't want the children.

He looked at her, his expression anguished. "Sally, how long do they have to stay here? The war is over."

Sally stared at her fingers. She didn't want the children to leave. How could she explain to him how she felt. Maybe she should stick to the facts. "The war with Germany is over but the search for their mother or other surviving family members has only just begun." She looked into his eyes, saying softly, "Nobody knows who survived the horrors that were the camps."

His eyes widened as he realised her meaning. He backed away a little, his voice unsteady and barely more than a whisper, "But you can't mean to keep them until they find their family. That could take months, years even."

Sally counted slowly in her head. Once she reached ten, she said quietly, "I want them to stay here forever. I never want to let them go."

There, she had said it. Finally admitted it out loud. She loved the kids and couldn't imagine not having them with her.

Derek looked as if he'd been struck. "Derek?" she prompted, but he stayed silent. The silence lingered, growing uncomfortable, but she restrained herself. She had to give him time to think, he'd only just met the children. But once he got to know them he would love them too, she was sure of it.

He finally looked up. "But … what if their real parents show up?"

"Tom's father died after *Kristallnacht*. He was beaten to death by the guards, at Dachau. His mother died soon after he was born."

"But he said Lisa was his sister."

"His half-sister. His father married a much

younger woman. She'd be about twenty-eight now. If she survived." Sally couldn't look at him for fear he'd read her mind. She didn't want Trudi to have died – she wouldn't wish anyone dead – but she couldn't think about giving the children up. Lisa belonged here in Abbeydale, this was the only home she'd known. She didn't even know how to speak German.

Derek looked incredulous. "But if she did, she would claim the children. You wouldn't stand in the way of reuniting the family, would you?"

Sally didn't want to answer yet. She wanted to scream *YES!* She would! She'd do anything to keep the children. But, in her heart of hearts, even though she loved Lisa, she knew that was wrong.

Derek looked at her intently. "What about when we have our own children?"

His question surprised her. She had given up on having her own baby. With her husband presumed dead, that dream had been filed away a long time ago. Feeling embarrassed, she turned her face away from him. "If that should happen, the children would see the baby as their sister or brother."

"My child wouldn't be related to Germans. Over my dead body."

She whirled around to face him; her hands clasped together.

"Derek, can't you see past their nationality? They are children, Jewish children. If the Nazis had their way, they wouldn't exist. SS men who murdered the men in that barn would have done the same to them. Those poor children have been through enough in their short lives. I can't abandon them now. You have no idea how hard things have been for them. Tom was distraught when he arrived; the Nazis not only killed his father but he then had to watch as his brother was arrested as an enemy alien and threatened with deportation. As it was, Harry spent time in a camp with others just like him. But the camp also held committed Nazis. Can you imagine the torment he endured?"

"I have some idea." Derek's sarcasm stung but she refused to rise to his taunting.

"Please, Derek, get to know the children. In time you will love them as much as I do. Lisa is such a gentle, sweet-natured child, always looking to please. She brightens up every room. Tom is a lovable rascal. He gets into trouble at school for saying exactly what's on his mind but he has a heart of gold. He's an intelligent chap; you should see how well he can repair things. And Harry ... well, he is different. You can't love him like a child, as he's an adult now. He won't be back for a long time. He's on a mission to hunt down the man who murdered his father. Until he finds him, he says he won't be back. But he writes regularly..."

Sally stopped babbling, conscious that her

husband had remained silent. When she glanced at him, she saw he was staring out the window, deep in thought, but she'd no way of knowing what he was thinking about. Then he turned.

"I need a bath and a kip. Is there hot water?"

"I can heat some up. The range has been on since early, so it won't take long. Tom found some wood for me, so I was able to make the coal last a bit longer."

She busied herself preparing his bath but didn't offer to scrub his back. Instead, she decided to make herself scarce. She didn't want to see her husband or give him any ideas of resuming marital relations. He was a stranger. She needed time to adjust.

"I'll leave you to it then. See you in a while." She was gone before he could react.

* * *

LEAVING THE COTTAGE, she turned right, in the opposite direction to Enid's. Enid could manage the children for a bit longer; she needed time to herself. To get used to the shock of Derek coming back. All her prayers for him to return had been answered. She should have been skipping down the street instead of feeling like she had the weight of the world on her shoulders. She didn't even see Maggie until she almost walked into her.

"Sally, you were away with the fa … Oh goodness, whatever happened to your face."

Sally lied, "I fell." Whatever issues they had between them he was still her husband.

"You're as white as a sheet and shaking. Come inside and have a cup of tea. I have some broken biscuits. A rare treat these days. Callaghan's shop got some in and Mrs Callaghan kept some back for the children. Kind old dear, she is." Maggie prattled on as she guided Sally up the path and into the vicarage.

Sally didn't resist. Her insides were frozen but not from the cold. She was reluctant to face Enid, never mind Lisa and Tom. Maggie wouldn't press her for details but would wait for Sally to tell her when she was ready.

They sat over a cup of tea and a plate of uneaten biscuits. Maggie filled in the silence with tales from the village. So-and-so was expected home soon, and somebody else had a letter to say their son was injured, not seriously, and would shortly be moved to Botley's Park. On and on Maggie chatted, while Sally stirred her tea. Finally, Maggie leaned forward and took the spoon away.

"Drink the tea – can't afford to waste good leaves."

Sally lifted the cup to her mouth and drank. Only then did she meet Maggie's gaze to see the concern in her eyes.

Maggie whispered, "What is it, love? Is it the children? Have they found their family?"

Sally shook her head.

Maggie waited but as Sally stayed silent, she prompted, "Harry? Has he been injured? Worse?"

Again, Sally shook her head. She whispered, "Derek … he's home."

Maggie's eyes widened as she processed the news. "That's a surprise."

At the understatement, both women exchanged glances and burst out in a nervous laugh.

Sally said, "Maggie, it's everything I ever wanted. I prayed so hard for a miracle. You knew I didn't believe Derek was gone, that I felt I would have known he was dead. But now…"

"Where was he? How come they didn't tell you he was alive?"

"It's a long story. He was at Dunkirk, Arthur was killed by a shell or something. When Derek surrendered, they were taken to a barn. Oh Maggie, they threw grenades at them and shot the ones the grenades didn't kill. He escaped but was badly injured. Another soldier stayed with him and they were both captured. What type of people do that?"

"I thought prisoners of war were protected."

"Seems not everyone signed up to the rules." Sally took a sip of tea, playing for time.

"What is it, love, tell me? You know it won't go

any further." Maggie moved her chair closer to Sally's.

Tempted to tell her friend, Sally battled with her conscious. Derek had behaved badly but he was her husband. "Derek, he's different, Maggie. He doesn't even look like the man I married…" She let the words 'He doesn't act like it either' hang in the air.

Maggie took her hands and pulled her into a hug. Then she gently rubbed her back.

"Sally, I don't know what happened but remember it's early days. You and Derek, you've lived completely different lives, and it's bound to take a while for things to settle down.

Sally nodded. She couldn't bring herself to say more.

CHAPTER 42

*S*ally felt a bit better as she walked back up the path into her cottage. She loved her home just as much now as she had done when they moved in after their wedding. Back then, it was the middle of summer and the windows of the cottage had been surrounded by blooming roses, making it look like something off a picture postcard.

She turned to close the wooden gate behind her, the original metal gate having long gone to the war effort. She didn't know why she bothered, as the children would leave it open again, but it was a habit. She forced the feelings of despair down as she took one step after another until she reached the front door. She opened it quietly. Maybe he was asleep. Even as she thought that, she felt guilty wanting to avoid her husband.

But she heard voices. It sounded like Derek and Tom. She moved quietly, not proud of wanting to eavesdrop, but her curiosity won out. She stood at the door to the living room, where they couldn't see or hear her. Tom was sitting on the sofa, his foot dangling over the side while Derek sat upright in the wingback chair Maggie had given them for a wedding present.

"Did you have Jews in your camp?" Tom was asking.

"Not the way you mean, no," Derek replied.

"What does that mean?"

"Some of our lads were Jewish, not that we told the Hun that. We learned that lesson early on in the war."

"What lesson?"

"The Nazis didn't have time for Jews. The usual rules didn't apply to those poor sods. Taken out and shot, if they were lucky."

Sally put her hand to her mouth. What was Derek doing? Tom was only eleven. He didn't need to hear these details. Yet Tom seemed engrossed and she hesitated to interrupt.

"Did you meet many Nazis? I mean real ones, not just guards wearing a German uniform."

Derek countered, "You mean there's a differ-ence?" But Sally heard the hint of respect and curiosity in her husband's voice. He also sat straighter.

"Of course there's a difference."

Sally winced at Tom's tone. Now was not the time for his know-it-all attitude, but Derek didn't seem bothered.

"Explain."

"The ones wearing the uniform are doing their duty. That's their job. They have to defend Germany and you, being British, are prisoners of war, right? So they have to keep you prisoner."

"I suppose…"

"But that doesn't make them Nazis. They could have been conscripted, for all you know. They did that. The Nazis ran out of soldiers, so they took grandfathers and cripples and even boys like me and put them in uniform. I don't think they put boys in as camp guards though."

A sound suspiciously like a laugh came from Derek but it was quickly smothered.

"My teacher explained it to me. I was in trouble for speaking out of turn. Again. And the head teacher told me I should be grateful for being allowed to stay in England, where it was safe. I told him he should have the boys who called me names in his office, not me."

"What did they call you?"

"A Nazi and a Hitler-lover. Shows they were

stupid, that did. How could I be a Hitler-lover? But the teacher took their side as usual."

"So, this head teacher, what did he say?"

"He explained to me what was happening in Germany. How boys like me were fighting against Russian tanks, sometimes without even a gun or anything. He said to remember that when someone called me names. Names couldn't hurt me but tanks – they are a whole other story."

Sally saw Derek nodding at that but his next words surprised her. "He's wrong, you know. Not about the tanks bit. And it's true, that many of the guards were conscripts or those you wouldn't usually expect in an army. Some were old and others were crippled in the first war."

"So, what was he wrong about? Aunt Sally says I should listen to the head teacher but if he's wrong then I should tell him, shouldn't I?"

Derek smiled at Tom, making Sally's heart flutter in a way she hadn't experienced for so many years.

"Let's not get ahead of yourself, young man. No adult likes a pup like you to correct him. As I said, your head teacher was right about a lot of things. It was telling you that calling you names can't hurt was where he was wrong. Never underestimate the power of what you say. People remember the words well after the injuries they suffered have long recovered."

"I guess." Tom didn't sound convinced. He stayed

silent for a couple of seconds before he started again. "So, what was it really like in the camps? Papa and my brother, Harry, were in one once. Harry wasn't in for long. Our stepmother got him out. But Papa … he didn't come home."

Sally restrained the urge to go to the child. She willed Derek to be careful in his reply, to hear the unasked question. What did they do to his father that he couldn't come home?

"I'm sorry to hear that, son. Your papa didn't deserve that. Nobody did. A lot of people got sick in our camp too and they died. The food was awful and there wasn't enough of it. We were always hungry..."

"Worse than Mrs Brown's?"

"Mrs Brown? Oh, you mean Enid. Ha! Yes, much worse. You would feed the pigs better than the stuff we got to eat."

"Harry said he and Papa didn't get good food so that's probably what happened. Papa would have given his food to Harry to keep him alive. He was like that. Always looking after other people."

"So, your papa, what was he like?"

Tom took a deep breath. "He was nice, at least to me. He had a lot of friends, as he was a doctor before Hitler came to power. Mother, my real mother, and him lived in a big house. Aunty Chana told me all about it. She said it was bigger than a palace but I don't remember it. We had to leave and live in a smaller apartment when I was born. Aunty Chana told me Mother didn't like it there and that's why she died."

"And your father remarried."

"Yes, to my nanny. She was mine before he married her. Then I had to share her. I didn't like that but then Lisa, my sister, came along. You know the girl who screamed when you came home. She does that a lot. Gets scared really easy, but that's girls for you, isn't it?"

"Not sure about that, son. From what I've seen, women can be very brave too. Is that right, Sally?"

Sally jumped. How had she given herself away?

Tom looked round and smiled at her. "Aunt Sally, you came home. I was keeping Uncle Derek company. It was all women at Mrs Brown's house." Tom rolled his eyes as he stood up. "Can I go find my mates now? I have some marbles to exchange. Would you like to come, Uncle Derek? Mark Clark has a pure black marble and I'm going to win it today."

"No, thank you, son, but good luck with your game. I have some talking to do."

"Can you come with me later? I want my mates to meet you. You are a real live hero and everything."

"Don't call me that. I'm no hero. The real heroes were left over there."

"That's not what Aunt Sally says. She says you were the first to volunteer to fight. Said you got a medal and everything. Will you be here when I get back?"

Derek glanced at Sally as if asking permission.

"Derek is tired, young man, so he might be asleep. Make sure you come home quietly."

"Yes, ma'am. See you later, Uncle Derek. Thanks for talking to me. You know, like a man, not a boy. Can I have a sandwich to take with me, Aunt Sally? I'm starving."

"Didn't you eat at Enid's?"

"Yes, but not your pie. She gave us something horrible. It was made out of vegetables but they were so mushed I don't know what it was. It was disgusting."

Derek's laugh prevented her from admonishing Tom for his rudeness. "Take an apple and go on with you. Be home for tea by six."

"Will do."

And he was gone.

Derek said, "He's a bright boy, that one. Need to watch what you say around him, that's for sure."

"Thank you for being kind to him, Derek. He's desperate for a man's attention. You know boys need a grown-up male to look up to. Harry's been away so long, and even if he was here, he would never have answered the questions about the camp."

"Can't blame him. Just glad Tom accepted my answer."

CHAPTER 43

*S*ally couldn't stop smiling. It was going to be all right now. Derek and Tom had got along and everyone loved Lisa. Then she thought, *Oh my goodness, Lisa's still at Enid's.*

She made to leave, saying, "I'd best collect Lisa. I don't think she likes being at Enid's much, either."

Derek stopped her. "Sally, wait a minute. I know it's a shock to you, me coming home like this. I should have sent you a telegram, but I was selfish. I thought you would run into my arms and..." Derek shrugged his shoulders as he lit a cigarette. "I'm not the same man as you once knew, Sally. I've changed."

She tried to fight her panic, stop her stomach from churning at his words. It sounded like he had given up on them.

"I've changed too, Derek. Five years is a long

time." She moved nearer to him. "I'm thrilled that you're home, though. I prayed for this moment every single night."

"You did?"

Her heart melted, as he looked at her in disbelief. Taking a few steps closer, she whispered, "Yes, darling, I did. I love you, always you and only you." She moved to kiss him but he held back.

"That's not the whole truth, though, is it?"

She didn't know what he meant. "Derek, I swear, I haven't looked at another man."

"I know that. I wasn't implying you had – but you have fallen for those children. They mean everything to you, don't they?"

Sally couldn't lie. She bit her lip, looking at him.

"I guess I understand why. He's a very bright boy, young Tom, and the baby was so young when she came here. You said you wanted a family and you got one."

"We've got one. I've shown the children your picture every day."

He looked startled at that. "What happens if they find their mother?"

"Tom's stepmother hasn't been in contact with the Red Cross. It's been months and they've heard nothing. Harry wrote to say he had toured a couple of the displacement camps but there was no record of a Trudi Beck."

"You think she's dead? I guess that would suit you."

Shocked, she choked back her hurt. "Derek! I would never wish another person dead." But yet, in her heart, wasn't she hoping Trudi wouldn't take Lisa and Tom away?

"If she doesn't come back, maybe Harry will take them."

Anger rushed through her, making her clench her fists. "No, he won't. Harry told me to look after them. He loves them but he's set on revenge." She forced herself to calm down. "I worry about him. He's consumed by hatred for the Nazis but in particular for one he blames for killing his father. He writes regularly but says he won't return until that man is dead."

Derek shook his head as if trying to find a way out, but knowing there was none. "So, the children have nowhere to go."

She fell to her knees beside his chair, trying to take his hands in hers, but he held back. She hated the pleading tone in her voice but she had to find a way through to the man she loved – her Derek, not this stranger. "This is their home, Derek, and has been for the last six years. Why should they go anywhere?

"This is our home, Sally. Yours and mine. What about our plans?"

"Derek, I meant what I said earlier. I love Tom and Lisa just as much as I will love our children."

Derek stood up, a look of pain and confusion on his face.

She stood too and moved closer to him, hoping he would take her in his arms and tell her it would work out. "Please, Derek, don't make any rash decisions. Give it time."

"I can't. I won't raise your hopes like that. I will never accept those children, Sally." He lit a cigarette from the one he was holding, before stubbing out the old one. He took a deep drag and exhaled. Then he said, "You will have to make a choice, Sally."

"Don't, Derek, please ... Not today."

"Those children or us."

Tears spilled down her face. "Derek, I'm begging you. Don't do anything rash, please. Stay here and get to know the children. Let us have time to find our way back to one another. There've been loads of programmes on the wireless and letters written into *Home Chat* from people in our situation. Men finding it difficult after being away fighting for so long, women trying to reconcile their new lives with the ones they lived when their husbands shared the home ... Just this morning, I read how one woman's son asked her when Daddy was going away again. See, it's going on all over Britain. We just need time to find our way..."

"Sally, that woman was talking about her son, with her husband. You want me to adopt two German children. The Germans stole the last five years from me, from us. They butchered the men in the barn, they killed Roland, Arthur and countless other people."

Sally countered, "They killed Tom and Lisa's father, and their mother too, most likely. Their grandparents, their aunts, uncles, cousins. I've seen the footage of the concentration camps. All those little children. And you want me to send mine back to that country where they know nobody. I won't do it. I can't do it."

Derek walked up the stairs. She heard the bathroom door shut.

Sally sank onto the sofa, weeping with her head in her hands.

After a few minutes, she heard the door close. She looked up; Derek stood in front of her, his bag in one hand, his hat in the other.

"I have to go to London. I have to see a specialist at St Thomas's. I will stay with Mother."

"Derek, please don't go. Not like this…"

"I'm sorry. I should have died out there in that barn. It would have been better for everyone. I will give you grounds for divorce."

She shook her head, she didn't even want to hear that ugly word.

"Sally, I can't adopt those children but I can behave as a gentleman." He turned on his heels and left, leaving the door open.

She watched him walk away – wanted to run to him, to drag him home, but she couldn't move. She watched through the window until he was out of view. How could he have said such a horrible thing? Not the divorce although that was bad enough. But wishing himself dead after so many had died. The pain was more than she could bear, worse than the day the telegram had arrived.

SHE DIDN'T KNOW how long she sat there but it had started getting dark before Tom returned. When she wouldn't answer him, he ran for Maggie. She could hear him calling her friend's name.

Maggie arrived, took one look at her and told Tom to get Rachel to collect Lisa from Mrs Brown and then to cook him his tea in the vicarage.

"Can Uncle Derek come too? He's so nice." Tom looked around. "Where is he?"

"Tom, go on now and leave me with Sally."

CHAPTER 44

*D*erek took the train to London. All around him, people were talking about the war but he made no effort to join in. He listened to two ex-servicemen sitting behind him.

"When we needed guns, the government found them. When we needed factories for making airplanes and bullets and goodness knows what else, the government built them. So, how come they find it so hard to build houses? I swear, I'll go mad if I have to spend another month in my mother-in-law's house. They should have set that woman on the Nazis and then the war would have been over in months, not years."

"Least you get to stay with your missus. Ain't no room for me, so my missus tells me. Neighbours say different. They said during the war, my missus had no problem putting up strangers. Had a fancy for Yanks, she did."

"She never. What you going to do about it?"

"What do you think? Down the divorce courts, I'm going. I ain't having that. Me away fighting for my country, and her entertaining the troops."

Amused, Derek watched a woman in her early thirties. She was wearing a faded-out dress, her face free of make-up. She looked up, and he was surprised to see she was younger than he'd first assumed. She had dark circles under her eyes and seemed strained.

She was getting more irritated as the men talked, until finally she spoke up. "Can you listen to yourselves? You had it good, you men. Off fighting the war. Seeing those exotic places like Paris and France and everything. While us women got stuck here, with rationing and flying bombs and all sorts. I haven't had a decent night's sleep in five years. I'm sick of hearing how you men had it so hard. Always complaining you are." The woman took a deep breath before continuing, "You think about all the kids this war has left as orphans. Who's going to look after them? Orphanages were full before the war, there won't be anyone able to take them in. Some of us don't have homes for our own families."

An image of Tom and Lisa flashed into his mind. Derek thought the woman had finished as she stood up to leave the train. But she poked her finger into one man's chest. "If I was your missus, I'd been happy to entertain the Yanks and anyone else that came my way, if it meant I didn't have to put up with your miserable old mug anymore. You're a disgrace. Your wife is better off without ya."

The woman left the men lost for words. Derek watched as she heaved her bags along the Clapham Junction platform. In the distance, where there used to be houses, all he saw were large areas of what looked like building sites. He saw youngsters playing in them, and it took a while to realise that was what was left of houses after the bombing. Was that where the woman had lived?

Her remarks about having no home hit him hard but not as much as her comments about orphans. The children had already suffered enough by living through the bombs, their fathers away with the forces, their mothers caught up in war work. Tom's face, as he'd sat telling Derek about the issues he had at school, filled his mind. Living as a Jewish refugee in England might not always be a bed of roses but it was heaven compared to what could happen if the children were sent back to Germany. Would there even be a Jewish community left alive to look after them? He shifted in his seat as his guilt weighed heavier on his mind.

When the train reached Waterloo, he decided to walk to his mother's home. He wasn't relishing the thought of seeing her. They'd never been close. He'd been measured against Roland and always found lacking. But it was his insistence on marrying Sally, a *commoner* according to his mother, that drove the final wedge between them.

Feeling thirsty, he stopped at a public house.

"Pint of lager, please, mate."

"Been away, have ye?" The bartender pushed the pint towards him. "You look half-starved. You weren't in one of those Jap camps, were you?"

He didn't look as bad as that, did he? "No, a German one."

"You were lucky. The things those Japs did to our boys. No wonder they landed those bombs on them."

Before Derek could answer, one of the men sitting at the bar spoke up.

"Shouldn't have done that, Charlie. They should have warned them first."

"Shut up, Stan, or I'll bar you. They got what they deserved and it finished the war, didn't it?" The bartender looked back to Derek. "From around here, are ya?"

"Not really. I live out near Chertsey. I came up to see my mother."

"She'll be glad to have you home. So many didn't get back." Charlie glanced at a picture of two boys in uniform. "Both my boys."

"Sorry for your loss."

"My missus too. She lost her reason when the first boy died, and then when we lost the second one, she just couldn't handle it. Turned on the gas. She was a great mother and the best wife a man could find. But her heart was broken."

Derek let the barman talk. Seemed like Charlie needed to chat as much as Derek needed to stay quiet. He sensed the barman wouldn't appreciate him saying he wished he'd died too.

"So, what will you do now you're home?" Charlie asked him.

The man called Stan answered for him. "He'll be like the rest of the others coming home. Same as in my day. No job, no home, no trade. If you're lucky, mate, you won't have a wife and a baby relying on ya. That was me when I got back in 1918, to a land fit for heroes. We were told the same lies you lot are being told now."

"Shut up, Stan. Nobody wants to hear the voice of doom and gloom." Charlie filled another pint and gave it to Derek. "On the house, lad. Wish you the best of luck."

Derek accepted the pint but took it to a table where he could sit alone and in peace. He wasn't there for long before a young girl came in and sat beside him.

"Looking for company?" she said.

He stared at her. She was about fourteen years old, if that.

He shook his head. "You're too young to be living a life like this."

"I'm old enough to give you what you want. Cheap too."

"What's your name?"

She moved closer. The stench of her unwashed body and rotten teeth turned his stomach. "What do you want it to be?" she whispered.

Charlie spotted her. "Oi, you. Get out of my pub. I told you before. Go on, clear off."

The girl retorted, "Keep your shirt on, granddad." Then she blew Derek a kiss and whispered, "I'll wait outside."

Charlie came over to wipe Derek's table down. "Sorry about that, lad, those girls are a menace."

"She's just a child."

"God love 'em, they grow up fast around here. Mothers and fathers gone, either in the bombs or in the forces. They rear themselves, and those unlucky ones end up on the streets with nobody to care for them. I wouldn't wish it on anyone to be an orphan these days."

Derek couldn't finish his pint. He waited until Charlie returned behind the bar and left. She was waiting, just as she said she would be. He searched in his pocket for some coins. She looked older in the dark but still skinny.

"I don't want anything. Get yourself some hot food. You look half-starved."

Her gaze raked him from his head to his toes. "Kettle calling the pot black, that is. Where you been then?"

"Germany. Listen, don't you have someone you can stay with? Get yourself a proper job?"

"You ain't been back long, have ya? There aren't any proper jobs, not for the likes of me. Soldiers are finding it hard to get jobs, never mind those with no education and no home."

Derek wished he had something more to give her but he had left most of his cash on the table in Rose Cottage.

"Be careful," he said.

The girl wandered off, leaving Derek staring after her. It was getting late and he should go to his mother's. On second thoughts, he decided he'd go straight to the hospital to find out what treatments the doctors wanted to do on his wounds. His headaches were worse than ever. Hopefully they would have a bed for him. He'd send a telegram to his mother. He didn't want her fussing over him.

CHAPTER 45

SEPTEMBER 1945

*L*ike everyone in the country, Sally was finding it difficult to adapt to life after the war. While the war was on, they knew they had to keep going. No matter what, they had to keep a stiff upper lip for the duration, until the war was over. They would rest when peace was declared, so they could deal with the mental, physical and emotional exhaustion that went with rationing, queueing for food and clothing, bombing raids, sheltering in Anderson shelters. They could survive anything as peace was coming. One day.

But now peace had arrived and yet there was still no let-up. They might not have bombing raids to cope with but the situation with food supplies was worse. Shopping queues were longer, food provisions smaller. People were snappy with one another. One radio host summed it up by saying: "At least in the war, you had the all-clear to look forward to."

She didn't know how Derek was. He'd sent a note to say he'd telegrammed his mother but had not seen her yet. He was a patient at St Thomas's. He didn't tell her the reason for his stay but he did say not to visit. She took his advice, not wanting to have to face the fact that it was over and he wanted a divorce. With him gone, she could pretend he had never come back and was still the man she'd married.

She pushed the door of the vicarage open, desperate for Maggie's good humour. Her friend could pull her mind out of the dark places it visited these days.

"Sally, come in." Maggie almost collided with her. "I was about to send Ruth to fetch you from your house. The kettle's on, and I've some carrot cake for you to taste." Sally could smell the scent of cooking in the air, making her stomach grumble. She moved to come inside but Maggie stood in the doorway and kept talking, her pace growing faster if anything. "It's a new recipe from the radio. Aren't I glad to see you! Rachel's had word from the Red Cross. Her mother's survived. Isn't that wonderful news?" Maggie's voice sounded strained, and Sally could tell her friend was struggling to sound positive. It would kill her to give up the girls; she loved them like daughters. "Come inside and stop letting all the heat out. What are you doing just standing there?"

Bemused, Sally pushed past Maggie and spotted Rachel standing on the other side of the kitchen. Walking over, she hugged Rachel, who was staring at the letter in disbelief. Maggie told Sally to take a seat. "The tea is fresh, although a bit weak as I had to reuse the tea leaves from this morning. When is this rationing going to end? The war ended six months ago, for goodness sake."

Sally ignored Maggie's grumblings.

"Rachel, tell us the good news. Is she well? Will she come here?"

Rachel picked up the letter.

"She writes in German, so I have to translate for you. She said she survived, thanks to Trudi, Lisa's mother. Mama didn't leave Berlin until the end of the war."

"She stayed there for the whole war?" Sally couldn't hide her disbelief. "That must have been so dangerous."

"She says it was but there were many who helped. A pastor called Erik Perwe helped her. The Swedish Church, where he was in charge, hid a few people in the actual church but had several other hiding places. Mother said she lived with Trudi and some other people for a while. That must have been when she wrote that last letter we got. Then Trudi took her to this Mr Perwe and he looked after her until he died in 1944."

"The one she sent in the summer of 1940 … It seems like yesterday, yet in other ways, those five years passed very slowly, didn't they?"

Rachel didn't answer Sally. She kept reading. "She says she was very frightened with the bombing and everything and was always hungry."

Rachel's mouth thinned.

"What?"

"She says the greatest danger was the Jew-catchers."

Sally thought that was a bit obvious but didn't like to say so. Rachel's next words surprised her.

"Not the Nazis or the German civilians, Sally, but other Jews."

"What?" Sally wasn't sure she'd heard correctly.

"Mama says there were a few Jews who worked with the SS. Those Jews denounced several brave people to the Gestapo in return for their own safety. The Jew-catcher would go to a suspected safe house and tell them they were on the run from the Gestapo. If the person took them in, the Gestapo would watch the house for several days to see who was coming and going. Only then would they swoop in and arrest everyone. Hundreds of good Germans and other nationalities, as well as the Jews they were sheltering, were murdered."

"Surely they wouldn't do that?" Sally couldn't hide her horror.

Maggie said, "Nobody knows what they would do to save themselves or their families, Sally."

Maggie's gentle reproof worked. Sally knew she would do anything to save Lisa and Tom. Wasn't she considering giving up on her marriage to keep them with her? Would she have denounced others to save their lives? She wanted to say she wouldn't but … could she honestly say that? Could anyone judge those who had lost all hope?

"Is Trudi with your mother? Are they going to come here?" Sally asked.

Rachel shook her head. "Mama says Trudi disappeared in early 1944. She says Trudi was always looking to help more people. Shortly before the Russians arrived, the Swedes got Mama and others out of Berlin."

Sally clenched her teeth together, trying to stop a gasp of horror escaping. They'd all heard how the Russian soldiers had treated any women they came across. Didn't seem to matter if they were Jewish, nor what age they were.

She reached across and put her hand over Rachel's. "I am so glad your mother survived."

Rachel didn't react; she wasn't crying, her face pale but almost expressionless. Sally exchanged a look with Maggie, seeing the concern in her friend's face too. Rachel was reading the letter as if it were a textbook.

"She is going to Palestine. She says she's heard rumours Gavriel is with Izsak. She wants me and Ruth to go to Palestine too."

Sally glanced at Maggie, who was staring at her shoes. Losing the girls would break Maggie's heart.

"Palestine? How will you get there? I know Maggie put the Jewellery you brought with you from Germany in the bank deposit box. Could you sell it to pay for the travel costs? Will the Red Cross help you get past the restrictions on travel?" Sally asked.

Rachel stood up and threw the letter on the table. "No, they won't. I already enquired, as I wanted to go even before I heard Mother was going there. The British government doesn't want to send any Jews from here to Palestine. They are afraid of upsetting the Arabs. Palestine is our promised land."

"When did you enquire?" Maggie said, barely disguising the anger in her voice. "I thought you liked living here."

Rachel implored her, "I do, Maggie. I love you, but when they took Harry away, I got scared. Then Mrs Brown and Mrs Shackleton-Driver kept saying things and I didn't feel safe." Rachel took a deep breath but it didn't stop her sobbing. "I'm sorry. The last thing I want to do is hurt you, Maggie."

"You didn't do anything to me, Rachel. I should

have protected you more. I should have kept those women away from you."

Maggie was crying too. Sally stood and gathered Rachel to her.

"Rachel, you're bound to be emotional. Your mother survived the war and you should be over the moon. It's horrible you won't be able to see her for another while. I understand you're frustrated but maybe you could see this as a chance for you. You and Harry, maybe?"

"Harry didn't consider my feelings when he stayed in Germany set on revenge. I shall not think of him either." But her expression of sadness and loneliness belied her words.

Now was not the time to discuss the merits or lack thereof of Harry's choices. "Stay for your own sake then."

"Why? How will it benefit me to stay here?" Rachel looked at her suspiciously.

"You said you wanted to be a doctor or a nurse. Now you have found your mother and know she's safe you can concentrate on achieving your dream."

Rachel stared at her. "You mean, study here?"

"Why not? I'm sure Maggie and the reverend would look after Ruth if you had to go away to study. You have good experience from working at Botley's Park. Have you thought about asking Matron for help in getting started?"

Rachel's eyes widened, her deep sadness fading. "You really think I could?"

"Of course Sally does. I do too. So does the reverend. We've been making enquiries for you." Maggie pulled Rachel back to her seat. "I'm thrilled your mother survived, love, but we were so worried she wouldn't. We wanted to make sure you had a future, no matter what the news from Germany was."

A tear slid down Rachel's face. "I am so ungrateful. You have done so much for me and all I could do was moan about Palestine. You must think I am horrible."

"Never. I think you are a very brave, wonderful young woman who can achieve her dreams. All of them. If you want to qualify as a doctor, do it. Palestine will need doctors and if they don't, your people surely will. It's going to take years to help those poor creatures who survived the war, either in the concentration camps or elsewhere. I'm sure you could volunteer to help in the camps now with your VAD training."

"I never thought of doing that." Rachel's eyes lit up. "Maybe that's what I should do. There is plenty of time later to choose a career." Then her face fell. "What about Ruth? She's too young to travel to Palestine."

"Ruth can stay here for as long as she wants."

A little voice said, "I want to stay here forever. I

don't want to go to a new country. I want to stay with Maggie."

The adults turned at once to see Ruth standing in the doorway, her hands on her hips.

"I am almost twelve and nobody thinks to ask what I want. I'm really glad Mama is alive but if she really wanted me, she would come here. She put us on that train and sent us away. She only cares about the boys. If you want to go to her, Rachel, go. Leave me alone. I don't care."

Maggie's eyes glistened. "Ruth, darling, come here and sit down."

"I'm not a child."

"I know that, love, you're a young woman. But come and sit down anyway. You've the wrong idea about your mother. When she put you and Rachel on that train, she made the most difficult decision any mother could make. You're not my flesh and blood, yet I don't think I could bear to put you on a train to another country even if I knew it was to save your life. I love you, child, but you are part of your mother. She did what she did because she loves you more than she loves herself."

Ruth hiccupped but didn't say anything.

"Rachel has protected you and loved you in your mother's place, ever since that train pulled out of the Berlin platform. She's done a wonderful job and I hope you will always be as close as you are. But it's time for Rachel to live her own life, Ruthie."

Maggie's use of her pet name made Ruth lean into the older woman. Maggie put her arm around her and pulled her closer. "Rachel has to make her choices but even as she makes them, she's still thinking of you. She wants you to be safe and happy."

"I am safe and happy here. I don't want to go away. Not again."

Maggie looked to Rachel.

"Ruth, Mama loves us both. She knows we are safe, that's why she has to look for the boys. She doesn't know what happened to them, if they are even alive. That's why she is going to Palestine first. You're her baby, if anything, her favourite."

Ruth looked mutinous. Her voice shook as she insisted, "I don't want to go."

"I am not forcing you to go to Palestine but I think you should write to Mama and ask her if you can stay here."

"What if she says no?"

Rachel took her sister's hand in hers. "I don't believe she will. She won't want you making that journey on your own. She will want you to finish school."

At Ruth's face, Rachel laughed. "Do you think Maggie will let you leave school?"

Ruth glanced at Maggie.

"Not on your life, child. Education is the key to freedom, particularly for girls. You will finish school and then head to university, if I have my way."

"Maggie, I hate school!" Ruth protested. "I want to leave and get a job as soon as I turn fourteen."

"Not on my watch, love. You'll stay in school for as long as they'll have you. Agreed, Rachel?"

Rachel nodded.

Ruth stood up. "Maybe I will go to Mother, after all," she announced, as she flounced out the door.

Rachel rose to follow her but Maggie held her hand.

"Let her go, love. She doesn't know whether she's coming or going. She knows your mother saved her life but she feels abandoned. That will take some time for her to figure out. You've done your best for Ruth. It's time to concentrate on Rachel now."

"Listen to Maggie, Rachel. She's a wise, old woman."

"Less of the old, thank you very much, Sally Matthews."

CHAPTER 46

"*E*vening, Mother." Derek stood in front of the fire in the main drawing-room. He'd been released from St Thomas's earlier in the day.

His mother, dressed in a long wine-coloured gown, as if she was going to an opera or dinner at the Savoy, walked into the room. Diamond earrings and a matching necklace danced in the light from the flames. He couldn't see her face but her figure was as perfect as always. She'd had her hair cut; the shorter style made her look older although he doubted that was her intention. She smelled just as he remembered, the lavender perfume overpowering his senses.

She glided across the room to light the crystal lamps on either side of the fireplace. She wouldn't dream of turning on the main ceiling light, for fear it would highlight her age.

"Darling, why didn't you let me know you were coming? I would have arranged a dinner with friends."

Derek knew she wasn't dressed like that to stay home.

She poured them both a drink, handing him the smaller measure. "It's much easier to go out these days. Rationing is such a trial. Goodness knows when the staff will supply a decent meal."

Derek let his mother's complaints roll over him. He'd already eaten in the kitchen, much to the consternation of Cook. As far as he could see, his mother and her staff wanted for little. There was plenty of gin and whisky in the decanters. Mother must have good contacts on the black market.

"It's so difficult to find good staff these days. Those munitions factories have ruined it for everyone with the wages they paid. Do you know, I interviewed a young girl to come in as a daily maid, she wanted half a crown an hour! When I asked her what her rate would be if she were to live in, the young madam said it would be three pounds, ten shillings, provided she got food and board. Well, I can tell you, I sent her on her way with a flea in her ear. Honestly, I don't know how I will manage. The money your father left me doesn't rise every day, unlike the prices of everything else."

Derek didn't comment. His mother had a beautiful

home, when more than half of London was a bomb site. Her dress probably cost six months' wages at least; it was real silk and not the rayon many were wearing. If she was starving, it was by choice, not necessity. She was doing just fine.

"Derek, you must have some other clothes. Those look like rags. I know you like to pretend you are a common villager but must you act like one? It would scandalise my friends to see you dressed like that."

Derek looked down at his demob suit. "Courtesy of the government, Mother dear. The only suit that will fit me now. My old clothes hang on me."

"Yes, you are far too thin and you look so old."

Derek lit another cigarette. The doctors had warned him about smoking so much. "Thanks, Mother. Charming as always."

"I say it as I find it. I am glad you are home. Now, you get on with divorcing that common trollop of a wife and finding someone more suitable. Lady Lancashire's daughter, Penelope, lost her husband in the war. She has two young boys but they are off to boarding school shortly. She would be perfect."

"I have a wife, Mother."

His mother muttered something.

"Mother, Sally said you'd been to visit her. Something about selling Rose Cottage."

"Well, I wasn't letting her have it. That cottage has been in our family for years, and it's bad enough those Jewish brats had to live there during the war. But now they will go back to where they came from, and you can pay Sally off. It's rather charming, isn't it? Or at least it would be if that wife of yours hadn't dug up the whole lawn and planted vegetables. The woman has no class." His mother took a drag of her cigarette before continuing, "The village is much bigger than I remember. I met a wonderful woman, Jane Shackleton-Driver, at the Women's Institute. She lives on a large spread just outside of Abbeydale. She filled me in on your wife's antics during the war. Imagine carrying on with a man barely out of short trousers. Thankfully, Winston had the right idea and arrested the enemy aliens. They shipped him off before too much damage was done."

"Harry was a sixteen-year-old boy on the run for his life. He's now serving in the British Army. I rather think he lied about his age to get in."

His mother sniffed. "It's not decent for a young widow to parade her by-blows for everyone to see."

"You mean the children rescued by the Kindertransport?"

"Who rescued them? We have enough children in Britain already. Mrs Shackleton-Driver had to take in five of them. Unruly lot they were, covered in lice and not one toilet-trained among them. Makes me feel faint to even think about it."

Derek coughed to hide a laugh. He doubted his mother had ever felt faint in her whole life.

"I didn't know Mrs Shackleton-Driver took in refugees."

"She didn't take in *foreigners*." His mother's face screwed up with distaste as she almost spat out the word. "She took in some evacuees from London, the worst parts of the East End. She got rid of them fairly fast. Sent them back as soon as she could, and I don't blame her one bit. Horrid little creatures."

"The war devastated the East End. Sending children to the country probably saved their lives, not that that would trouble you much, Mother."

She turned her glacial stare on him.

"Be careful, Derek. I'll make allowances for your mood based on your considerable suffering in that camp. Now, sit down and tell me your plans. With Roland dying, you're now heir to a vast fortune. Give up this salesman business and take your rightful place in the family business. Harold – you remember Harold Echols – he's been with us for donkey's years and will show you all you need to know. First, I will call your father's tailor and have him make up some new suits. You can't be seen in that."

"What about rationing?"

"Darling, don't worry about things like that. I don't. There is always a way to secure what we need. We have no time to lose. Your brother's remembrance service is next week. Then we have to go to collect his medal. They have awarded quite an honour to your brother."

"I'm sure Roland would prefer to be still alive."

He ignored his mother's glare and excused himself on the basis he was tired.

*a*s he walked to his room, his father's old manservant climbed the stairs behind him.

"Sorry, Master Derek. These old legs of mine aren't used to walking as fast as they used to."

"I didn't ring for you, Smith. Why aren't you resting in the kitchen?"

"Your mother said I was to attend to you while you were in residence. Only, nobody told me when you were coming, so apologies for not being here when you arrived."

They reached Derek's old room.

Smith said, "Not in there. I moved your things to Master Roland's room. It's yours now, being the bigger room."

Derek didn't want his brother's room or his inheritance. He closed his eyes. He knew what he wanted, and that was Sally. Only, she came with two children now.

"Sir, are you all right? You look rather pale."

"I'm fine, Smith. I should worry about you. You should have retired by now." Derek waited, hoping the servant would tell him why he hadn't. The man wouldn't return his gaze, his eyes shifting right and left.

He called him by the name he'd used as a boy. "Sam? Come in and sit down and tell me what's really been happening since I've been away. For starters, you can tell me about the black market."

Sam paled even more, if that was at all possible for a man who looked like he never went outdoors. He followed Derek into the room but only sat when Derek insisted.

Derek glanced around. The room looked like Roland had just left. All of his brother's things were laid out in perfect position. If he opened the wardrobe, no doubt he would find it full of the best suits a man could wear. Meanwhile, out in the streets, men who had returned from fighting froze.

"Sam, tell me. I won't let on to Mother."

Sam looked uncomfortable. "Your mother took the news of your disappearance badly, sir, but when Master Roland died, I think she might have lost her mind. For a while, at least. She had some funny guests call to the house."

"Funny?"

"The Mitford sisters, amongst others. They said some things that would make your hair stand on end. If it wasn't for our age, and the fact that we had nowhere else to go, Cook and I would have left. Then your mother insisted we find everything she wanted for her guests. Champagne and caviar and stuff like that, when you can't even buy sugar, a packet of ten smokes or a tin of pears. I miss my tinned pears something dreadful. They were my treat, like, on a Sunday."

Derek wasn't interested in tins of pears but he said nothing. The old man was uncomfortable enough.

"Cook and me, we didn't know anyone who could get this stuff. We tried telling the mistress but she wasn't having any of it. One of her friends came to the rescue, and every couple of weeks we got a delivery. Cook was all of a tither, convinced the coppers would come to arrest her. That's why she was so nervous when you walked in the door. She thinks you might hold her responsible and fire her. She doesn't have a soul in the world, except for me, and I can't afford to put a roof over our heads. Not now."

Something about the way the man said "not now" made Derek ask, "Why not now?"

Sam didn't look up.

"Sam, tell me. Why not now?"

"Well, there's nowhere for us to go, for a start. All

those servicemen coming home from the war who have no homes, they get priority. Only right that is, really. And if we could find something, we don't have the money."

Derek raised an eyebrow. His father had paid his servant well and they lived in.

"Your father, God rest his soul, always said he would give us a lump sum if we stayed with him until we reached retirement age. He promised it to all his servants but the younger ones didn't care. They got paid better in the munitions factories. Me and Sarah, I mean, Cook, we had plans. We was going to get married and buy a nice cottage somewhere in the country. I would go fishing and she was … well, I don't really know what she would do but she wouldn't skivvy for anyone no more. But…"

"Father died and the money went to Roland, only he was too busy with the RAF. And when he died, they tied the money up, as I wasn't around?" Derek prompted when the silence lasted longer than a few seconds.

"Not exactly. Yes, you were away but Roland was home a few times. Only, he didn't have time to see to things. Your mother was desperate to get her hands on Rose Cottage. I'm not rightly sure why; she'd had no interest in it when your father was alive."

"What happened?"

"I wasn't being nosy, sir, but sounds travel in this

house. Cook and myself heard them having a big old argument. Your mother was furious with your brother for not getting rid of your wife. She wanted him to throw her out but your brother wasn't having any part of it. He said your Sally was a lovely, kind lady who had taken in two delightful children. He said, well, he said some horrible things to your mother. Called her quite a few names, which made my Sarah blush scarlet."

"Roland did?" Derek couldn't believe his ears. Roland had always been his mother's favourite.

"Yes, sir. Then he told her he was changing his will. He said he was going to leave some money to your wife, for if you didn't come back. But he always said he thought you'd get home. He was sure you were in a camp somewhere. He made several enquiries, not just at the Red Cross but through the War Office and everything. He told Cook it worried him what your mother would do to Sally if he died. I think he knew he wouldn't make it. Said something about outflying his number or something. Master Roland was a brave man, a kind one too."

Derek blinked rapidly, so the tears in his eyes wouldn't disgrace him. He'd never been close to his brother, who'd been sent away to school before Derek had been born. Father had insisted Derek attend a local school, for which he'd always been thankful.

Roland had told him some horror stories about his time away at school.

"Roland was very fond of Cook. Didn't he look after her in his will?"

A furious expression took over Sam's face.

"I believe he was going to, Master Derek, but the will hasn't been read. Your mother kept putting it off. Said she would deal with it later."

Shame engulfed Derek – and sadness. He wished his brother had lived. Maybe they could have reconciled. He was grateful to Roland for looking out for Sally.

Sam coughed. "Have I said too much? My Sarah said I should keep my mouth shut."

"Not at all, Sam. You've not only given a lifetime of service to this family but you fought side by side with Father during the first war. You and Sarah deserve to spend the rest of your days in peace." He ran his hands through his hair. "I'm rather tired now, as I'm sure you are. Tomorrow, if you could help me find more suitable clothes, I'll call on Father's solicitors. I'll get this sorted, just have a little more patience, please."

"I'd do anything for you, Master Derek. You're the image of your father, God rest him. If you forgive the intrusion, I think your mother is dead wrong about your wife."

"You heard?"

Sam nodded.

"Miss Sally, she was very kind to us during the war, after the time I visited the cottage. We wouldn't touch the black-market stuff, not when so many of our men were drowning, trying to get us food. Your Sally, she sent my Sarah a parcel every now and again when she had a friend coming to London. She gave us eggs, some vegetables and the best blackberry pie I ever tasted. Don't be telling Sarah that though." Sam winked.

Derek couldn't stop himself. He put his hand on the old man's arm. "Thank you, Sam. I think I've been rather blind lately."

"You and the rest of the country, lad. We all thought liberation would free us all but it didn't, did it? You can't forget the things you saw and did. The scars you can't see can be harder to deal with. I still have nightmares about what went on in my war. If you ever need someone to talk to, over a pint maybe, you just say the word."

"Thank you, Sam. I just might take you up on that."

CHAPTER 48

*D*erek found some letters from Sally in the top drawer of the dresser in the dining room. They hadn't been opened, and the last one was postmarked a month ago. Why hadn't his mother sent them on to the hospital? He picked them up and went into his old room to read them.

DEAR DEREK,

I hope you are feeling better. I tried to call the hospital to see if I could visit you but they said you were not allowed visitors. I hope this was true and not just your way of avoiding me.

I have news of a sort. Harry wrote to say he hasn't found any members of his family alive. He's traced most of them to Auschwitz. It's somewhere in Poland.

He hasn't been able to trace Trudi, Lisa's mother. He wrote to tell me to start the adoption process as he's worried Lisa and Tom might be sent back to live in Germany. He said he has been to some of the camps for displaced people and couldn't bear it if his siblings ended up there.

Rachel, the girl who lives with Maggie Ardle, she got a letter from her mother. Mrs Bernstein survived the war but is trying to get to Palestine. She thinks her sons might have gone to live there. Maggie has written to suggest Ruth and Rachel continue to live with her. Rachel wants to study to be a doctor although she has mentioned she might volunteer overseas with the Red Cross first. Ruth wants to stay with Maggie and be near Tom. They are like brother and sister, that pair. At least, they fight like siblings.

Oh, Derek, how did we come to this? I love you and I don't want a divorce. I want you to come and live at Rose Cottage and raise a family with me. I can't give up the children and I beg you to reconsider. It's not that I love them more than you. I do love them but even if I didn't, they don't have another home. They need me. Quite honestly, I need them too. They kept me sane when I thought I had lost you. If it hadn't been for the children ... well, I'm not sure I'd have been here when you did get back.

The pain now is worse. Knowing you are alive and less than fifty miles away but not being able to

see you or touch you is driving me insane. Please,
Derek, I will beg if I have to.

Give our marriage a chance.

I love you,
Sally

HE HELD THE LETTER TIGHT, noting the places where
her tears had smudged the ink. His kind, soft-hearted
Sally. Her kindness was what had drawn him to her,
after the initial physical attraction. She went out of
her way to be nice to people, to see the good in them.
Her experiences, growing up illegitimate, in a place
where everyone knew all about you, could have
turned her into someone hard and uncaring. Someone
filled with anger against the world.

Someone like him.

* * *

AFTER A SLEEPLESS NIGHT, Derek got up knowing
what he had to do. He dressed and walked downstairs
to the kitchen.

"Morning, Cook … can I call you Sarah? Morning, Sam. Are you free this afternoon?"

The old couple looked at each other, Sarah's eyes
filled with fear.

Sam took Sarah's hand. "Yes, Master Derek."

"Sam, please call me Derek. As of this moment, you no longer work here. I am going to get you the money Dad promised you and find you a place to live. You will stay here in the meantime. Sarah, if you can find someone to cook for mother, I will pay you to train them."

Sarah sat down. "You want to sack us."

"Not at all. I want you to retire. To live a little. Sam wants to go fishing. I aim to make that happen. I have to pop out for a while but while I'm gone, Sam, could you clear out Dad's old suits? Roland's too. I want to take them down to the centre. There's far too many servicemen walking around in suits too big or small."

"Sir – I mean, Derek. It'd be my pleasure. We know a couple who are looking for work. He was with bomb disposal and lost a leg. His missus is a good cook, not as good as my Sarah, but good enough."

Sarah looked fit to cry, so Derek hastily retreated. Whistling, he grabbed his hat and went in search of his solicitor.

* * *

HE TOOK a cab and asked the cab driver to take the long way down to Victoria, where his father's solicitors were based. Derek couldn't get over the damage.

Almost every building seemed to have been hit by a bomb.

"It's going to take years to rebuild this mess, isn't it?" Derek remarked.

"It is but it's a good reminder of what our families went through while we were off fighting. My Nellie had to send our kids down to Wales. Couldn't visit them neither. I could tell you some stories of how hard it is to control them now they're back. What about you, got kids?"

"My family lives in Chertsey," Derek replied, staring out the window once more. "St Paul's looks magnificent, doesn't it?"

"Even Hitler couldn't destroy that. Here you are, that's the office you were looking for."

Thrilled to see Cecil Tones' office in one piece, Derek paid his fare and gave the driver a tip to treat his kids.

As he'd expected, Cecil was relieved to see him, confiding he found Mrs Matthews rather difficult to please.

"Don't worry about my mother from now on, Cecil. I will invite her this afternoon too. I want her to know I'm in charge now. She will live on the money father left for her or she can get a job. Or even marry one of the landed gentry she is so keen on."

Cecil's eyes nearly bulged in their sockets but he didn't agree or disagree.

"I want you to look into something else for me. Do you think Dad's firm could be sold? It would have to be on condition that the current employees, Harold Echols, in particular, be retained."

Cecil took off his glasses and laid them on his walnut desk. He rubbed his head as if to relieve a headache.

"Certainly, Derek, it's a valuable business – but are you sure you want to sell?"

Derek eyed up the solicitor. Would he be interested in buying the thriving practice?

"Absolutely. I spent five years planning my future, and working as solicitor never entered my mind once. That was Dad's role. Maybe Roland would have been happy in the office but not me. I'm a country boy at heart."

"Are you looking for a quick sale?"

Derek caught the gleam in Cecil's eyes. The cunning businessman was still very much alive behind the stately airs and grey hair.

Derek pretended to think about the question.

"Only at the right price, Cecil. You'll earn one percent of the price for completing this work for me, in addition to your usual fees. We can arrange for it to be paid privately if your business wants to acquire Dad's old clients."

Derek smiled at the look on the solicitor's face.

The one per cent would ensure he got the best price for the business.

"Now, is there anything we need to clear up before the wills are read this afternoon?"

"No, I don't think so. But there is something else, Derek. You haven't made a will. You should. You left your wife unprotected by not having one in place when you went missing."

Derek sighed. Yet another reminder of his failings as a husband.

"Can you draw one up in time for the meeting this afternoon?"

"It's complicated, Derek."

"No, it isn't and we both know it. Everything goes to Sally if anything happens to me. I want that airtight, no interference from my mother. Agreed?"

"Agreed."

CHAPTER 49

*D*erek left the solicitor's office to return home and face the music with his mother. She wouldn't be happy, but he didn't care. She didn't love him, didn't want him around. She never had; he was the spare son to ensure the family name carried on if anything happened to Roland.

Roland. How he wished he could tell his brother he missed him. Why hadn't he made an effort to get to know him when he was alive? It was too late now.

As he walked, he found himself watching children play in the bombed-out remains of people's homes. A child, about Tom's age, was kicking a ball, or something that once resembled a ball. He kicked it in Derek's direction.

"Kick it back, please, mister."

"Haven't you got a proper ball?"

The child put his head to one side, looking at Derek as if he was an idiot. "Don't you know there was a war on. Nothing in the shops for us kids. They used rubber and leather for other stuff."

Amused at being told off by a child, Derek remembered there were some footballs at home. They'd belonged to him and Roland. They were probably still there.

"Will you be here long?"

"Me? I live here. Over there!" He pointed at what looked like a pile of bricks.

"Is your mother home?"

"Why do you want my ma? I ain't done nothin'. I was just playin'."

"You're not in trouble, son. I want to ask her something. Or your dad."

"He's in the pub. He came back from the war but he left his brains behind him. Least, that's what Ma says."

Derek didn't comment.

The boy yelled, "Ma, some rich fella in a fancy suit wants ya."

His mother came out of a door behind the rubble, a child on her hip, balancing on the bump of another pregnancy. She looked haggard and weary as if she carried the worries of the world on her shoulders.

Derek smiled politely. "Excuse me for interrupting you, but I was wondering if your son could come home with me for a few minutes. I don't live far away, just off Grosvenor Square."

Suspicion clouded her eyes. "What do you want with our Mikey?"

"I have a football and some other things he might want."

"We don't take charity, mister. We may be poor but I'm an honest woman."

"It's not charity. I'm moving to Chertsey and need to empty the house. He'd be doing me a favour."

"You sure?"

"Please, Ma, let me go. I can protect myself. I'll kick him hard if he tries anything funny."

"Go on then, pet, but don't be long."

* * *

MIKEY WALKED beside Derek as they made their way to the house.

"You like living in the country?"

"I do. I can't wait to get back."

"I lived in the country when they sent us away. I didn't like it. All those animals made such a racket I couldn't sleep. I prefer it now we're back with Ma."

"Your mother seems like a nice lady."

"She is. She'd be better off if Da didn't come back from the war. Any money she has, he just beats her and takes it. He goes down the boozer and spends everything. We ain't got food but he gets to drink plenty."

"What public house?"

"The one we just walked past. Why? Do you like drinking? Do you leave your kids hungry?"

Derek was about to say he didn't have children, but he did. Or at least he would have if Sally took him back.

He shook his head. "No, lad. Right, this is where I live."

"Cor blimey, this is one house?" Mikey stood staring at the building. Derek tried to see it as the child did. It was large, but to him it was a prison and he couldn't wait to get rid of it.

"Yes, it is. Come inside." Derek pushed open the front door, expecting Mikey to follow him. Mikey was too busy staring at everything to move. "Come on. Sarah, our cook, will have something in the kitchen. You can take some back to your mother and sister too."

"Are you Santa Claus or something?" Mikey asked him. Derek didn't get a chance to answer, as his mother appeared and shrieked.

"Good heavens above, Derek? What are you doing with that … that…? What's he doing in my house?"

"This is my friend Mikey, Mother, and I invited him to *my* house. I'm glad you're up. We have a meeting at the solicitors this afternoon."

"Impossible. I have plans."

"Cancel them. You're expected, and the will reading will go ahead regardless of whether you are there or not."

Derek didn't wait to see his mother's reaction. "Come on, Mikey, let's go down to the kitchen."

He saw Mikey poke his tongue out but didn't say a word. He didn't blame him. Mother had been rude.

"Mikey Brennan, what are you doing in here?"

"Sam. You live here?" Mikey's eyes grew wider.

"Sam, you know Mikey?" Derek asked, stating the obvious.

"Sure I do, I fought alongside his grandfather. A better soldier you never did see – ain't that right, Mikey?"

Mikey agreed, before pointing at Derek. "He told me to come here and get a football. Then he said I could have some food and bring some home for Ma. I asked him if he was Santa Claus."

Sam burst out laughing, as did Sarah. Sarah took out a bowl and filled it with soup. She put it on the table along with some bread.

"There you go, lad, eat up. I have apple pie for afters."

Mikey didn't need asking twice.

"Sam, could you help me find Roland's old football?"

"I can show you exactly where it is. Come this way."

They left Sarah and Mikey happily chatting in the warm kitchen.

CHAPTER 50

*D*erek followed Sam up to the attic. Once they were out of earshot, he asked him, "What do you know about Mikey?"

"He's a good lad but given how desperate things are for his family, he'll fall in with the wrong crowd, soon enough. His ma, Dee, is from Ireland. Mick, her husband, is a bad'un. He came back from the war worse than he left. He beats her and the young'uns too. Heard she'd go back to Ireland if she had the money. Has family back there."

"Mikey says his dad is always in the pub."

"That would be right. Only time he isn't there is when they shut the doors and kick him out." Sam pushed open the door to the attic. "There you are."

Derek tried the light switch not expecting it to work but it did. He whistled as he looked around. It appeared nothing had been given away or thrown out since he was a child. In fact, some things looked old enough to have come from his mother's family, Mother having grown up in this house.

"Sam, look at all this stuff. There must be two or three of everything. Grab that ball, will you – Mikey will like that. Now, what could we give him for his sister? This?"

Derek picked up a train set.

"Won't stay in her hands very long. Mick will sell it. Dee would be better off with some food, cans of something or other."

Derek scowled and put the train set back.

"Do you think she really would go to Ireland?" Derek couldn't stop himself from wanting to help the woman. Mikey was about ten or eleven, a victim of the war, like Tom.

"You mean, run off?"

"Yes. I can't think of any other way to keep Mikey safe. The streets are no place for a boy – and his mother, well, she seems overwhelmed and tired."

"Worn out, she is, the poor woman. I think she'd go but being Catholic they don't agree with divorce." Sam fell silent.

As the silence continued, Derek prompted, "What are you thinking?"

"She's got brothers back in Ireland. She told me they would kill Mick if they lived nearby."

"So, maybe if we got the family to Ireland, we could leave Mick to her brothers."

"You'd have to buy the tickets and give them to Dee. If you gave anything to Mick, he'd sell it."

"You can do it. I don't think she would take it from me."

Sam's eyes glistened as he turned away, his voice quivering with suppressed emotion. "You're a decent man, Derek. Your father would be right proud of you."

Derek wasn't at all sure his father would be proud, given what he had done and said to Sally, but that was going to change. He took the football down to Mikey, told Sarah to pack up a basket of food and they would drop it off on the way to the solicitor. Mikey rubbed his face on his shirt a couple of times. When they dropped him at his home and he handed the basket of food to his mother, he surprised Derek by giving him a hug.

"I wish my da was a man like you."

"Maybe in time, Mikey, your da will learn to value you and your mother. But, remember you are not him. You don't have to end up like him."

Derek watched Mikey's mother as Sam whispered to her. The tears ran down her cheeks and she made no attempt to clean them off. She muttered something to Sam and moved closer to Derek.

"I don't know why you're doing what you are, but

thank you. I can never repay you but I'll pray for you every day."

"Please pray for my family. We have some work to do on getting over the war."

She touched his arm, understanding written over her face. "Nobody said coming back from the war would be the hardest bit for you men. If I had a shilling for every man I've heard say they miss the war, I'd be rich."

Derek gave her a small smile and replied, "I don't miss the war itself but the comradeship and the understanding. Us men don't appreciate how bad you women had it at home. How much stress and strain you were under and how courageous you all were. I hope things work out the best for you in Ireland, Dee. Write to Sam if you ever need anything. He can contact me."

"I won't be needing your help again; I've got my family over there ... but thank you."

Derek nodded and turned to Sam. "Sam, we have to go. The meeting starts soon."

Derek, Sam and Sarah sat in the solicitor's office. Derek wished he could say something to make the old servants look more at ease. Cecil barely looked at them, but he kept fawning over Derek.

It would take a few weeks for the sale of the business to go through and for Derek to clear out his old things from the house. He looked at Cecil as the solicitor gave them the details of the will.

"Your father left everything to Roland as the eldest son, apart from an annual allowance to your mother and a stipend to the servants."

Sam looked up at this but said nothing.

Cecil continued, "Roland had already accumulated a sizeable sum of money in his own right. Your brother purchased quite a large plot of land in Chertsey, close to Rose Cottage. He also had a small rental portfolio. I will have to check if all the properties have survived the war and whether any need repairs."

Derek nodded, trying to hide his surprise. He had no idea Roland was so wealthy.

"Everything passes to you, Derek. Roland had a good knowledge of investments; if you keep his choices, you could comfortably live off the income they provide."

Derek couldn't believe his ears. He didn't have to go back to travelling for work, he could live the rest of his life in Chertsey with Sally. If she'd have him.

"Thank you, Cecil. I will discuss the investments with you another day. Can you pay the money to Sarah and Sam with immediate effect? They have waited too long already."

* * *

SAM TOOK Sarah out for a celebratory meal, leaving Derek to face his mother alone. When he returned, she was sitting in the drawing room, a large glass of wine at her side.

"We missed your presence, Mother. Cecil passed on his regards."

She didn't reply.

"Cecil will write to you with the details of your annual income but expect in the region of £8,000."

His mother stood so suddenly she almost lost her balance. "Have you lost your mind?" She moved closer to him, a wild look in her eyes. "I can't live on that. There has to be more money. Your father had many investments."

"He didn't have as much as you think, Mother. His money went to Roland. Roland left everything to me."

His mother tried tears next, staggering into the seat – but without knocking the glass beside it. She started crying into a rather conveniently found hanky. He waited for her to recover her composure; it didn't take long once she saw he wasn't falling for the fake tears.

"I don't know how I shall manage. This house costs a lot for a start. Your father should have done better by me."

Derek let that comment pass. "Mother, this is my house so I'll pay for its upkeep. You're free to live here as long as you wish, on one condition. You treat Sam and Sarah with utmost respect."

His mother opened her mouth, but Derek ignored her. "Mother, I'll stand as best man for Sam when he marries Sarah. After the ceremony, they'll live here while I work on finding them alternative accommodation closer to Rose Cottage."

"You expect me to live with servants?" His mother held her hanky to her nose as if she was about to get an attack of the vapours.

"You have always lived with servants, Mother. Only this time, they'll use Roland's room as a bedroom. I have told them to turn my bedroom into their private sitting room."

His mother paled. "I won't agree to this."

"That is your choice. But with accommodation so difficult to find, give it some thought." Derek decided his mother needed a firm reminder. "Sam and Sarah have worked for us for most of their lives. They are entitled to retire, something Dad promised them, but you reneged on that promise. This is my way of making it up to them. My decision is final."

She looked at him with hatred in her eyes. "Why did Roland have to die?"

Derek heard the unsaid words: *and not you?*

"I wish Roland hadn't died, but he did. So this is the way things stand. You have another option."

His mother stared at him, waiting.

"You could marry again but I must warn you, your allowance would cease."

"You are insufferable, Derek. You always were."

Derek left the room. He itched to go to Chertsey but he knew he had to delay his trip by two days while he finished what he'd started. He could have gone and come back to London but sensed that wasn't the correct thing to do. Instead, he sent a note to Sally telling her he would be there soon.

* * *

THE TWO DAYS seemed to last forever, but finally he arrived at Chertsey station. He got out of the train and walked towards Rose Cottage. He took the back lane in the hope he wouldn't meet anyone he knew.

He repeated what he was going to say over and over again. It sounded good to him but what would Sally think...

He pushed the gate open, hearing sounds coming from the back garden. Walking around the cottage he saw Sally playing ball with the children. Looking closer he saw it looked like the football was flat. Grinning, he was glad he had kept one football back for Tom.

Tom spotted him first.

"Look, it's Uncle Derek." Tom came racing towards him. "Are you back for good now? Are you really home? Aunt Sally has cried so much, I thought she might drown."

He glanced up at Sally. She'd turned pink hearing Tom's comments.

He held out his hand to Tom. "Nice to see you again, Tom. I know I upset your Aunt Sally, and I must have frightened your sister." He sensed Tom would react badly if he'd suggested the boy was scared too by his actions. "Do you think I could try again to make friends with Lisa?"

Tom looked at him, uncertainty in his eyes, then he turned towards his sister. "Lisa, come here and meet Uncle Derek."

The girl walked over slowly, her blue eyes holding his gaze. She didn't seem to blink. He had a feeling she could read his soul.

"Nice to meet you, Mr Derek." Her voice and manners were perfect but he felt like she was addressing a stranger. Which in fairness he was.

Tom turned towards his sister. "Uncle Derek, silly. He's Aunt Sally's husband." Lisa just stared.

"Nice to meet you, Lisa. You're very pretty. I love your dress."

"Mum made it for me. She's good at that. Are you

here to stay? Where's your case?" Lisa looked behind him.

"I have to check with your mum first. Tom, do you think you could take Lisa to Callaghan's and buy her something?"

"A gobstopper?" Tom gave Derek a hopeful glance, but Sally intervened.

"No, Tom. Last time she had one, she got a toothache. Buy her some liquorice or whatever Mr Callaghan has. The ration book's in the cupboard."

"I know. Come on, Lisa, let's go before they get all mushy."

"Why will they get mushy?" Lisa stared at Derek before Tom dragged her away.

"I wish we could get mushy," Derek said lightly, but the look on Sally's face told him not to try joking. "Sally, I ... oh heck, I had it all laid out in my head, and now I can't remember what I was going to say."

"What are you doing here? Did you bring papers?" Her lovely face showed signs of strain, large black circles under her eyes, her mouth thinned. The hurt in her eyes. All of this was his fault.

He didn't follow what she was saying at first but then it dawned on him.

"No, Sally. I don't want a divorce. I want to be your husband."

"Derek, I want that too, but I can't..." She turned

away from him. He took her by the arm and held her gently.

"Listen to me. I want you and the children. I've been so stupid. I didn't know my backside from my elbow. I'm such a fool. Please tell me it's not too late."

"You want the children?"

"Yes."

She didn't look convinced. "But what if we have children of our own?" Her cheeks turned pink. His Sally, still embarrassed, after all they had been to one another.

He rubbed her hands in his, wanting to hug her but sensing it was too soon.

"Then we will have a big family like you said you wanted. I don't care if we have the two we have, or ten more. I want you, Sally – and the children."

Sally hesitated.

He took a step towards her. "I know I hurt you, and I wish I could take back every word I said. I was in a bad place. I should have gone to the hospital straight away."

"What was wrong? Why didn't you let me visit?"

"I had some shrapnel in an old wound. They had to operate to take it out. There was a chance I might not walk again, and I didn't want you to feel under a burden."

He almost stepped back from the blaze of anger in her eyes.

"Derek Matthews, I don't know if I want to slap you or hug you. I married you in sickness and in health."

"I'd like the second option."

But Sally seemed not to hear him.

"You're my husband. I wanted you back so badly I wouldn't have cared if you came back with one leg, one arm or one eye." Sally threw herself into his arms. He pulled her closer, wrapping his arms around her.

"Sally, forgive me."

"I love you, Derek. I always will."

He drew away from her but didn't let her go. "It will be hard at first. You and me, we aren't the same people we were all those years ago."

"I know that."

"I miss my docile little wife," he responded, grinning.

"Your what? I was never docile, Derek. You take that back."

He kissed her deeply, removing all ability for either of them to speak.

"See, I told you they'd get mushy." Tom's voice interrupted them.

Sally pushed him away, redder in the face than he'd ever seen her. She rubbed her hands on her dress as she said, "That was fast. We didn't expect you to come back so quickly."

"I wanted to make sure he didn't disappear again, like last time."

Tom's look made Derek feel like a heel.

"Come here, son. I have something to ask you."

Tom came closer, holding Lisa by the hand.

"I'd like to come here and live with you. Would that be alright with you?" Derek asked, watching Tom's face closely. He hadn't realised until this minute how much he wanted the boy to agree.

"You mean forever?"

"Yes. Or at least until you find your own girl, move out and have a home of your own."

"Yuck! I'm never getting married. Are you really going to stay? You aren't going to disappear again if I go to Maggie's or somewhere. You did that last time." His accusing look made Derek feel lower than a snake.

"Yes, I did. I can't give you any excuse, other than to tell you I'm sorry. I was a fool. But give me a second chance and I won't let you down. I may mess up sometimes, but all dads do that."

At the look on Tom's face, he realised what he had said. "Sorry, I didn't mean…"

Tom spoke over him, the hopeful look in his eyes tearing Derek apart. "You want to be my dad. Like, for real?"

Sally slipped her hand into his as he choked on the lump in his throat.

"Yes, I would. I can never take the place of your papa but I'd like to be your dad."

Tom looked at Sally. "Does that mean I could call you Mum, like Lisa does?"

Derek heard Sally's hard swallow before she spoke. "I'd love for you to call me Mum. I see you as my son, Tom."

Lisa put her hands around Derek's waist. "Dad."

Derek pulled Tom into the group. "Family."

Sally kissed his cheek. "Our family."

"Will Harry call you Mum and Dad too?" Tom asked, after a few minutes.

Derek and Sally exchanged a glance.

"He could but I guess he might feel too old to call me anything but Derek."

Tom shrugged his shoulders. "Can we go tell Ruth and Rachel we have a new dad?"

"Take your time doing that, son. I'll wait here with your mum."

"You're going to get all slushy again." Tom picked up the pace as he ran, holding Lisa's hand, almost lifting Lisa's legs from the ground as she tried to keep up with him.

Derek held Sally's hand until the children had gone down the lane.

Sally turned to him and whispered, "Thank you, Derek."

He put a finger under her chin, forcing her to look up at him.

"No, Sally, thank you. Not just for this, but for everything."

EPILOGUE

June 1947 Abbeydale

*M*aggie's voice rang out. "Sally, where are you?"

Sally heard the back door shut behind Maggie. She called back, "I'm here, just giving the front room a good dusting." As Maggie entered the room, Sally looked at her friend and frowned. "You're breathless again. Have you been to the doctor yet?"

Maggie waved away Sally's comments as she had every other time she mentioned the doctor. Sally was worried about her and the effect the long war years had on her. Even now, two years after the war had ended, they had to queue for rations. People all over the country were suffering.

In London and other cities there was no accommodation to be found. The houses destroyed by bombs were left the same way they had been when Derek had returned. There was no money to rebuild them. Every penny seemed to be going to repay loans to America or help those in Europe. Sally thanked God over and over for the fact that Derek's money meant they had a comfortable standard of living and gave them the opportunity to help the less well off in their community.

"Maggie, you're out of breath. I'm calling the doctor." Sally moved to pick up the telephone. They'd had it installed a month ago. Derek had insisted, as he was worried about Sally going into labour when he was out of the house. He'd waived aside Sally's concerns about the cost, reminding her his brother had left them comfortable. By law, they had to join a waiting list and share a line with a neighbour. Sally had yet to use the device as nobody she knew, apart from the doctor and the police station, had a telephone in their house.

"Don't fuss." Maggie took a seat at the table. "Sally, I'm old enough to say when I need a doctor."

Sally didn't like it, but she couldn't make Maggie do anything she didn't want to do. She gave Maggie a glass of water and then put the kettle on.

"Sally, I met the postman, he had a letter from Rachel. I'm dying to read it but have to wait for Ruth to come home. He gave me these for you." Maggie took a breath as she handed Sally her post.

She rifled through them, her heart skipping a beat as she spotted Harry's writing. "It's from Harry. The children will be so excited."

"Why do you think I hand delivered it? I want to hear all the news, me being a gossipy old witch and all."

"You aren't a gossip. Maybe I should wait for the children."

Maggie shook her head. "No, read it first. Where are they anyway?"

"Derek took the kids down to the river to go fishing with Sam. That old man is such a blessing, he and Sarah are like grandparents to the kids."

"Less of the old thank you, that couple are younger than I am. How are you feeling?"

Sally patted the bump of her stomach. "He kicks a lot."

"He? I'd say you're carrying a girl from the look of you."

"I don't care what it is, so long as it's healthy and doesn't come early. I'm not ready yet."

"You'll manage. Now, are you going to read Harry's letter, or do I have to steam it open?" Maggie's tone was teasing but her eyes held concern.

Sally turned the letter over and over. She didn't want to open it, yet she was desperate to know. Harry had told her in his last letter he was searching for Trudi. He was happy to support Sally and Derek in their bid to adopt Tom. It was a fairly straightforward procedure as they knew Tom was an orphan.

But Lisa was different; she might not be an orphan. Had Harry found Trudi? Did the woman want her child back? How could Sally give up the daughter she considered hers?

Sally's eyes stung. "What if he's found Lisa's mother? I couldn't bear to give her up. I just—" Sally's voice broke. Her hand shook as she gave the letter to Maggie. "I can't. Can you open it?"

"You've got to have faith. Whatever the news is from Harry, you and Derek will deal with it. You're not alone. You have a family who love you to the moon and back."

Maggie's hands were shaking almost as badly as Sally's. She seemed to take forever to open the letter and scan the contents.

Her face crumpled and Sally stopped breathing. Trudi was coming back. She would take the children because Tom wouldn't be separated from Lisa, and Sally couldn't stop her. She stifled the urge to run and find Derek so they could smuggle the children away, somewhere the authorities couldn't trace them.

"Sally. Sally, you're not listening."

"She's alive, isn't she? Maggie, I know I'm horrible, but I can't give up my children. I know she's Lisa's birth mother but I…"

"Trudi's dead, Sally. She won't be coming."

Sally couldn't breathe through the thick, heavy feeling in her chest. "Oh my God, what have I done? I prayed I could keep those children. I killed her – or as good as…"

Maggie frowned with concern. "Stop that, Sally. You didn't kill anyone, and you love those children from the bottom of your heart. You didn't want anyone to die when you prayed you wouldn't lose them."

Sally's tears trickled down her cheeks. "How? When? Is he sure?" Harry's face was as clear as day in her mind. "Poor Harry."

"Harry confirms what Rachel's mother hinted at in her letter. Trudi was helping Jews and other refugees of the Nazis. She found them hiding places, food and papers. Someone denounced her to the Gestapo, and they captured her in 1944. She was shot on the first of May, 1945."

"Days before the war was over. Why? Why would anyone do that?"

Maggie didn't answer but stared at the letter. Sally put her head in her hands and cried. She didn't hear Maggie get out of her chair and come to put her arms around her.

"Sally, love, none of this is your doing. Trudi took

a big risk putting the children on the Kindertransport. She did it out of love, hoping they would live through the war. They did more than just live, they thrived – and you are to thank for that. Tom and Lisa – Harry too – have a future. A good one. Trudi and their father are looking down on you and smiling. You have to believe that."

"Maggie, I can't. I feel so guilty. I wanted those children to be mine. I didn't think about the consequences of my prayers. What it would mean for Trudi … How can I look Tom and Lisa in the eyes?"

Maggie released her hold and stood, straightening her shoulders. "That's quite enough of that. You don't sit there feeling sorry for yourself, Sally Matthews. You have to break the news to those children and hug them if they cry. Tom is bound to feel a little guilty over what he said about hating Trudi."

"We know he didn't mean it; he was just jealous of her relationship with his father."

"We know that. But for all his thirteen years, he's still a child. So, wipe your tears and go and fetch your family. What about asking Reverend Collins to say a few words for her? I know Trudi was Jewish, but we don't have a rabbi."

Sally wiped her tears away; she could cry later. Maggie was right as usual. The children needed her.

"I think that's a lovely idea. Can you tell Ruth for me? I'll write to Rachel, but I think Harry may have done that." Sally couldn't help bursting into tears once more. Maggie pulled her close. Sally sobbed on Maggie's shoulder for a few minutes before taking a deep breath and forcing the tears to stop.

"What would I do without you, Maggie? You've been like a mother to me. Always there, never judging me."

"I love you like a daughter. Families aren't always blood. Some of the best have no blood connection at all. Tom and Lisa will love this little one as much as they love each other." Maggie took a second before continuing, "Your family will get over this news, just like they survived the war and all that entailed. You are the glue that sticks this little family together."

Maggie left to go back to the vicarage. Sally washed her face and hands and left to find her husband and the children.

* * *

THE FOLLOWING EVENING, the children, including Ruth, gathered near the old cherry tree at the edge of the garden. Come spring, they would plant a tree in Trudi's memory but for now the old tree would have to do.

Derek had dug a small hole at its base, before taking his place holding Sally's right hand. Maggie stood on her left.

Each child had written a letter thanking Trudi for saving their lives and promising never to forget her. Reverend Collins said a few words, and then everyone watched the children as they placed their letters in the small hole.

Tom stepped forward. "Can I please say something, Reverend?"

"Of course."

Tom looked from the hole to his sister and then to the adults.

"I owe my life to Trudi. She was the one who got Harry out of Dachau and got us on the Kindertransport. I never thanked her. In fact, I thought she just wanted to be rid of us. I know now, what she did was the hardest thing a mother should ever have to do." Tom gulped.

Sally ached to go to him, but he wouldn't want that.

In a shaky voice, Tom continued, "I thought Trudi stole my father and loved her baby more than me. I know now I was wrong. She saved me. I will never forget her. I swear now my children and their children will know about this wonderful woman, Trudi Beck. When Lisa used to ask 'When's Mummy coming?', I said my mother could never come back as she was dead. I hurt my sister and myself by telling a lie. Trudi was as much a mother to me as she was to Lisa."

Sally's tears flowed down her face as Tom spoke, her heart breaking as she watched the anguished expression on his face. She couldn't look at Lisa.

Tom swallowed hard. "I am very lucky. I have had three mothers in my life, the woman who gave birth to me, Trudi who saved me and Sally, the woman who took me into her home and treated me as her son. I believe that makes me one of the luckiest children in the world."

Sally broke away from her husband and friend, and rushed to gather Tom in her arms. Seconds later, Lisa joined them.

Sally said, "I love you both very much and I'm thankful to Trudi for sending you away. She gave me the greatest gift a woman could ever have."

The sun broke through the clouds at that moment, bathing the little group in light.

Lisa looked up and gasped, before saying, "I think Mummy sent us a sign. She's happy with Papa up in heaven. She knows we have a good home and a new mum and dad."

Derek picked the little girl up in his arms. "We should all listen to Lisa. My daughter is a very wise old soul."

"Dad, I'm not old. I'm only eight. You're old. Your hair is all grey."

Sally and Derek exchanged loving glances. Derek

put Lisa down and, taking her and Tom by the hand, they went to fill in the hole in the ground.

Sally walked towards the kitchen. Maggie slipped her hand into her arm and walked with her.

"Are you feeling a little better than yesterday?" Maggie asked.

"I feel blessed, Maggie. Thanks to Trudi, I have two beautiful children. I have a good husband and wonderful friends and a charming home in a country at peace." Sally thought for a second. "All I need now is to deliver this baby safely and get Harry and Rachel home."

Maggie turned to face her. "Harry won't be coming home any time soon, Sally love. He has his own demons to chase."

Sally frowned. "I hope he knows what he's doing. I know he hates the Nazis and blames them for the death of his father, but taking a life won't bring him peace, will it?"

Maggie put her hand on Sally's arm. "He's got to figure that out for himself, Sally, you know that. The war isn't over for him yet. But with any luck, he'll find his way back home to you, just like Derek did."

AUTHOR NOTES

The Wormhoudt massacre isn't as well known as it should be. The members of the Waffen- SS 1st Division Leibstandarte SS Adolf Hitler, responsible for the murder of the English and French prisoners of war, were never held accountable for their actions. Hauptsturmfuhrer Wilhelm Mohnke, the man in charge of these murderers, denied he had ever given an order to execute prisoners of war.

After murdering some wounded who couldn't keep up with the marching prisoners, the Waffen- SS ushered approximately one hundred men into the barn. They threw two grenades. Sergeant Stanley Moore and Company Sergeant Major Augustus Jennings, threw themselves on the grenades, sacrificing their lives in an attempt to preserve those of their mates. But the SS hadn't finished.

They called out the men in groups of five and those remaining behind heard shots. That proved too slow a method of execution so the Nazis opened fire into the barn with machine guns.

Private Bert Evans recollected the senior officer, Captain James Lynn Allen, told them to run – every man for himself. Captain Lynn-Allen was murdered when he went to Evan's aid, saving his life.

Evans was shot behind the ear and left for dead. He was found by regular German army soldiers who took him to a hospital and after treatment there, he was sent to a German POW camp. He remained there until he was repatriated back to the UK in a German prisoner exchange program. Although I have mentioned him in my book, Private Evans didn't rescue anyone from a stream, he was too badly injured himself. This hero, who tried his best to have his mates remembered, died at the age of 92. Approximately ten men survived this ordeal.

Mohnke, who joined the Nazi party in 1933 i.e. voluntarily not because he had to do so, became one of Hitler's most senior Generals. He surrendered to the Red Army and was imprisoned in a Russian POW officers camp until 1955. He is alleged to have been involved in the murder of Canadian POW's in 1944, a charge he also denied. He died of old age in Germany.

ACKNOWLEDGEMENTS

These books wouldn't have been possible without the help of so many people.

The ladies from my reader group on Facebook, Rachel Wesson Readers, who always cheer me on. They keep me smiling and I am so grateful for their support.

Special thanks go to Marlene Larsen, Meisje Sanders Arcuri, Sherry Parks, Dawn Bafta, and Jackie Knight Cline. And of course, the three Janets who are always cheerleading my books :-)

My editor, Vicky Blunden, who understands what I am trying to say even when I use the wrong words. She corrects my Irishness lol. My copy editor and proofreaders are also important parts of my team. Without them, this book wouldn't exist.

The fabulous readers and authors in the Second World War Club on Facebook. If you love to read about the war, please join us.

Last, but by no means least, huge thanks and love to my husband and my three children.

Printed in Great Britain
by Amazon